NICK FITTED A LARGE EVIDENCE BAG OVER THE FIRST ONE AND SEALED IT WITH DUCT TAPE.

He made a small incision in the top of the second bag with a scalpel, then inserted the scalpel through the hole and used it to slash an opening in the bag beneath. He pulled the scalpel out quickly and slapped a duct tape patch over the hole in the outer bag. "Come out, come out, whatever you are," Nick muttered.

A second later, something did.

Two long feelers attached to a black head the size of a pea tested the air. A second later, a segmented black body fringed with orange legs flowed out of the hole, followed a second later by another. And another. And another.

"Centipedes?" Riley said.

"Millipedes, I think," Nick said. "Grissom would know for sure." He sniffed the air. "You smell that? Almonds."

"Cyanide?" Riley said. "So our suicide poisoned himself, sealed a bag full of bugs around his head then cuffed himself to the bed?"

"Whatever this is," Nick said, "it's no suicide."

Original novels in the CSI series:

CSI:
CRIME SCENE INVESTIGATION™

THE KILLING JAR
a novel

Donn Cortez

Based on the hit CBS series CSI: Crime Scene Investigation produced by CBS PRODUCTIONS, a business unit of CBS Broadcasting Inc.

Executive Producers: Jerry Bruckheimer, Carol Mendelsohn, Anthony E. Zuiker, Ann Donahue, Naren Shankar, Cynthia Chvatal, William Petersen, Jonathan Littman

Series created by: Anthony E. Zuiker

POCKET STAR BOOKS
New York   London   Toronto   Sydney

Pocket Star Books
A Division of Simon & Schuster, Inc.
1230 Avenue of the Americas
New York, NY 10020

This book is a work of fiction. Names, characters, places, and incidents either are products of the author's imagination or are used fictitiously. Any resemblance to actual events or locales or persons, living or dead, is entirely coincidental.

First Pocket Star Books paperback edition December 2009

POCKET STAR BOOKS and colophon are registered trademarks of Simon & Schuster, Inc.

For information about special discounts for bulk purchases, please contact Simon & Schuster Special Sales at 1-866-506-1949 or business@simonandschuster.com.

The Simon & Schuster Speakers Bureau can bring authors to your live event. For more information or to book an event contact the Simon & Schuster Speakers Bureau at 1-866-248-3049 or visit our website at www.simonspeakers.com.

Cover design by David Stevenson

Manufactured in the United States of America

10 9 8 7 6 5 4 3 2 1

ISBN 978-1-4391-5370-3
ISBN 978-1-4391-6688-8 (ebook)

AUTHOR'S NOTE

This novel takes place during the ninth season of CSI: Crime Scene Investigation, prior to the introduction of Ray Langston.

1

THE RED BABOON SPIDER HISSED at the showgirl.

"She's a little nervous," Gil Grissom said. "I don't take her out in public very often."

On Planet Showgirl, evolution had clearly favored sequins and feathers, while gravity was obviously much less of a factor. The showgirl leaned in closer and peered at the cage. "Hairy, irritable, and poisonous," she said. "Reminds me of my ex. Nice to see you, Gil." She strutted off on absurdly high heels, an exotic alien who somehow seemed completely at home.

Grissom glanced around the lobby. He often felt like an outsider in "normal" society, and his usual environment—working graveyard shift at the crime lab in Las Vegas—was anything but. Not only was it one of the busiest labs in the country; Grissom had helped it attain one of the highest case clearance rates as well. His world was one of high contrast, of bodies found in high-roller penthouse suites and in back-alley Dumpsters, of prostitutes who ODed on a thousand dollars' worth of cocaine, and homeless men frozen to death in the desert. Vegas was its own world, where all the rules were different and cash was king, where people came for the sex and the buzz and the shows and the slots, and everybody knew that beneath the city's bright neon smile were the sharp, hungry teeth of a shark. Vegas was a river, a shiny twenty-four-hour current of brilliant color and chiming bells, with the nets that let the fish through while separating them from their money so cleverly designed that people hardly noticed them—and were too enthralled with the glitz to feel their pockets getting lighter. You could meet literally anyone in Vegas, from a celebrity throwing away his signing bonus at the craps tables to an elderly tourist couple from Iowa, from sharp-eyed hustlers honing their skills at poker to fresh-faced drunks eager to do something they'd regret tomorrow.

The town attracted many a convention-goer, too. Grissom had investigated his share of weekend warrior misadventures; the combination of booze, peer pressure, and sudden disconnection from their everyday lives pushed people to extremes of behavior they never would have considered at home.

Everyone needed to blow off steam; he understood that. Grissom himself rode roller coasters, the intense visceral rush so completely different from the cool calm of the lab. He sometimes wondered what sort of release his scientific colleagues indulged in—not the ones he worked with every day, but other entomologists.

He supposed he was about to find out.

The sign board in the lobby read WELCOME ELEVENTH ANNUAL CONVENTION OF INTERNATIONAL ENTOMOLOGICAL RESEARCH PROFESSIONALS! They'd misspelled *entomological*. Grissom had already told the front desk, but they hadn't gotten around to changing it yet.

"Grissom? Gilly!" The voice was loud, Australian, and familiar: Grissom recognized the tall, lanky man who strode across the lobby toward him immediately. Jake Soames was from Melbourne, one of the foremost experts in the world on poisonous insects. He was dressed the same way he'd been the last time Grissom had seen him, in tan cargo pants and a jacket with too many pockets, a matching Tilley hat pinned up on one side of his head bushman-style. His face was wide and ruddy, his abundant red mustache streaked with gray.

"Hello, Jake," said Grissom. "Good to see you."

"You too, mate. How about this, eh? Guess we're on your turf now!"

Grissom smiled. "I suppose you are."

"It sounds," a polite voice from behind Grissom said, "as if you're conceding him the home-field advantage. Setting the stage for your inevitable admission of defeat?"

Grissom turned. The speaker was a short, trim Asian man, dressed in a conservative blue suit. Grissom knew him, too: Khem Charong, a researcher from Thailand. They'd met at a conference in Duluth, where Charong's entries in the cockroach races had just edged out Grissom's.

"Not bloody likely," said Soames. "I've got some real beauties this year—though I'm sure Gilly's boys will give 'em a run for their money."

"Hello, Khem," said Grissom. They shook hands. "I don't know how much competition I'll be able to give you this year. Things have been extremely busy at the lab—I'm afraid my breeding program's suffered as a result."

"I fail to be relieved, Mr. Grissom. A halfhearted effort on your part is simply not a credible premise."

"Well, thank you. I'll try not to embarrass myself."

"What have you got there?" asked Soames, peering at the cage. "Looks like a *Harpactirinae*."

"*Citharischius crawshayi*, actually," said Grissom. "I promised a colleague I'd bring her along. I'm supposed to meet him here, but he's late." Grissom glanced around the lobby once more.

"Well, we're all a bit early," said Soames. "Conference doesn't start until tomorrow, after all. I asked if anyone else had arrived, and the hotel told me so far us three were it."

Grissom frowned. "He hasn't checked in yet? That's odd."

"Never keep a man with a tarantula waiting, I always say," said Soames. "Could be a good thing you brought it, though. We can feed it the losers, give 'em a little incentive."

Just then, Grissom spotted whom he'd been looking for, standing at the front desk and looking through a pamphlet. "Ah, there he is. If you gentlemen will excuse me, I think the person I was waiting for just arrived."

The man looked up as Grissom approached. "Dr. Quadros?"

"Yes. Dr. Grissom, I presume?"

Dr. Roberto Quadros was a Brazilian man in his forties, his skin tanned by field work, his neatly trimmed beard and slicked-back hair pure white. His eyes were dark behind tinted, thick-framed glasses, and he wore a gray blazer over a T-shirt with a *University of Rio de Janeiro* logo on it.

"A pleasure to finally meet you," said Grissom. "I've greatly enjoyed our correspondence."

"As have I," Quadros said. His smile was wide but brief, his attention immediately turning to the cage Grissom held. "Ah. This is the specimen we discussed?"

"Yes." Grissom handed him the cage.

Quadros brought it up to his face, staring at the spider from no more than six inches away. "Beautiful," he murmured. "And one of the largest I've ever seen."

"Did you just get in?"

"Hmm? No, I arrived yesterday. Been looking around. Don't much care for the place so far. Too bright, too busy."

"Parts of it are. Vegas can be something of a shock to the system."

"I'm sure. Fortunately, we'll be too busy this week for such distractions. I'm looking forward to your paper."

"And I yours."

Quadros sighed. "I hate most conferences. Tele-communications are so advanced today that face-to-face meetings seem unnecessary; staying in the field and swapping files via a good satellite connection seems much more efficient."

"Well," said Grissom, "even a spider can't spend *all* its time on the web . . ."

Captain Jim Brass wasn't a cynic. He was the person cynics studied when they needed a role model.

"Yeah, okay, fine," he said to the motel desk clerk, a heavyset man with long, greasy black hair. "All you remember about who rented the room is he was a guy. Average height, average build, hair brown or possibly blond. Somewhere between twenty-five and forty-five years old. I'm gonna have to ask you to slow down—I don't know if I can keep up with this blizzard of details."

The clerk, Manny, looked at him with eyes a little too bloodshot to be attributed to the late hour. "He was just this guy. I think he was black, or maybe Hispanic. Or he could have just had a good tan."

"Well, that narrows things down. You sure he wasn't Chinese?"

Manny thought about it. "I guess, maybe."

"Thanks for your help. I'll let you get back to your eagle-eyed observation of the immediate environment."

Brass left the motel office and climbed the stairs to the second level. The crime scene was in room 219, now guarded by a uniformed officer. As a homicide detective, Brass was usually the second official to arrive on the scene, after the beat cops who originally investigated the call but before the medical examiner. This led to Brass sometimes saying he was middle management in the death business, but nobody ever seemed to laugh.

The ME had arrived while he was talking to Manny. Doctor Albert Robbins stood just inside the doorway to the room, leaning against the arm crutch he used to help him get around.

"Hey, Doc. How are you doing?"

"Damn stairs," Doc Robbins grumbled. "I hate these two-level motels. They never have an elevator."

"Yeah, too bad the vic didn't have the consideration to die on the first floor. You open the bag?"

"No. And I'm not going to, either. I'll let Grissom do it."

"Grissom can't make it," Nick Stokes said, walking up with Riley Adams at his side. "He's at a conference."

"Where's he gone this time?" Brass asked. "The wilds of Duluth again?"

Nick shook his head. "No, this time it's right here in town. Some big bug expert thing. He's pretty pumped up about it."

"Well, he's going to be sorry he missed this," said Brass.

"What have we got?" Riley asked. She was a slender, pretty blonde with her hair tied back in a ponytail.

"Well," Robbins said, "at first glance I thought it might be a suicide." He moved aside to let Nick and Riley get a better look.

The body on the motel bed was that of a young, well-built white male, wearing only a pair of boxer shorts. His arms were spread, wrists handcuffed to the bedposts, and his head was covered with a white plastic bag secured around his neck with a plastic zap strap.

"Suicide?" said Riley. She adjusted the focus on the camera she held and started taking photos. "With his hands cuffed like that?"

"Oh, sure," said Robbins. "A lot of suicides are afraid they're going to lose their nerve at the last minute, so they try to impose a point of no return. I call it hesitation insurance."

"Can't back out once that cuff locks into place," Nick murmured. "But you said 'at first,' Doc?"

"Yes. I was going to remove the bag from his head, get a look at his face—"

"But you didn't," Riley said. "Why not?"

"Poke the bag," Brass said. "You'll see."

"Gil Grissom," Roberto Quadros said, "I'd like you to meet Professor Nathan Vanderhoff."

Grissom shook the hand that was offered. Vanderhoff was a slender man with coffee-hued skin, his curly hair cut short against an elegant skull. He wore an expensive-looking pale green suit that looked far too warm for Vegas in the summer, and a bright yellow tie.

"A pleasure, Mr. Grissom," Vanderhoff said. His accent was Dutch Afrikaans. "I see you have one of my countrymen with you."

"Countrywomen, actually," Grissom said with a nod at the cage. "Her name is Elizabeth."

"A fine name for a king baboon spider," Vanderhoff said, chuckling. "Or perhaps I should say a queen?"

"I don't name my specimens," Quadros said. "They're not pets."

"Mine is," Grissom said mildly. "I'm quite fond of her."

"Come now, Roberto," Vanderhoff said. "Don't tell me you've never named a subject you've been studying—we've all done it, especially in the wild. If nothing else, it makes them easier to differentiate."

"I find numbers work just fine," Quadros said. "Objectivity must be upheld."

"Objectivity is for physicists," Vanderhoff insisted. "We deal in the study of life; surely a little subjectivity is allowable, even desirable, in our field. A biologist should never forget he is a biological organism himself—don't you agree, Mr. Grissom?"

Grissom blinked. "I think," he said carefully, "that all science stems from a desire for knowledge. And that's a very . . . *human* characteristic."

Quadros shook his head vehemently. "I can't believe I'm hearing this. We study *arthropods,* do we not? The biological equivalent of machines. They have no psychology, no culture, no advanced cognitive functions. Seeing them through the filter of human experience does nothing but distort data."

Vanderhoff grinned, clearly enjoying himself. "You are even more passionate in person than online, Dr. Quadros. Quite the contradiction, considering that what you're arguing for is the cool, detached perspective of objectivity."

Quadros's scowl deepened, then broke into a grudging smile. "Hah! You're right, Nathan. Damn it, you can always get me going."

"And speaking of going," Grissom said, checking his watch, "it's getting late. Shall we?"

"You two go ahead," Vanderhoff said. "I've got a few things to do."

* * *

"Never could resist a dare," Nick said. He took out a penlight and prodded the bag with one end.

The bag moved.

Nick jumped and Riley took a step back. It wasn't so much the suddenness of the movement as the quality; the bag *squirmed*.

"What the hell?" Nick said. "What's in there, a snake?"

"No way," said Riley. "I saw the outline of legs. Lots of tiny little legs."

"Cockroaches, maybe?" said Brass. "Though the way it's moving does seem kind of snake-like."

"You're right, Grissom is gonna hate missing this," said Nick. "Okay, whatever's in there, we've got to get it or them out. I've got an idea."

Nick fitted a large clear evidence bag over the first one and sealed it with duct tape. He made a small incision in the top of the second bag with a scalpel, then inserted the scalpel through the hole and used it to slash an opening in the bag beneath. He pulled the scalpel out quickly and slapped a duct tape patch over the hole in the outer bag. "Come out, come out, whatever you are," Nick muttered.

A second later, something did.

Two long feelers attached to a black head the size of a pea tested the air. A second later, a segmented black body fringed with orange legs flowed out of the hole, followed a second later by another. And another. And another.

"Centipedes?" Riley said.

"Millipedes, I think," Nick said. "Grissom would know for sure." He sniffed the air. "You smell that? Almonds."

"Cyanide?" Riley said. "So our suicide poisoned himself, sealed a bag full of bugs around his head, then cuffed himself to the bed?"

"Whatever this is," Nick said, "it's no suicide." He pulled out his cell phone and hit a button.

"Who you calling?" Brass asked.

"Who do you think?" Nick said. "If I didn't let him know about this he'd bust me back down to a level one. Hello, Grissom? Yeah, I thought you'd be up. Listen, there's something you're gonna want to see . . ."

"Really?" Grissom said. "Can you describe them?" He listened for a moment, then said, "Yes, you're right, it's probably best if I see for myself. Thanks, Nick. I'll be there shortly." He closed his cell phone and put it back in his pocket.

"It sounds as if you're leaving us," Nathan Vanderhoff said. He, Grissom, and Jake Soames sat at a table in one of Vegas's quieter lounges, the torch singer having just finished her set and left the small stage. Grissom didn't generally avail himself of such places, but he'd heard good things about the performer—plus, his colleagues had pestered him to take them out and show them around his town. Being wide awake despite the hour—one of the perils of night-shift work—Grissom had given in.

He was actually enjoying himself; he didn't get the chance to talk shop with fellow entomologists face-to-face very often.

"I'm afraid so," said Grissom. "Work."

"You told me you were off for the whole of the conference," said Soames. "You're not just ditching us, are you, Gilly?"

"I'm not actually on the clock," Grissom admitted. "This is more of a personal interest."

"Nobody you know, I hope," said Vanderhoff.

"Not exactly. More like a species I'm familiar with."

That got their attention. "Oh?" said Soames. "Flies? Maggots?"

Vanderhoff shook his head. "They wouldn't bother him for something so mundane. Beetles? Something poisonous, perhaps?"

"I'm not sure," said Grissom, getting to his feet. "But it's definitely unusual."

"Unusual?" said Soames. "Oh, no, mate. You can't do that to us. That's like dangling a nice plump rabbit before a croc and then snatching it away."

"I can't really talk about an active police investigation."

"We're not asking for gossip," said Vanderhoff. "We understand the need for discretion. But we *are* your colleagues—couldn't you share a few details in a purely professional sense?"

Grissom hesitated. Many were the times he'd

discovered some particularly fascinating aspect of bug life related to a case and either had no one to share it with or had been met with raised eyebrows and squeamishness when he brought it up. "I'll see what I can do," he said. "I can't promise anything, but I might be able to discuss the insects themselves. In a purely scientific way, of course."

"Good enough," Soames declared. "Go get 'em, Gil. Bring us back some juicy tales tomorrow."

"Yes," said Vanderhoff. "Do return with something interesting . . ."

Grissom showed his CSI ID to the uniform at the door and stepped into the motel room. He hadn't brought his kit, but he had slipped on a pair of gloves as a precaution.

"Knew you couldn't stay away," said Brass. "Pay up, newbie." He held out his hand to Riley.

"I'll get you later," said Riley.

Grissom raised an eyebrow at her. "You bet against me?"

"Against you driving to a fleabag motel in the middle of the night on your own time? Seemed like a pretty safe bet to me."

Behind her, Nick Stokes tried to suppress a chuckle. Grissom gave him a look. Nick suddenly found something very interesting to examine on the other side of the room, though he didn't bother getting rid of the wide grin on his face. He'd known Grissom a long time.

Grissom nodded hello at Dr. Robbins, then approached the bed. They'd removed the bag from the head and transferred the millipedes to a plastic evidence container with holes punched in the top. Grissom ignored the bugs and studied the corpse's face instead.

"Gris?" said Nick. "Creepy-crawlies are over here." He tapped on the lid of the evidence container that stood on the table next to him.

"They're probably *Harpaphe haydeniana,*" said Grissom. He pulled a penlight out of his pocket and shone it on the vic's face. He looked like a high school or college student, his hair brown and cut short. His skin was a bright pink.

"You know that without looking?" said Riley. She sounded skeptical.

"I could be wrong," Grissom admitted. "But the color of the skin and the petechial hemorrhaging in the eyes point to death by cyanide poisoning. *Harpaphe haydeniana* are more commonly known as cyanide millipedes, because they emit hydrogen cyanide gas as a defense mechanism. They're common in the rain forests of the Northwest, but not in Nevada."

"So the bugs were actually the murder weapon?" Brass asked. "Means he and they were sharing that bag while he was still alive. Nasty."

"It's like a killing jar in reverse," said Grissom.

"Killing jar?" said Brass.

"It's what entomologists call the container they

put specimens in—specimens they don't want alive. It has a thin layer of plaster of paris on the bottom as the absorbent substrate for whatever poison is used. These days, chloroform or ether is the most common—but some collectors will actually use these very same millipedes to generate cyanide gas. You have an ID?"

"Keenan Harribold," said Riley. "Found his wallet in his jeans. Pile of clothes at the side of the bed. He's seventeen, goes to Plain Ridge High. I've got a cell phone, too—looks like the last place he called was home."

"Desk clerk—and I use the term *clerk* loosely—was no help," Brass said. "Name in the register is L. W. Smith. Doesn't remember anything about the guy—it could have been our boy here or someone else."

Grissom scanned the room. "A teenage boy in a motel room—any sign of alcohol, drugs, or condoms?"

"Yeah, found a brand-new box of pre-lubricated love gloves in his pocket," said Nick. "Looks like he came prepared to party. Didn't happen, though—no sign of sexual activity."

"Whoever he was meeting had a very different agenda than he did," said Riley. "And they didn't leave much behind, either. We've been through this room and the bathroom and found nothing. Neither the soap nor the water glasses have been used."

"So our killer probably wasn't staying here," said Grissom. "This location was probably chosen for its privacy. Easier to control someone young and strong—he could have threatened him with a weapon to get him to put on the cuffs."

"And then bagged and bugged him," said Riley.

"Yes," said Grissom. "A very deliberate—if un-usual—way to kill someone. The killer obviously has some knowledge of entomology."

"Sorry, Grissom," said Brass, "but I'll have to take you in now. You had a good run, but your homicidal tendencies have finally gotten the better of you. Thanks for making it so easy, though—I ap-preciate it."

"It's the least I could do," said Grissom. "The thing is, while normally I'd agree with you about the identity of your prime suspect, at the moment I'm not the only one in town who holds those par-ticular qualifications . . ."

"Damn," Greg Sanders said, turning on the AC of the Denali. "It's gonna be a hot one today."

"Yeah," Catherine Willows agreed. "Sun's only been up an hour and it's already over a hundred degrees. But look at the bright side—we're almost at the end of our shift."

"There's something seriously wrong with work-ing graveyards and still being at risk for sunburn."

"Baseball hat and sunglasses, Greg." She tapped the brim of her own cap. "Also useful for hiding bad hair and bags under your eyes."

She checked the dashboard GPS and then pulled

off the highway onto a narrow dirt road. They were a few miles west of the city, the terrain uneven and rocky. They hadn't gone far when Greg spotted the telltale blue-and-red flashing lights of a parked cruiser.

The coroner's wagon was already there. David Phillips, the assistant coroner, was talking to a tall black officer, both of them drinking coffee from paper cups.

Catherine parked. "Hey, David," she said as they got out. "What do we have, guys?"

The officer nodded at both of them. "Well, it's a little strange—"

"Uh, do you mind if I explain it?" David interjected. He smiled a little nervously. "It's just—I probably won't get a chance to do this again."

The officer shook his head. "Be my guest."

"What's up, Dave?" Greg said. "You got something special for us?"

"You could say that." David smiled. "Okay, first thing I have to tell you is that I'm pretty sure our vic is a Pacific Islander." He motioned for the CSIs to follow him as he led them around a house-sized outcropping of granite. "And the second is that he's probably a virgin."

Catherine mock-frowned as she walked along, her CSI kit in one hand. "Virgin as in the Virgin Islands? Or as in—"

They rounded the corner and all of them stopped.

"—virgin sacrifice," Greg finished.

Only one arm and the head of the body were visible. The hand ended in five red stumps—his fingers were gone. The rest of the corpse was embedded in a mass of pitted black rock with veins of vivid scarlet running through it. A thick scarlet sludge was edging its way across the desert floor, bits of black matter floating on top.

"Lava," Greg said. "This guy was killed by his own personal volcano, in the middle of the Nevada desert."

"Kind of looks that way, doesn't it?" David said.

"But looks," said Catherine, "can be deceiving." She crouched down beside the slowly spreading ooze and stuck a gloved finger in it. She pulled it out again, then rubbed her finger and thumb together. "This isn't lava—unless you're talking about the lamp variety. It's wax."

"Right," Greg said. "Only the stuff in the sun is running. I guess that black stuff isn't hardened magma, either."

"Pretty weird, huh?" David said. "Hiker found him. No obvious COD, but there's a large contusion on his forehead."

Catherine walked around the semicircular pool of wax, getting as close as she could to the body without walking on the wax itself. She bent down and studied the corpse while Greg began to take pictures. "I think you're right about him being a Pacific Islander," she said. "Could be a hotel worker."

Greg nodded. "Yeah, there's a big Hawaiian population in Vegas—some people even call it the ninth island. You know those ABC Stores you see in Vegas? Those are based out of Hawaii."

Catherine examined the ground. "Guess they have a lot of experience with tourism . . . I've got some tire marks here. Looks like a truck, maybe an SUV. I'm thinking this is just a dump site."

"Or," Greg said, "the remains of a luau gone horribly wrong . . ."

2

GREG TOOK CASTS of the tire marks. He remembered the first time Warrick Brown had shown him how to do it.

"All right, that's a good consistency," Warrick had said. "You don't want it too thin or it'll crumble on you. And don't use the same stuff you'd use for a shoe print—those come in two-pound bags, and you'll wind up without enough coverage. You want a tire cast to be three feet long, minimum. Dental stone is best; don't use plaster of paris. Takes about thirty minutes to set—don't rush it. You want a cast with a high compressive strength, one that won't fall apart on you when you clean it."

"Okay, I got it. How strong is this stuff, anyway?"

"Nine thousand pounds per square inch, give or take."

"Wow. That's pretty strong."

Warrick had given one of his wry smiles. "Just make sure you do it right the first time," he said. "Worry about the strength of your evidence, not the materials you're using. When you're casting a track, you only get one shot."

One shot.
Greg made sure he did it right.

They moved the body, wax and all, to the lab to be processed. Once it was there, Catherine checked it for prints but had no luck. "Too bad," she said. "Wax holds a print really well. But before we can do anything else, we have to get all this wax *off*. Suggestions?"

Greg crossed his arms and studied the large, waxy mound in front of them. "Heat lamps?" he said. "We can raise the temperature just enough to melt the wax and then collect and process all the runoff."

"Sounds good. Let's make it happen."

They positioned four large lamps over the body. "Kind of like an Easy-Bake Oven," said Greg.

Catherine gave him an amused glance. "And how would you know about Easy-Bake Ovens? Shouldn't you have been playing with *Star Wars* figures?"

"Hey, it was one of my first pieces of forensic equipment. You could bake more than cakes in it, you know."

"I don't think I want to, actually."

It went fairly quickly. Before too long they could pry open the vic's pockets; they didn't find any ID but did get a crumpled receipt.

"It's from the ABC Store on the Strip," said Greg. "Looks like he bought some dried green mango at around two thirty this morning."

"So he died sometime after that." Catherine took off her lab coat and hung it up.

"Where are you going?" asked Greg.

"You can babysit the wax man while he melts. I'm going to go talk to whoever sold him the snack food."

At first glance, the ABC Store looked like any other Vegas souvenir shop; lots of T-shirts, key chains, and baseball hats up front, most of them emblazoned with the Vegas logo or something related: dice, cards, even the name of a popular TV show set there. Catherine picked up a hat and checked the tag on the inside: MADE IN CHINA.

"Nothing like a genuine Las Vegas memento," she muttered to herself.

Toward the back of the store, though, the merchandise underwent a definite shift. Suddenly she was surrounded by old-fashioned ham jerky, Maui-style potato chips, and more products featuring macadamia nuts than she'd known existed.

"Excuse me," she said, walking up to the cashier. "I'm Catherine Willows, with the Las Vegas Crime Lab. Were you working last night?"

The clerk, a sleepy-looking woman with jet-black hair and dusky skin, nodded. "Still am, in fact. Day guy phoned in sick, so I'm pulling a double."

"My condolences. Do you remember this guy? Came in around two thirty, bought some dried green mango?" She showed the woman a photo of the vic.

"Uh-huh. He seemed pretty wired, made me kind of nervous. Paid with a hundred-dollar bill."

"You know who he is? He ever been in here before?"

She shrugged. "Not that I can remember. He was a *kanaka*, fo'shua. Said he had to get some of that green mango ono. I told him get choke, we ain't gonna run out—*haole* never buy 'em."

"I'm sorry?"

"You no speak pidgin, brah?" She smiled. "Hawaiian slang. He was from the islands, you know? Had a craving for the mango—I told him we had plenty, the tourists never buy it."

"Ah. You remember if he was on foot or in a vehicle?"

"Sorry, I didn't notice."

She talked to the clerk for a few more minutes but didn't learn anything else. The woman said, "Aloha," when Catherine left.

"As you can see," Doc Robbins said to Catherine, "cause of death was asphyxiation." The body of the Pacific Islander lay open on the autopsy table. Robbins had just cut into one of the lungs, revealing it was packed solid with red wax.

"Like an inside-out version of Madame Tussauds," Catherine said. "He must have been completely immersed in the stuff."

"I'd have to concur. I found it in his nose, his throat, even his ear canals—though those generate their own, of course."

"We didn't find the fingers, but the cuts looked clean. Postmortem?"

"Definitely. The other hand—the one completely encased in wax—was intact, so we've still got prints."

"The killer was probably trying to hide the vic's identity but lacked either the time or the tools to dig through the wax and finish the job. How about the contusion on his forehead?"

"Not just a contusion—a burn. He was struck with something both hard and hot. I took a closer look and pulled this out of the subcutaneous layer." Robbins handed her a small clear evidence vial.

Catherine took it and studied what it held: a small black sliver, no more than half an inch long. "I'll get it to Trace. Any idea what it is?"

"Well, it seems to be a shard of mineral or metal, which doesn't support my first guess." He paused.

"And that would be?" Catherine prompted.

"A wick."

Catherine rolled her eyes. "Somebody told you to switch from rock and roll to comedy, Doc?"

Robbins shrugged. "At least it wasn't a pun. I found something else interesting when I X-rayed the body—take a look at this." He limped over to the light box on the wall and pointed. "See this? He's got a cyst growing on his spine—it's called a syrinx."

"Cancerous?"

"No, from the condition of the surrounding vertebrae I'd say it was caused by an injury, possibly a car accident or a fall. Not a recent one, though—from its size, I'd estimate the syrinx was between six and eight months old."

"What sort of symptoms would that produce?"

"It's possible he wasn't even aware of it. Many syrinxes generate no symptoms at all for months or even years; then they can produce pain, weakness, numbness, and sensory impairment—especially the ability to detect heat or cold with the extremities. Advanced cases can affect sweating, sexual function, and bowel and bladder control."

"Sounds nasty."

"Even . . . wick-ed?"

She sighed. "I'll see you later, Doc."

Greg ran the tire prints through the database. He'd found marks from both the front and rear tires, which gave him a wheelbase; that combined with the tread told him he was looking for a 1994 Ford F150 Supercab truck.

He caught up with Catherine in the hall outside the main lab and told her what he'd found.

"Well, I just got the tox screen," she said. "Our vic was high on meth when he went to that great tiki bar in the sky. And Post found a shard of something stuck in his forehead. Looks like he took a smack to the noggin before going volcano diving." She told Greg about the wax in the vic's lungs.

"That's a lot of wax," he said. "What was this guy doing, running his own candle factory?"

"You might not be too far off. Wax is used in a number of industrial applications—especially in manufacturing."

"And those waxes tend to have very specific for-mulations," said Greg. "Find the formulation and we can find out what this was supposed to be used for—and hopefully where it came from. I'm on it."

Catherine got an AFIS hit on the vic's fingerprints almost immediately: Hal Kanamu. He'd been ar-rested for possession of methamphetamine two years ago in Honolulu, but his current driver's license listed an address in Vegas. She jotted it down, then went to find David Hodges.

Hodges looked up from his microscope as she walked in. "Don't tell me," he said. "You're here about the shard found in Don Ho's skull."

"Hal Kanamu's skull, actually. Can you tell me what it is?"

"Sure. What's big and hot and likes to blow its top?"

She grinned despite herself. "It's volcanic?"

"Yes, indeed. Nevada is littered with deposits of volcanic rock, due to its geologic history. You know how tectonic plates push against each other and create mountains in the middle? Our whole state is like that in reverse—we're being pulled apart. That makes all kinds of interesting things rise to the surface, some of them volcanic. The black rocks of the Black Rock Desert are, in fact, obsidian—and so is this shard."

Catherine nodded. "Any chance you could narrow its origin down a little further?"

Hodges knew how to smirk and chose that moment to prove it. "As a matter of fact, I think I can. Think of a volcano as a giant pot of chili; the ingredients are all the different kinds of minerals that are melting and mixing together. There are a lot of different kinds of chili in the world, but every cook has his or her own favorite recipe."

"Analyze the ingredients and you can ID the chef?"

"Not only that, I may be able to tell you which batch this came from. Individual eruptions produce individual results." Hodges got a dreamy look on his face. "I have very fond memories of a batch I produced in the fall of '06. Fiery, but with a lovely creamy consistency."

She raised her eyebrows. "You made . . . lava?"

"What? No, chili. I still have some frozen at home—I know fresh is best, but when you produce something of that quality it's hard to let it go."

"Uh-huh. I'll talk to you later, Hodges."

Catherine joined Greg in the lab. "Any luck on the wax?"

"Yes and no. I ran it through the GC mass spec, and here's what came out." He handed her several sheets of paper.

She scanned the one on top, then the next, and frowned. "This isn't wax—this is *soup*."

"I know. Wax comes in three basic varieties. I'll give you . . . twenty-one tries to ID them."

"Animal, mineral, and vegetable?"

"Exactly. Animal waxes come from bees and other insects, sheep wool, and the foreheads of sperm whales—hey, did you know that no one knows exactly why sperm whales are full of the stuff? Up to three tons per whale, and the best guess is that it helps them control their buoyancy. People used to think it was actually sperm, which is where the name comes from—"

"Greg."

"Sorry. Vegetable wax comes from certain palms, Mexican shrubs, Japanese berries, African reeds, rice bran, and jojoba trees. Mineral waxes are derived from petrochemical sources like lignite. There are also synthetic waxes made from long-chain fatty acids, but I left those out because they spoiled the punch line."

"And which of these did our fake lava contain?"

"Most of them. Well, not the sperm whale wax—that's been mainly replaced by the jojoba tree—but a good eighty percent of the others are present. That doesn't correspond to any industrial process I know of."

"No, but it does remind me of something else," said Catherine. "Not so much soup . . . as chili."

Greg grinned and shook his head. "Okay, I'll go with the flow. Why chili?"

"Something Hodges said. Some cooks try to throw in every possible ingredient, and apparently Mother Nature's one of them. Real lava is a mix of many different elements."

"So our magma maker was trying to mimic the actual geologic process? When I was in school, we just used vinegar and baking soda."

"Accuracy is clearly important to someone. How about the black flecks embedded in the wax?"

"Ash from charred paper. I found a couple of chunks that weren't completely carbonized—they had a high lignin content."

"Newsprint. Probably old newspapers or flyers."

"Yeah, and almost impossible to trace. We'll have better luck with the wax."

"I guess we need to see how many local manu-facturers use wax in their business—"

Greg offered her another sheet of paper before she could finish. "One step ahead. Cosmetics, in-dustrial casting, waterproofing for cardboard boxes, food producers . . . and a whole lot more."

Catherine scanned the new list with a frown. "Terrific. There's even a ranch on here."

"Yeah. The butcher, the baker, and the candle-stick maker—I'm just glad we don't have to visit a whaling ship."

*　　*　　*

There were times that Catherine appreciated being a CSI level 3. For one thing, it meant that she could delegate canvassing the local wax-using industries to Greg, while she concentrated on Hal Kanamu's apartment.

According to records she'd dug up, Kanamu had been briefly employed as a busboy when he first moved to Vegas six months ago. If he'd been employed by a hotel or casino since then, she couldn't find any record of it. She didn't know what he'd been doing, but the forwarding address the hotel gave her for his last paycheck surprised her: the Braun Suites, a set of luxury apartments often used by celebrities when they were in town. Catherine knew the hotel often comped those suites to high rollers.

Her CSI ID was enough for security to let her into the suite, and the fact that she was Sam Braun's daughter didn't hurt, either. Sam had been one of the Vegas giants, a casino owner renowned as much for his connections as his wealth; she hadn't known him when she was growing up, but he'd done his best to connect with her before he died.

"Well, well, Mr. Kanamu," she murmured to herself as she stepped inside. "Quite the upgrade in living accommodations. You must have been one hell of a busboy."

The suite was large and opulent, with an impressive view of the Strip through a glass wall that ran the entire length of the main living area. A padded conversation pit in the middle of the room held a round gas fireplace in its center, a wet bar made entirely of chrome and Lucite gleamed to one side, and the flat screen on the wall was the size of a garage door. It was on, too, cycling through a slide show; shots of Kanamu's native Hawaii, it looked like. The brilliant greens and bright blues painted the room in vacation Technicolor, a more evolved version of motel neon.

The room was neat and clean; clearly the maid had been in recently. That was bad news as far as evidence went, but she knew from experience that the cleaning staff didn't always get everything. Though the level of service at the Braun Suites was high, guests who stayed for extended periods often designated certain areas off-limits. No matter how nice the hotel, it was still a hotel—people needed to claim personal space in order to make it a home.

The suite's bedroom featured a hot tub, king-size bed, and walk-in closet. It was just as clean as the living room but revealed more of Kanamu's personality; rock-climbing gear was piled in a corner, an expensive camera sat on the nightstand, and Catherine was pretty sure the three poster-sized, framed photographs on the walls hadn't been put there by the hotel.

She studied the closest picture. It had apparently been taken at night, and the subject was a robot giraffe with a huge fireball erupting from its mouth.

The next was of a woman wearing only an elaborate horned headdress, stilts so tall they extended past the bottom of the photo, and body paint accented with glitter; the artist had used an astronomy theme, swirling galaxies and fiery comets chasing themselves across the woman's body. She was framed against a perfect blue sky, no clouds or horizon visible.

The third was the outline of some sort of temple in the distance, rising out of a thick cloud of mist. In the foreground, a man wearing a gas mask and a huge pair of white angel wings stood with his arms extended.

She found what she was looking for in the walk-in closet, which Kanamu had turned into a small office. A desk at one end held a laptop, and a comfortable chair was parked in front of it.

She turned on the laptop and wasn't surprised when it asked her for a password. *Only one reason a man locks himself in a tiny room with no windows and a laptop: porn.*

No wastepaper basket, though. She opened the top drawer of the desk, expecting Kleenex and a bottle of hand lotion—and found something else instead.

Plain Ridge High School in North Las Vegas enrolled just under three thousand students. It had slightly more male students than female; 40 percent of its student body was white, 12 percent black, 15 percent Asian, and 33 percent Hispanic. Its chess club regularly placed in the state finals, it had a drama department fond of producing all-Spanish versions of Shakespeare plays, and its sports program included soccer, volleyball, baseball, basketball, and bowling.

But none of those activities compared to football.

Plain Ridge High's long-standing rivalry was with Carston High, located only a few blocks away. While the two schools competed in almost every possible arena, their most fervent battles were always on the gridiron. In past years, both schools had been subject to toilet papering, mascot stealing, trash-talking graffiti, and the occasional brawl due to the intense rivalry between the Plain Ridge Rockets and the Carston Enforcers. Blood had been spilled before, both on and off the field, and would be again.

But nobody at either school knew just how much.

Keenan Harribold had been their star player. Only hours after his death, graffiti was discovered sprayed on the exterior wall of Plain Ridge High's gymnasium. It provoked anger from the students and concern from the faculty; while scrawled obscenities were nothing new, death threats were. The administration of both schools agreed to a meeting later that day to discuss the situation and decide what to do about it.

The news of Keenan Harribold's death surfaced midmorning. It spread throughout Plain Ridge High like a shockwave, followed closely by a surge of rising fury.

Bad news always traveled faster than good. The students at Carston knew about the murder almost as soon as the ones at Plain Ridge did, and expressed shock, dismay, and a complete denial of responsibility. Despite their historic rivalry, there were still friendships that linked students at both schools; a flurry of cell phone calls as intense as any high-level diplomatic negotiations followed. They were not successful.

As a result, the retaliatory attack was anticipated, though not prepared for. Then again, the mob of students from Plain Ridge—around a thousand strong, a good 30 percent of the student body—was not highly organized, either.

But they were angry.

"It's on," Tyler Pullam said to Ryan Dill. The noon bell had just rung. "They're on their way." He'd just come from PE, and he'd brought a baseball bat with him. Alarms vibrated in the social web, but no one had informed any of the teachers; the social dynamics at work were primitive, violent, and instinctive. The colony was under attack.

Ryan and Tyler were two of the students who rushed outside as the mob approached; they were joined by hundreds others. People had grabbed bats, two-by-fours from the wood shop, tire irons; some of them had knives.

The two groups converged. War had begun.

Grissom was eating breakfast at a diner when the phrase "student at Plain Ridge High School" caught his ear. He asked the waitress to turn up the television and for another cup of tea.

"—bizarre twist to this tragedy," the anchorwoman said. Her solemn face was replaced by a shot of a white concrete wall with a message spray-painted on it in bright crimson: HOW YOU GONNA WIN WITH A DEAD QUARTERBACK? "This graffiti was found on the wall of the Plain Ridge High School gymnasium, only hours before Keenan Harribold, the starting quarterback for the Plain Ridge Rockets, was found dead in a Las Vegas motel room. News quickly spread throughout the school, leading to an impromptu march at noon to nearby Carston High, Plain Ridge's longtime rival in many areas, including football."

Jittery amateur footage replaced the graffiti shot. It showed a horde of angry teenagers rampaging through the hallway of a school, tearing posters from walls, smashing glass, and attacking other students. Some carried baseball bats.

"The riot lasted half an hour and resulted in multiple injuries, including three knifings and one shooting. Eleven people are in the hospital this afternoon, three of them in serious condition, though no fatalities have been reported at this time. So far, the police have declined to give any details concerning Harribold's death."

Grissom finished his tea, paid the bill, and left.

Nick Stokes wasn't crazy about bugs.

This had less to do with any sense of squeamishness than the fact that he'd once been buried alive by a psycho with a grudge against the Las Vegas Crime Lab. The crate he'd been buried in had been sealed up tight—but not tight enough to prevent it from being invaded by fire ants. Nightmares had woken him up for months afterward, his skin burning with phantom bites that had long since faded from his body. He wasn't too fond of enclosed spaces after that, either.

The experience had marked him on a deeper level than just the physical, and now he found certain cases affected him, maybe more than they should. When he'd seen what had crawled out of that bag, he couldn't help but imagine what the boy's last moments had been like. Blind, suffocating, feeling the maddening tickle of a hundred legs crawling over your face and through your hair . . .

Grissom had known immediately that no one would choose to commit suicide in such a way, and so had Nick. The reason Nick was now searching Keenan Harribold's bedroom wasn't because he thought he'd find giant posters of millipedes on his wall and a pile of *Insect Hill* brochures on his bedside table; it was to try to glean some kind of clue about who would want to kill him.

The room was pretty typical for a teenage boy into sports: posters of girls in bikinis on the walls, a trophy on a bookshelf, an unmade bed, and piles of clothes on the floor. A small desk under the window held a stack of homework and a closed laptop.

Nick pulled out the wooden chair in front of the desk, sat down, and opened the laptop. It came to life immediately, still online.

"Looks like you weren't too careful about security," Nick murmured. "Let's see what you were up to . . ."

A few minutes sorting through Keenan's e-mails led Nick to something interesting: a message from someone named LW.

"Really looking forward to seeing you tonight," Nick read out loud. "I hope you're as hot in person as you are in your pictures."

There were more messages stored, all of them telling the same story of an online seduction. There were pictures, too, of a young and pretty blonde standing outside different Vegas landmarks: the Bellagio fountains, the MGM Grand, the Luxor. There was nothing terribly racy in any of them, nothing to suggest that they were anything but genuine.

Nick knew better. Photos were easy to find and copy on the Net, and wholesome teenage girls didn't lure you to a Vegas motel room and kill you with poisonous bugs. Usually.

He backtracked through the e-mails by date until he found their point of origin: a dating site. LW had her own page, with an extensive list of interests, hobbies, favorite movies, and music she liked. Nick found a page for Keenan Harribold, too; not surprisingly, his interests and LW's synched up nicely.

The e-mails went back six weeks. *So you stalked him online*, Nick thought. *Got into his head, designed the perfect lure. Took your time, didn't overplay your hand. And when Keenan was confident you were the real thing, you set up a meeting.*

Nick closed the laptop, unplugged it, and bagged it as evidence, even though he'd probably already learned all it had to tell him. The real trail didn't begin at the laptop, or even in Keenan's bedroom; it began in the vast electronic tangle of the Internet, where a predator had spun his own very specialized web designed to snare Keenan Harribold.

Grissom squinted at the program booklet while waiting for the next presentation to start. Most of the seats in the room were empty, the spotlight on the lectern at the front the brightest point in the room.

"Well," said Vanderhoff, taking a seat next to Grissom, "how did things go?"

"Yes," said Quadros, taking the seat on the other side. "Nathan has been telling me about you mysteriously disappearing in the middle of the night. Most intriguing."

"It was . . . unusual," Grissom admitted. "Though I'm not sure it's appropriate for me to comment further."

"Why?" Quadros demanded. "We are all men of science. Surely you're not afraid we're going to steal your data?"

Vanderhoff shook his head. "Now, Roberto, you know that's not fair. Mr. Grissom has to concern himself with legalities, not just peer review."

"I do not see the problem," said Quadros. "In São Paulo, scientific experts are often consulted by the police. Could you not take us into your confidence under the same conditions? I would be happy to sign any necessary document—and, of course, to offer my own expertise." He frowned. "Unless, of course, you feel you *need* no assistance . . ."

Vanderhoff sighed. "Nathan, Nathan—must you make everything about your stubborn pride? Can't you see—"

"Gentlemen," Grissom interjected. "It's not that I don't appreciate the offer. But at this stage of the case, the entomological aspect is fairly straightforward. If I needed help in a difficult classification or in analyzing data, you'd be the first people I'd turn to. I still may—and if that happens, I will ask you to sign forms promising not to share any sensitive information. Is that satisfactory?"

Quadros, somewhat mollified, said, "I suppose."

Vanderhoff raised his eyebrows. "You still may? That sounds promising. Are you expecting more late-night excursions?"

"In Vegas?" said Grissom. "You can count on it."

Jake Soames caught up with Grissom as he was leaving a slide show dealing with the effects of butterfly migration on bird populations. "Gil!"

Grissom stopped. "Hello, Jake. Enjoying the conference?"

"Haven't seen a lot of it so far—too busy enjoying the town. Haven't gotten a lot of sleep yet, if you know what I mean." He winked.

"If you're suffering from jet lag, I'd suggest melatonin. It's quite effective, even in very small doses."

Soames shook his head, then winced. "Ow. Shouldn't do that again, or the bloody thing'll come off. And how was *your* evening after you left?"

"Short. I visited a crime scene, then went to bed."

"All in a night's work, eh? Even when you're not working. Was it worth the trip?"

"I suppose it was. Saw something I've never seen before, in any case."

"Which you can't tell me about, right?"

"Not in any detail, no."

"I seem to always be arriving at the tail end of interesting conversations," Khem Charong said. Today he wore a suit of dark gray with a black tie. "I must endeavor to improve my timing."

"We were just talking about Gil's late-night activities," Soames said. "Got a phone call in the middle of our festivities, disappeared into the night. Seems the Vegas constables can't do their job without him."

Grissom did his best to smile. "It was more of a courtesy call. The people I work with thought I'd appreciate certain . . . *aspects* of the case."

"Oh? Such as?"

Grissom surrendered to the inevitable. "Millipedes. *Harpaphe haydeniana* were found at a crime scene."

Charong tilted his head quizzically. "In a dry, desert climate like this? Very odd."

"You understand that you can't repeat that," said Grissom. "It's confidential information in an ongoing case."

"I'll be the soul of discretion," said Charong.

"And I'll keep my gob shut," said Soames. "Until it's time to pour some more beer down my throat, anyway. What do you say we go get a drink?"

Riley Adams inspected the spray-painted graffiti carefully. She'd already taken numerous photos, and now she scraped off a tiny sample into a collection vial.

The wall was right next to a concrete path, one well traveled in the daytime. There was no convenient security camera nearby or even a light source. No one had seen the vandal.

She sighed. Though she was sure the two sites were connected, the perpetrator had left even less evidence at this scene. All she had was a vague description, a phony name in a motel register, and a bag full of millipedes. Oh, and twenty dollars less in her pocket after she paid off Brass.

She tried to think it through. Kill a football star to start a riot? Maybe, but why use such an esoteric method? The crime had clearly been carefully planned—but was the quarterback the real victim or just a means to an end?

It seemed to her like a revenge killing—the horrific means of murder, the taunting message left behind. She doubted if the rivalry between the two schools really ran that deep—and if it did, there was more at work than sports teams competing.

No shortage of deep-seated hatreds in high school, she thought. *And football players generate more than their share.* Spurned girlfriends, bullied geeks, competitors for the same position . . . if Riley's experience was any indication, Keenan Harribold probably had more enemies in his own school than at Carston High.

But how many of them could be into bugs?

She walked around the building and found the front entrance for the school. It was locked now, but she spotted someone moving around inside and knocked on the glass of the door. The custodian, a heavyset Hispanic man, let her in when she flashed her ID.

"Can you tell me where the science classrooms are, please?"

To her surprise, there was someone in one of them when she got there: a blond man in his thirties sat at the teacher's desk, intent on a pile of papers in front of him.

"Working late?" asked Riley, standing in the doorway.

The man's head jerked up in surprise. "What? Oh, I'm sorry. You startled me."

"I'm Riley Adams, with the Las Vegas Crime Lab. I'm investigating the incident that happened earlier." She walked into the room, looking around and noting details: models of molecules hung from the roof; large colorful posters of the periodic table and solar system were on the walls. In the corner, fluorescent light shone dimly from a glass terrarium with a sand-filled bottom, its only apparent occupant several plastic plants.

"I'm Colin Brady," he said, getting to his feet. "I teach science here."

"My favorite subject," said Riley. "Looks like you're catching up on your marking."

"Trying to." He paused. "I'm sorry, that sounded rude. I just meant I'm *always* trying to catch up— emphasis on the trying, as opposed to succeeding." He smiled. Despite his thinning hair, he looked young for a teacher.

"Yeah, marking is always the worst. I still have bad memories of working as a TA in college." She smiled back.

"How can I help you, uh . . . Detective?"

"Riley is fine. I was wondering if any of your students have ever shown a fascination with insects."

"The first student that comes to mind is Lucas Yannick," Brady said. "He's the one who convinced me to get our emperor scorpion. I wasn't sure at first—high school kids and a poisonous creature are a bad combination—but he told me he'd take personal responsibility for any problems."

"And have there been any?" asked Riley.

"There was one, yes. A few of the kids were horsing around and one of them decided to pick up the scorpion with a pair of forceps and wave it around, try to get the girls screaming. Lucas told him to drop it and when he didn't, he punched the kid in the stomach."

"I see. Who were the other kids who were involved?"

Brady leaned against his desk and crossed his arms. "Let me see . . . It was a while ago, so the details aren't terribly sharp. I'm pretty sure it was a few of the guys on the football team."

"Would that include Keenan Harribold?"

Brady stared at her for a second before answering. "No. No, I'm pretty sure he wasn't involved."

"What kind of student is Lucas otherwise?"

"Very bright. Not terribly social, but he has a small circle of friends he hangs around with."

"Does he get picked on a lot?"

"Not in my classroom. But yeah, he's the kind of

kid who winds up being a target if he isn't careful."

Riley had a little game she liked to play in her head. She called it the WTAA game, and the rules were very simple: she counted how many questions she could ask a subject before she got the question "What's this all about?" or something similar. It didn't matter if she'd started the interview with an explanation for why she was there— sooner or later, anyone trying to project an air of innocence asked it, as if being unable to see the obvious meant they were clearly incapable of any crime. It didn't necessarily mean the person she was talking to had done anything wrong; it was simply an indicator that they were nervous, a common reaction to being questioned by an authority figure.

"I have to ask . . . ," Brady said.

"Yes?"

"Would you like to see our scorpion?"

She blinked. "Okay."

He led her over to the terrarium. Crouched in one corner under one of the plastic plants was a huge black scorpion, its barbed tail curled over its back. It didn't move at their approach; it was so still it could have been made of stone.

"Here's what finally persuaded me," said Brady. He hit a button on the top of the tank, turning off the fluorescent. "Get the lights, will you?"

Riley hesitated, then walked over to the switch beside the door and turned it off. A second later a small UV tube flickered to life in the roof of the terrarium—and suddenly, the black scorpion was no longer there.

It had been replaced by one that glowed an eerie electric blue, like the world's most intricate neon sign. Only the tiniest twitch of its claws told Riley she was looking at a living thing—though it looked more like it belonged in a video game than a classroom.

She got closer and knelt down. "That's pretty amazing," she said.

"Yeah. Younger scorpions don't do it, only adults."

She straightened up. "I guess there are some things kids just aren't ready for . . ."

As Nick expected, LW's dating website page led nowhere. It was hosted by a server in the Philippines, one that wouldn't give him access to its personal files. Not that it mattered—a cursory check of some of the information on LW's page proved she was almost completely fictional. She didn't go to the school she listed, the organizations she said she belonged to had never heard of her, and even the pictures of her looked suspiciously dated when examined closely—Nick spotted the corner of a billboard behind her in one and recognized it as having been from an ad campaign in Vegas at least five years ago. Keenan Harribold would have still been in elementary school.

*   *   *

"Hey, Grissom," said Brass. "Am I interrupting?"

Grissom looked up from his untouched drink. "No, not at all," he said.

Grissom, Nathan Vanderhoff, Jake Soames, and Roberto Quadros were sharing a booth in the hotel lounge. A mediocre comic had just left the stage to scattered applause and widespread indifference.

"Hi," said Brass, smiling at each of them. "Captain Jim Brass." He offered his hand and got an introduction from each of them in turn. "I hate to bother you, Gil," said Brass. "I know you're technically not on the job, but we could really use your help with this one. I mean, come on—this case is tailor-made for you. You're our bug guy."

Soames leaned forward, his eyes bright. "Actually, Captain Brass, at this table we're *all* 'bug guys.' If Gilly is too busy to help, maybe we could."

Brass glanced over at Grissom. "Gilly?"

Grissom gave him a warning look. "My team is perfectly capable of handling the case without me."

"No offense, 'Gilly,'" said Brass, "but your team, good as they are, just doesn't have your expertise when it comes to things that scuttle around and hide under rocks. We need help on this one—I'm almost tempted to take your friend up on his offer."

"And why not?" said Vanderhoff. "I'd also be happy to volunteer my services while I'm in town. Roberto, of course, is far too sophisticated for such an endeavor—"

"Shut up, Nathan. I'm just as interested as the rest of you."

Grissom put up his hands. "All right, I surrender. I'm clearly in the minority here. Jim, if you're that desperate, I suppose my colleagues—and I—are willing to offer our advice. But I warn all of you—forensics work isn't as glamorous as you might imagine."

"Fantastic," said Brass. "Well, this turned out better than I could have hoped. I went out hunting one expert and bagged three."

"Better make it four," said Soames. "Khem will want in, too."

"I'll have the nondisclosure forms drawn up right away," said Brass. "Grissom, can I grab you for a few moments? There're a few details I'd like your take on right away."

Grissom nodded and got up. "Excuse me."

As they walked away, Brass muttered, "Think they bought it?"

"I guess we'll see," said Grissom.

Greg looked around nervously. The gun he gripped in his right hand wasn't his own; it was an old-fashioned six-shot Colt, the kind of long-barrelled revolver Wild Bill Hickock or Wyatt Earp might have owned. It was fully loaded—but then, so was the gun of the man he was hunting.

He leaned against the weather-beaten wall, listening for the crunch of boots on gravel, and tried to get his breathing under control.

Remember your CSI training, Greggo. This guy might think he's a killer, but you've got a fair bit of range time under your belt. Don't get spooked.

A hard voice called out, "Hey! Kid! I'm getting tired of this. You know you don't stand a chance—why don't you just face me and get this over with?"

"If that's the way you want it," Greg called back. "Let's see how good you are . . ."

Greg whirled around the corner, gun held straight ahead of him, already aiming at where the voice had come from. He snapped off a quick shot—

Two bullets slammed into his chest. The first caught him in the breastbone, right over the heart; the second smacked into his shoulder.

As he collapsed, one thought flashed through his mind: *This hurts a lot more than paintball . . .*

3

Grissom studied the body of the millipede with a magnifying glass. He'd hoped to find something that might tell him where the arthropod had originated, some trace on one of its many legs perhaps, but so far his search had proven disappointing.

"So," said Brass, strolling into the lab, "this is the part where you tell me the bug you're examining is found solely in one corner of North Africa and is only eaten by blue-crested finches."

Grissom glanced up. "I'm afraid not. The cyanide millipede is extremely common in the Pacific Northwest, found in forests from California to Alaska. They may not be from around here, but that doesn't mean they're difficult to obtain."

Brass shrugged. "Worth a shot. You really think one of your fellow experts could be our killer?"

Grissom shrugged back. "It's certainly possible. Their presence here at the same time a very singular method of homicide turns up—well, the coincidence seems unlikely."

"Uh-huh." Brass looked away. "And how are you doing? You okay with all this?"

Grissom frowned. "You mean deceiving my colleagues?"

"Yeah, that."

He considered the question for a moment before answering. "Jim, you know as well as I do that any time an outsider tries to involve himself in an investigation that the probability he's who we're looking for shoots up. It's why we take pictures of crowds at arson fires or funerals of homicide victims. Besides, only seven attendees arrived for the conference early—and the alibis of the other three checked out, correct?"

"I know it makes sense. But still—they are your peers."

Grissom shook his head. "That's irrelevant. If one of them is a killer, lying in order to catch him hardly seems like a breach of professional ethics."

"And how about the two—sorry, three—who aren't?"

"They'll have experienced being on the inside of a police investigation into a murder. I doubt they'll be offended." He paused. "Well, maybe Quadros will. He seems a little touchy."

"Which brings me to my next question: how well do you know these guys?"

"Not well, I suppose. I've known Jake Soames for years, but we see each other only at conferences. I've met Khem Charong only twice before.

Nathan Vanderhoff and Roberto Quadros I've only corresponded with online."

"Any of them strike you as the homicidal type?"

"No. But we both know it's hardly ever that easy." Grissom frowned. "I've never understood the psychology of protecting your own social circle at all costs. I've seen it many times—especially in law enforcement—but it still seems counterintuitive. You'd think that if one of your own went bad, you'd see their removal as desirable."

"That's because you have no guilt in your soul," said Brass. "It's a lot easier to chuck rocks when your house isn't made out of glass. And, Grissom, you practically live in a bunker."

"That's not true, Jim." Grissom's frown turned into a wry smile. "You know perfectly well I live in a townhouse."

Greg opened his eyes.

The first thing he saw was a woman standing over him. She wore red cowboy boots, jeans, a plaid shirt, and a red Stetson over long, honey-colored hair.

"Are . . . are you an angel?" said Greg.

The woman grinned, then turned and called over her shoulder, "Hey, Neal! I think you musta shot him in the head!"

"Nah, Miss Tracy. I got him right in the ticker. Twice."

Greg propped himself up on an elbow and

pulled off the protective mask that covered his face. "Technically, you only got me once in the heart. Your other shot was wide."

The man who'd shot him strolled up, twirling his own six-gun on one finger. He was dressed much the same as the woman but favored black over red; that included a black leather vest, a black hat, and a ferociously bushy black mustache. "Technically? Kid, dead is dead. Ain't nothin' technical 'bout it—the word you want is *technique*. As in mine is unbeatable and yours just got beat."

"All right, you got me," Greg admitted as he got to his feet. "But to be fair, I'm not used to this gun. If I'd been using my own, things would have been different."

"Mebbe," Neal said. "Guess we'll never know."

Greg glanced around. He, Neal, and Miss Tracy stood in the middle of a broad, dusty street. Ramshackle wooden buildings lined either side, with hitching posts outside most of them. "Wind's picking up," said Tracy. "Reckon we should head indoors."

"Lead on," said Greg.

"Indoors" was the interior of a 2005 Suncruiser Winnebago, complete with kitchen, shower, and satellite TV system. It was decorated in an Old West motif: knotty pine wallpaper, antique table and chairs, saloon doors in the hall between the bedrooms and the living area. Tracy sat down at the table, while Neal put on some coffee.

"I gotta say," said Greg, "that when I got up today I didn't expect to be getting shot. Even by wax bullets while wearing a vest—which, by the way, is more painful than I expected."

Tracy chuckled. She was a tall, rangy woman with a spray of freckles across her nose. "Well, you said you wanted to know what it was like. Now you do."

"Yes, I do," Greg said ruefully. "But it was worth it—how many times does a guy get a chance to actually play cowboy?"

"If you're us," said Neal, "all the time." He drew his pistol, twirled it around in a complicated and impressive way, then stuck it back in its holster.

"Quit showing off," said Tracy. "You already killed him, remember?"

Neal nodded, looking pleased with himself. "Don't take it too hard, kid. I spend as much time practicing my draw as you probably do flossing your teeth."

"To give you a proper answer," said Tracy, "the Quick Shooters Society does not actually endorse shooting cowboys. In fact, we'd probably get in a fair bit of trouble for what we just did, so we'd appreciate it if you didn't spread that around. Gunfights are fun, but they're dangerous unless you know what you're doing. Mostly we shoot at targets."

"Fair enough. Now that we've gotten that out of the way, how about telling me about your ammo?"

Tracy nodded. "We use wax bullets, loaded with black or smokeless powder for the primer. Once the bullet's pressed into place, you stick a shotgun primer into the hole that's been countersunk at the base of the shell."

"Or you could use a twenty-two blank," said Neal. "There, the hole's drilled off to one side—twenty-two's a rimfire."

"Okay. Now, the bullets themselves—you two make them in bulk, right?"

"Sure," said Tracy. "Have a nice little mail-order business going. Approved by the World Fast Draw Association and the CSS. Wax bullets are cheap and easy to make—we turn 'em out by the hundreds."

"And they make you a whole lot less dead if you accidentally shoot yourself while trying out a fancy new draw," said Neal. "They don't penetrate walls, so you can even use 'em indoors."

"Can I see where you make them?"

"Follow me, greenhorn," said Neal.

He led Greg out of the RV and to a wooden shack in a little better shape than most of the other buildings; it had a hand-lettered sign over the door that read BLACKSMITH. Inside, cartons of cardboard boxes labeled PARAFFIN were stacked against one wall, while a pair of propane camp stoves with several large iron pots on them rested on a plain wooden table. The casts for the bullets were on another table, just two long wooden boards clamped together with a row of holes drilled along the seam so that the bullets could be removed easily when the boards were unclamped.

"We like to keep it simple," said Neal.

"Ever had any of your wax stolen?"

Neal shook his head. "By who? Candle rustlers?"

"How about the excess? How do you get rid of it?"

"What excess? The only thing that gets lost is a few scrapings here and there, and we just sweep 'em up and put 'em back in the pot. About all that goes to waste are the shards that spray when the slug hits a target—and even that mostly sticks to the surface; we scrape off what we can and reuse it."

Greg sighed. "Thanks for your time. Looks like *all* I'm doing today is shooting blanks . . ."

"Greg," said Catherine. "How'd your field trip go?"

Greg groaned and sank into a chair next to the layout table. "I'll never be able to watch *The Karate Kid* again. Wax on, wax off, wax up and down and inside out. I now know far more about the furniture polish, artificial fruit, and turbine-blade industries than I ever wanted to."

"And?"

"No leads. My best guess is that our lava cook was scavenging leftovers from industrial Dumpsters— wax isn't terribly toxic stuff, so regulations concerning its disposal are pretty lax. Lax on wax, those are the facts."

"Well, I just got back from Kanamu's residence—and it wasn't what I expected." She told him about the suite.

"So," Greg said, "Kanamu obviously moved up in the world in the last six months. Any idea how?"

"Nothing obvious. I did find these, though."

She looked down at the objects on the layout table: a small butane torch, a pill bottle, and a glass pipe, the bubble at one end charred from use.

Greg straightened up in his chair. "A meth pipe. Well, we already knew he was a user."

Catherine picked up the pill bottle. "Triazolam."

"A benzodiazepine? Lot of meth heads use it to ease their comedown."

"True—but not many have a prescription for it, at least not in their own name." She tapped the bottle with a finger. "I recognized the prescribing doctor, Henry Oki. He was involved in a case last year, hooker who overdosed on sleeping pills. Seems like Dr. Oki isn't too choosy about who he hands scrips out to."

"Guess we should have a talk with him. Think his high level of professional ethics extends to patient confidentiality?"

"He's not going to want to implicate himself, obviously. But I'm betting he'll be pretty quick to point us in another direction if we ask nicely—especially if it'll take the spotlight off him."

Greg grinned. "A little sweet talk, a few implied threats? Works for me. You bring the carrot, I'll get the stick."

Catherine smiled. "Try again."

Greg's smile turned rueful. "Okay, you bring the stick. Hey, if I have the carrot, does that mean I can say 'What's up—' "

"No."

"I really want to thank you once again," said Brass. He smiled at Nathan Vanderhoff, who was seated on the other side of Brass's desk. "I mean, it's kind of phenomenal, having these kinds of resources to draw on. We're very lucky."

Vanderhoff nodded and leaned back, crossing his legs. "Again, we're happy to offer our assistance. Is Mr. Grissom going to be joining us?"

"He'll be here in a few minutes—had something to do in the lab. I thought I'd take the opportunity to talk to you first, before everyone else shows up."

Vanderhoff's smile was friendly but puzzled. "Oh?"

"Yeah. See—and don't tell Grissom I said this— I sometimes feel as if, well, as if I don't know whether or not Grissom's as good as he seems."

"I don't follow."

Brass leaned forward, put his elbows on the desk. "It's not like there are a *lot* of bug experts available, you know? So we use what we've got. I'm not saying Grissom isn't good, but—well, you guys are *world-class*. I've looked at your credentials, and they're impressive."

Vanderhoff chuckled. "Thank you for the compliment, but I assure you that Mr. Grissom is a highly respected member of our community. He's certainly 'world-class' himself."

"I guess. Still, a fresh perspective can be invaluable. You've been given the rundown on the case—what's your take?"

Vanderhoff nodded. "Most intriguing. There are many poisonous insects the perpetrator could have chosen, yet he picked millipedes. He clearly has some knowledge of entomology, but he—or she, I suppose—is not necessarily an expert. *Harpaphe haydeniana* may seem exotic to the layman, but they're quite common. The fact that they were used at all seems significant to me—after all, the plastic bag itself would have been lethal, would it not?"

Brass nodded. "We noticed that, too. Obviously, the bug thing has some symbolic value."

Vanderhoff shrugged and spread his hands wide. "Perhaps. Unfortunately, I'm an entomologist, not a psychiatrist . . ."

"Dr. Charong," said Brass, "I understand you're interested in helping out the Las Vegas Police Department."

Khem Charong nodded. His posture was stiff and formal, his hands folded demurely in his lap. "How could I resist? My colleagues will talk of nothing else."

"I see. Well, thank you for coming in. I just have a few quick questions, if you don't mind."

Charong cleared his throat. "Of course not. Go ahead."

"You're a researcher in Thailand?"

"That's correct."

"Must be a lot of bugs in the jungle out there."

"Yes, Thailand has some of the richest biodiversity on the planet. It is a fascinating place in which to work."

"You must go to some pretty remote locations, am I right?"

"I suppose that I do. It is very rewarding, though."

"I'm a city boy myself. Don't think I could give up the bright lights for a tent and a campfire. Still, I guess you've got a good excuse to cut loose when you get back to civilization."

"I'm sorry?"

"You know, make up for lost time. Party like a wild man."

"That is . . . not really my style."

Brass frowned. "No? Sorry, my mistake—in Vegas, we learn it's always the quiet ones who tend to wind up making the biggest noise. You didn't have any problems entering the country, did you?"

Charong blinked. "What?"

"You know—scientist, bioterrorism, twenty-first-century paranoia? You wouldn't believe some of the horror stories I've heard, people being denied entry for the most ridiculous reasons."

"I—no, I had no trouble."

"Well, that's good." Brass favored him with a big, friendly smile. "I mean, if you had, you wouldn't be here, would you?"

"Where is Dr. Grissom?" Roberto Quadros demanded.

"He'll be here in a minute," Brass said. "Why don't you sit down—"

"What is this? Why am I being treated so rudely? I expected Dr. Grissom to be here to greet me. And where are my colleagues?" Quadros shook his head, his bushy white beard bouncing from side to side. "He's already discussing the case with them, isn't he! Just because I disagreed with him on the overwintering capabilities of *Acherontia atropos*!"

"Calm down, Doctor. Grissom'll be here soon. I had no idea there was bad blood between you two."

Quadros took a deep breath and let it out. "I apologize. I have nothing but the utmost respect for Dr. Grissom. I'm afraid I'm simply . . . not very good with social situations. Never have been."

"Then you and Grissom have something in common—though he does tend to go more the internalization route."

Quadros sighed. "Indeed. A true scientist—one in control of his emotions, instead of the other way around."

"Oh, everybody needs to blow off a little steam now and then—even Grissom."

Quadros shook his head. "A scientist doesn't

'blow off steam,' Captain Brass. That would be a waste of thermodynamic energy . . ."

"I gotta thank you once more for helping us out," Brass said.

Jake Soames grinned and shook Brass's hand before sitting down. "Glad to help."

"Good, good. Y'know, Grissom's a real smart guy, but honestly, sometimes what he says goes right over my head. It'll be nice to have some-one around to explain things to me in plain lan-guage . . ."

"How'd you play it?" Grissom asked.

Brass blew on his coffee, took a sip before an-swering. He and Grissom were in the CSI break room, while the four entomologists waited in the reception area. "Different for each guy. You know how it is with suspects; learn as much as you can about them beforehand, then see how they act and trust your instincts."

"How'd they do?"

"Let's see. Charong's uncomfortable around authority, Quadros has a chip on his shoulder the size of the MGM Grand, Vanderhoff thinks he's the smartest guy in the room, and Soames is just a good ol' boy who wants everyone to like him. That's about all I got. Ready for your part?"

"'All the world's a stage, and all the men and women merely players. They have their exits and their entrances; and one man in his time plays many parts.' "

Brass got to his feet. "Come on, Shakespeare. Showtime."

Lucas Yannick's home wasn't much to look at, a ranch-style bungalow with peeling paint, missing roof tiles, and a yard that was more weeds than lawn. Plastic toys were scattered on the sidewalk leading up to the house, and a bicycle with a flat tire was chained to the front porch.

Riley knocked briskly on the front door. She could hear kids yelling inside and a TV blaring. A woman's voice yelled, "Lucas! Get the door!"

The boy who opened the door was pale and skinny, his dark hair in the pointy style known as a faux-hawk. He wore glasses with cheap plastic frames and a black T-shirt with a heavy-metal band logo on it. He took in Riley's CSI vest and cap and frowned. "Uh, hello?" he said.

"Hi. You must be Lucas. Can you tell your mom I need to talk to her?"

Lucas blinked. If he was nervous, it didn't show. "Mom!" he yelled over his shoulder. "There's a policewoman here to see you!"

"Actually, I'm a crime scene investigator," said Riley.

"Yeah?" Lucas said. "Cool. You guys have to know about insects, right? Like, in bodies and stuff?"

"That's right," said Riley.

Mrs. Yannick appeared, holding a baby in her arms. She was a tall, bony woman, wearing pajamas, and looked both wary and tired. Her nose was very red, and she clutched a tissue in one hand.

"What's this about?" Mrs. Yannick asked. Lucas had already disappeared.

"Actually, it's about Lucas," said Riley. "I need your permission to talk to him. I'm investigating the incident at school."

"Lucas wasn't involved in that. It was all a bunch of jocks and hotheads." She blew her nose. "Excuse me."

"I know he wasn't directly involved in the riot," Riley said carefully. "But we collect a lot of information in the course of an investigation and never know which piece of the puzzle will turn out to be important. You can be present while I talk to him—"

Mrs. Yannick sneezed, then said, "Sorry. Look, I don't want to give you this cold, so just go ahead and talk to him. He's a good kid, he won't give you any attitude."

"Thank you."

Riley followed the direction his mother pointed in and found Lucas in his bedroom. His interest in things that crept obviously extended to more than just scorpions; there were three terrariums along one wall, though none of their occupants were visible at the moment.

"Hi, Lucas. Can I come in?"

He was sitting upright in bed, reading a comic—*Spider-Man*, of course. "Yeah, sure."

She looked around for somewhere to sit down, saw only a chair heaped with clothes, and decided to stand. "What's in the tanks?"

He pointed at each in turn. "That one has a striped scorpion, that one a Chilean rose-haired tarantula, and the one on the end's empty. It had a praying mantis, but it died."

"Gonna replace it?"

"I dunno. Maybe. I was thinking about getting something different."

"Like a millipede?" She kept her face neutral but watched his carefully.

He thought about it, then shrugged. His face gave away nothing.

"So. I guess you know all about what happened at your school."

"I heard about it, yeah. All the jocks were really angry about Keenan. A lot of girls were crying. I don't know whose idea it was to go over to Carston, though." Now there was an edge of nervousness in his voice.

"Did you see the graffiti?"

"Yeah. I mean, it was right there, everybody saw it. Nobody thought it was serious, not at first. Then someone heard the news."

"How are *you* taking all this?"

"I'm okay. I mean, they say they're gonna have

counselors come in and talk to us, but that's—I guess that's for people who really knew him."

"You didn't?"

"Not really." He hesitated.

Riley waited; it was one of the best methods she knew of to get someone to talk.

"Actually, he was kind of a jerk," he said after a moment, glancing at her to see how she'd take it.

"Not a big surprise," she said. "Football star, right? I knew a few guys like that in high school. None of them impressed me."

"They all act like they own the world and you're supposed to pay rent," he said. A little anger had sparked in his tone. "It's like, they already have everything, but they have to find something of yours to take away. Even if it isn't something they want—they just like taking it away."

"I know. Well, Keenan's days of taking things away are over."

"He wasn't the worst. I mean, yeah, he was a jerk, but he didn't go out of his way to make my life hard. Not like some of the other guys." He met her eyes. "You know what? When I heard he was dead, I felt sad just like everybody else. But then I started thinking about it, and I was glad. Not that he was dead . . . but that all his friends were hurting. Because somebody finally took something away from *them*."

"Gentlemen, this is Nick Stokes," said Grissom. "Nick, this is Professor Nathan Vanderhoff, Doctor

Roberto Quadros, Doctor Jake Soames, and Doctor Khem Charong."

Nick smiled broadly and shook everyone's hand in turn. "Grissom tells me you're going to be lending us a hand. We appreciate the help."

Nick knew what was going on and understood the reasoning behind it. They were taking things one step farther than normal, though, by actually letting suspects into the lab—it was Brass who'd come up with the idea of giving the killer enough rope to hang himself with by allowing access to the inner workings of the investigation. *This guy obviously has a scientific bent,* he'd said. *We let him roam around and touch the equipment, he might give himself away.*

Nick had suggested they could do even better. They could lay a trap.

"Over here is our fingerprint lab," said Nick, leading the experts through the facility. "That's Mandy, one of our techs. And here's where we analyze DNA."

Wendy Simms, an attractive, brown-eyed brunette, looked up when they entered. "What's up, Nick?"

He performed another round of quick introductions. "They're here to consult on the Harribold case—you know, the one with the millipedes."

Wendy nodded. "Right. I was just running the DNA on that." She held up a glass slide, then carefully set it aside.

"Yeah, we got lucky," said Nick. "Found a hair caught in one of the handcuffs that didn't match the vic. We're hoping we can match it to one of our databases."

"Excuse me," said Khem Charong. "Isn't it quite difficult to derive a DNA sample from human hair?"

Wendy smiled. "It depends. In this case, we got a follicular tag, a layer of skin around the root. It should give us all the information we need."

"Sounds like you might not need us after all," said Soames.

"Don't sell yourself short," said Nick. "Grissom thinks you'll be a big help . . ."

"And this," said Nick, "is Hodges."

Hodges crossed his arms. "What are all these people doing in my lab?" he said with a pleasant smile.

Nick took him by the arm and led him a short distance away. "Look, don't make a fuss, okay?" he said under his breath. "This is only temporary—"

"What's only temporary? What's going on?" His eyes widened. "OMG. They're outsourcing my position, aren't they?"

"No, that's not it." Nick paused. "Did you just say *OMG*?"

"I've been texting a lot lately. Is the lab being sold?"

"It's a government facility, Hodges."

"So what—everybody knows privatization is the wave of the future. Are those our new corporate masters?"

Nick rolled his eyes and gave up. "Yes, Hodges, that's who they are. One of them's an eccentric billionaire with a passion for science, and the other three are his entourage. Treat them nicely or they'll make you play the new corporate mascot."

"We're going to have a mascot?"

They rejoined the others. "Mr. Hodges is our expert when it comes to trace. He's currently busy on another case, so—"

"I'd just like to say," Hodges blurted, "that I really admire Richard Branson."

They all stared at him.

"And that if the application period isn't over, I'd appreciate being allowed to offer a few ideas in the mascot arena. I mean, something obvious like a talking DNA spiral or giant fingerprint might seem like a good idea up front, but something based on trace evidence offers *far* more possibilities—"

Grissom, who'd been standing in the back, stepped forward and cleared his throat. Hodges shut up.

As the scientists filtered out of the Trace lab, Nick whispered to Grissom, "Maybe we should have told him."

"Have you ever seen Hodges act?" said Grissom. "The real thing may be odd, but at least it's genuine."

*   *   *

Grissom thanked all of them for coming in and assured them he would keep them apprised of the investigation. They filed out together, Soames already suggesting they adjourn to a bar. Only Nathan Vanderhoff lagged behind, turning at the last instant to retrace his steps to Grissom's office.

"Gil? A moment of your time?"

"Of course, Nathan. What is it?"

"Something that occurred to me about the case. I was hesitant to bring it up while the others were around; it seemed presumptuous of me. Foolish, I know—you did say any insights were appreciated."

"That I did. You have one?"

"Perhaps. It has to do not so much with the method of homicide as the resulting effect."

"The riot."

"Yes. And how the news of the murder was disseminated: the graffiti. Many social insects like bees and ants use chemical markers to communicate, and that's what the graffiti reminded me of."

Grissom nodded. "Leading to the victim's school attacking its rival—like one anthill raiding another."

"Yes. It may simply be my admittedly biased perspective as an entomologist, of course, but I thought I should mention it."

"Thank you, Nathan. I appreciate the input."

"My pleasure." He nodded his head good-bye and left.

Grissom kept his eyes on Vanderhoff's back until he was out of sight.

"Dr. Oki," said Catherine, "thank you for coming in. Saves us the trouble of a warrant."

Oki looked at Catherine. Then he looked at Greg. Then he looked back at Catherine. His face held as much expression as an ice cube held heat. He wore a short-sleeved brown shirt, and his hair was dyed a reddish blond.

"No problem," he said.

"Oh, I wouldn't go that far," said Catherine. "Another one of your patients has wound up in our morgue. I'd say that's a problem."

"People die," he said. His voice was as impassive as his face.

"Good thing, too," said Catherine. "Otherwise I'd be out of a job. But your job is supposed to be keeping them alive. Not very good at it, are you?"

"I get by."

Catherine gave him a slow smile. She loved a challenge. "Right. So far, that's exactly what you've done. But I'm about to put up a big red stop sign, Doctor—one with you on one side and your medical license on the other. Think you'll still be able to get by after that?"

His expression didn't change—but he didn't reply, either. She chalked that up as one for her side.

"But it doesn't have to be that way," said Greg.

"All we're after is a little cooperation. We get it, you can go back to prescribing diet pills and sleep aids to Z-grade celebrities."

"What do you want?"

Catherine pushed a photo at him. "Hal Kanamu. We know you were supplying him with triazolam, and we know why. We were hoping you could supply a little context, too."

Something tugged at the corner of Oki's mouth, like an invisible fishing hook trying to pull him toward the ceiling. He fought it bravely. "What do you want, his biography? I didn't know him that well. I knew The Story"—Catherine could hear the capital letters—"but everyone knew that. His one claim to fame."

"Enlighten us," said Catherine.

Two more unseen hooks snagged Oki's eyebrows and pulled. "You don't know? Huh. Well, okay. I can't tell it the way he could, but then I'm not trying to charm my way into your pants."

"Good call," said Greg.

"It's like this. Kanamu was a loser—or used to be, anyway. But then he makes this crazy-ass bet and it pays off."

"What kind of bet?" asked Catherine.

"A props bet. You know, like what'll come up at the coin toss for the Superbowl, heads or tails. There's all kinds of things you can gamble on, including some really bizarre stuff."

"Sure," said Greg. "I heard a guy bet a vegetarian

ten grand he wouldn't eat a cheeseburger. He lost."

"Yeah, well, Kanamu didn't. He placed an entertainment bet—you know, like who'll win *American Idol* or get voted off the island first—at five hundred to one."

"What was the bet?" Catherine asked.

"That the teen actress Kendall Marigold would not only lose her virginity out of wedlock before the end of the year, she'd announce it on national television."

"He predicted *that*?" Catherine asked. "Talk about a long shot—she was the spokesperson for the Save Yourself for Marriage organization."

"Emphasis on *was*," said Oki. "It was tabloid gold for about two weeks, but it made even more money for Kanamu. He went around telling everyone he'd had a vision, which is why he placed the bet. The sportsbook who took the wager tried to say he must have had inside information, but an investigation couldn't find any link. They paid up."

"So Kanamu stopped hauling bus pans," said Greg.

"And started popping pills," said Catherine.

"Hey, I was just trying to help him out. I met him at a party and he was all wired on meth. Told me he wanted to get clean, but he needed a parachute, give him a soft landing."

"You're a real humanitarian," said Catherine. "But now he's dead. Any idea how that might have happened?"

"I thought that was your job."

"It is," said Catherine. "And unlike you, I'm very good at mine. Any idea where he was getting the meth?"

"I'm a doctor, not a dealer. I don't have any connection to that kind of world."

"Except for the hookers and junkies you meet at parties," said Greg.

"Are we done?"

"For now," said Catherine. "We'll be in touch."

After Oki had left, Greg turned to Catherine and said, "Well, well. The specter of the virgin sacrifice rears its head again."

"It's just a coincidence, Greg."

"Offered on the altar of public media. Thrown into the volcano of . . . okay, the metaphor kind of breaks down there. But it is interesting."

"Only to someone who watches too much *Entertainment Tonight*. And what was with that 'hookers and junkies' crack? I'm the one who was supposed to be carrying the stick, remember?"

"Right. Sorry. I guess I forgot about my carrot." He paused. "And now I'm really, really sorry I just said that . . ."

The sportsbook who had taken Hal Kanamu's longshot props bet was located in the Las Vegas Golden Sapphire Casino. There were over one hundred and fifty legal sportsbook operations in the U.S., and every one of them was run out of a Nevada casino. The Diamond had a reputation for taking some of the more outrageous or unusual props bets, especially ones dealing with Hollywood or music celebrities; Catherine remembered reading that the sportsbook gave odds last year on which female celebrity would be the next to have a photo published displaying a personal disdain for wearing underwear in public.

The room the sportsbook was based in was high-ceilinged and resembled a NASA control room; panels of high-definition monitors gridded one wall, while row after row of computers were lined up facing them. The computers were for online betting, while the TV screens showed everything from horse races to hockey. Betting windows lined one wall, and computerized odds boards another. A lounge with comfortable chairs took up one corner.

Catherine stood in the doorway and looked around for a moment before going in. She smiled, then dug a tissue out of her pocket and wiped her eyes. Places like this might look like they were getting ready for a shuttle launch, but that wasn't what they made her think of.

She found the man she'd come to see at one of the tables in the lounge area. He was a stocky man with curly blond hair, dressed in gray sweatpants and a New York Yankees jersey, watching one of the games playing out on the wall of screens. It was hard to tell which one; his eyes kept shifting from one side to the other, his head tilting first up then down.

"Come on, come on," he muttered. "No, don't put him in, that's suicide—shoot! Shoot, damn it! No, don't throw it to him, are you *nuts*?"

"Excuse me," said Catherine.

His glance flickered to her for all of half a second, then back to the screens. "What can I do for you? Go, baby, go! Yeah!"

"How about giving me your undivided attention for a minute?" she said, and waved her badge in front of his eyes like a dog owner dangling a treat.

It worked. He looked over sharply, seemed to really see her for the first time, and gave her a cheerful, disarming smile. "Right! Sorry, I'm at work; it can get a little hectic here in the office."

She smiled back. "I'll bet."

"Yeah? How much, and on what?"

"You're Frankie Thermopolis, right?"

"Hey, that's a gimme. No odds on that one, except maybe the exact day my heart gives out. Give you five to one it's on a weekend—even money if we're on a date."

She laughed. "That your idea of romantic, Frankie? Offering odds on expiring while you're getting busy?"

Frankie grinned. "It makes 'em try harder. Now—what can I do for Las Vegas's finest?"

"I was wondering about a props bet you took— guy named Hal Kanamu."

Frankie's eyes rolled up in anguish. "Ah! The Hawaiian hophead. I couldn't believe that one, I really couldn't. Thought it was an easy thousand bucks and I wound up paying out seven hundred and fifty grand. I'm still in pain."

Catherine frowned. "I thought you gave him five hundred to one. Should have been an easy fifteen hundred, no?"

"Hey, you think I don't know about due diligence? Any time someone tries to blindside me with a bet like that, I make sure it's on the up-and-up first. Got a PI that checks things out for me, makes sure the guy placing the bet doesn't have some inside information."

"You must have been pretty sure."

Frankie shrugged. "I've used this guy before; he's really good. What he told me was the guy was a flake—a meth head who was trying to get clean, worked as a busboy. I thought hey, maybe he overheard something at his restaurant, almost didn't take the bet. But Hardesty—that's the PI—tells me that he looked into Kendall Marigold, and she's about as clean as Snow White in a nunnery. She's eighteen, she's not dating, she's never even set foot in Vegas. Plus, he knows someone on her security team, and his contact says her parents guard her so close she's practically under house arrest."

"Yeah, teenagers will always surprise you."

Frankie shook his head in sorrow. "Putting a dent in the family car, sure. But announcing she's having a secret affair with her yoga instructor on *Oprah*? I'm surprised her dad didn't just stroke out right there in the green room."

"So you paid out."

"Not right away. I threw a few more grand at Hardesty, hoping he could find something, anything to link Kanamu to the yoga instructor or one of his friends. Nada. And before you ask, yes, I trust Hardesty. He's looked into bigger payoffs than this one, and no one's ever been able to buy him. Much as I hated to do it, I had to give Kanamu his money. If he scammed me, I couldn't prove it."

Frankie's eyes were already flicking back to the monitors. Catherine moved between them and him. "Where can I find this Hardesty?"

"He's in the book—HardLook Investigations."

"One more thing, Frankie, and then I'll let you get back to work. How did Kanamu justify making the bet in the first place?"

He snorted. "Said he had a dream. Kendall Marigold being thrown into a volcano, then getting spat back out because she wasn't 'pure.' And that the whole thing was part of an episode of *Dog the Bounty Hunter*, which I guess is a show Kanamu watches a lot."

"Watched. He's dead."

Frankie's eyebrows went up. "Hey, you don't think I had something to do with it, do you? I may hate losing, but whacking the winners is bad for business."

She shook her head. "Relax. I checked with casino security before I came here—you were right here all night long."

"Yeah, office hours are a pain." He chuckled. "But hey, it's what I do, right? Couldn't quit if I tried . . ."

After she'd said good-bye and walked away, Catherine paused again at the threshold and looked back. Warrick Brown had loved to gamble, loved it a little too much. But there was one time—years ago, before it became obvious he had a problem— that she'd met Warrick for a drink at a sportsbook. He'd put some money on a football game, and she'd watched the last quarter with him. What she'd seen then wasn't the desperation or fervor of an addict, but the engagement of someone enjoying himself. Laughing, joking, watching every play intently while still talking to her, explaining why he thought a particular play had been chosen over another. He'd been animated, lively, just a little more pumped up than Warrick's usual laid-back manner. She'd found it incredibly appealing, an intriguing counterpoint to a man she already considered attractive.

Even when he lost, Warrick hadn't seemed to mind; he'd just laughed and said there was always tomorrow.

She'd thought about initiating something that night. Thought about it carefully, weighing the pros and cons, and eventually decided against it. She wasn't willing to take the gamble.

Thinking back on it, she was pretty sure that Warrick would have.

But she'd never know. Warrick's tomorrows had run out.

HardLook Investigations was located above a pawnshop. Despite that, it didn't have the run-down, film noir look of a hard-boiled detective's office—in fact, it was bright and sunny, with several ferns in the reception area, a skylight, and posters of McGruff the Crime Dog on the walls. The receptionist was a friendly, chubby black woman with tinted glasses who told Catherine to take a seat—Mr. Hardesty was with a client but should be done shortly.

Catherine could almost have imagined she was at the dentist's if it weren't for the magazines in the waiting area—*PI Chronicle, Detective Magazine*, a newsletter from the International Bodyguard Alliance. She was halfway through an article on body armor when the door into the other office opened and a woman clutching a manila envelope in one hand and a handkerchief in the other walked out. She strode right past, her face angry and her eyes blinking back tears, and slammed the door behind her.

"You can go in now," said the receptionist, who didn't seem surprised at all.

The man sitting behind the desk in the next room was not what Catherine had envisioned. He was young, clean-cut, wore glasses with stylish, stainless steel frames and a short-sleeved white shirt with a blue tie. He was so nondescript her eyes practically slid off him—which, she had to admit, was probably the point.

"Hi," she said. "Catherine Willows, CSI." She showed him her badge, which he examined a little more thoroughly than she was used to while shaking her hand.

"Darwin Hardesty," he said. "Have a seat. What's this about?"

"Hal Kanamu. He just turned up dead."

Hardesty frowned. "Overdose?"

"Surprisingly, no."

"Robbery?"

"Doesn't seem to be. You investigated him, right?"

He nodded. "Yeah. You know about the bet? Well, I was sure he must have had some sort of inside information. Couldn't prove it, though."

"Any leads?"

"I think the closest thing to a link I dug up was a second cousin he hadn't seen in ten years who once worked at a resort Kendall Marigold's dentist stayed at. When she was six."

"What's your gut say?"

He sighed. "I don't know. It was such an out-of-left-field, weird prediction . . . but not only did I not find any proof, Kanamu himself came across as on the level. A slightly off-the-wall, drug-using kind of level, but essentially honest. He really believed the information came to him in a dream—I had experts interview him. He even passed a polygraph."

"How did Frankie Thermopolis take the news?"

Hardesty smiled with a mouth full of even white teeth. "Not too well. But he's a professional gambler and knows there's no such beast as the sure thing. He may not like it, but he takes the bitter with the sweet. I think he'd recouped his losses within a couple of weeks, anyway."

Catherine nodded. "You turn up anyone else who might have wanted him dead?"

"Not around here, but he hadn't been in Vegas that long."

"How about in Hawaii?"

"Some small-time drug stuff. I guess one of his former buddies might have gotten wind of his win and shown up demanding his share, but Kanamu didn't seem to hang with a dangerous crowd. He was even trying to clean up—before his big score."

"Yeah, that much money could push anyone off the wagon." Catherine got to her feet. "Thanks for your time. Think I could take a look at your files?"

"Sure. I'll have Cindy fax them over to your office. Willows, right?"

"You got it."

Catherine had to admit that Darwin Hardesty seemed to know his stuff; the file he sent over on his investigation into Hal Kanamu was thorough and professional. It also seemed to confirm exactly what he'd told her—if Hal Kanamu had inside information on the status of Kendall Marigold's virginity, he hadn't been able to uncover it. Catherine sighed, put down the file, and went in search of other information.

She found Hodges hunched over a table in his lab; he seemed to be sketching something. "Taking up cartooning, Hodges?"

Hodges looked up, startled. "What? No, I was just brainstorming a few ideas for—never mind."

Catherine glanced at the pad Hodges was doodling on. "Is that a microscope with legs?"

Hodges flipped the pad over. "What can I do for you, CSI Willows?"

"I was wondering if you had anything new for me on that shard of volcanic rock."

"Ah. You mean you need information on a *mineral* sample?"

"Isn't that what I just said?"

"Then I can't help you." Catherine had seen that smirk too many times to think he was finished. "However, if you would like my findings on a *mineraloid* sample, I have some news for you."

"The rock . . . isn't a rock?"

"Not exactly. It's obsidian, a very interesting substance. As a glass, its structure isn't crystalline. It's highly felsic, but with too many elements to be considered a single mineral. It's mostly silicon dioxide, though."

"Okay, so it's volcanic glass. Where did it come from?"

"That's the interesting thing. I checked a geologic database and got a match. It's not from Nevada at all—it's from *Hawaii*. Not only that, but—despite the fact that the Hawaiian Islands are basically *all* volcanic—there's only one site on any of them that produces obsidian: Puu Waawaa."

"Excuse me?"

"That's the name of the place, Puu Waawaa. It's a volcanic cone on the north side of the Hualalai volcano. Primitive tribes used it to make things like arrowheads or knives—obsidian holds an edge right down to the molecular level. In fact, it's still used for surgical scalpels today."

"So our vic probably brought it with him."

"Or his killer did." Hodges paused. "Catherine, I want your honest opinion—which do you think is sexier, a centrifuge or a gas chromatograph?"

"Hodges, you really need to get out of the lab more often."

4

"NONE OF THEM went for it?" asked Brass.

Nick and Grissom glanced at each other on the other side of the desk. "No," said Grissom.

"We gave 'em every opportunity," said Nick. "We paraded them around the lab, put crucial evidence in plain sight, then made sure each of them was alone with it at least once. Hidden camera showed that none of them so much as glanced at it."

"They all seemed genuinely interested in the millipedes," said Grissom. "A fistfight almost broke out over a disagreement about the species."

"Quadros?" said Brass.

"And Jake Soames. Though to be fair, I don't think Jake would have swung first."

Brass leaned back and sighed. "So much for the direct approach. How about the subtle? Did any of them ask inappropriate questions?"

Grissom frowned. "They're scientists. There's no such thing as an inappropriate question."

"Then I guess we're back to square one," said Brass.

"Maybe not," said Nick. "None of these guys are local, but the U.S. has pretty good relations with Australia, Thailand, Brazil, and South Africa. I might be able to dig up some background with a few phone calls and e-mails."

Brass raised his eyebrows. "You've got connections I don't know about, Nick?"

Nick laughed. "Everybody comes to Vegas sooner or later. I've made a few friends."

"Then start running up that phone bill," said Brass.

Riley found Grissom in his office. "Got a minute?"

Grissom peered at her over the top of his glasses. "Yes?"

She leaned against the doorframe, her arms crossed. "I just talked to a possible suspect in the Harribold case."

"And?"

"He's a minor. But he could be who we're looking for."

Grissom frowned. "Did you speak with him with a legal guardian present?"

"No, but his mother gave me permission. He didn't say anything incriminating."

"But you feel he could be responsible."

She shook her head. "I don't know. He's only sixteen, but he has motive and possibly the means.

I thought I'd talk to you first before bringing him in for a formal interview."

Grissom thought for a moment, then pointed to a jar on a shelf to his right. "You see that?"

Riley took a step into the room and tilted her head. "Is that a brain?"

"Yes. Specifically, the brain of an *Oryctolagus cuniculus*—a domestic rabbit. I dissected and preserved it myself—when I was fifteen."

"Uh-huh. So you're saying you'd like me to bring him in?"

"I'm saying I'd like to be present when you talk to him."

Nick Stokes was a friendly guy, and he knew the value of networking. While many people these days relied on e-mail, Nick had found that a phone call was more likely to get results than a line of text on a screen. He put out feelers to various agencies in various countries, talking to people when he could and leaving messages on voice mail when he couldn't. He'd been at it for over an hour when he finally got a call back from Mongkol Sukaphat, an officer with the Royal Thai Police. One of the oddities of Thai culture was the use of a nickname, usually bestowed in childhood, that then followed the person throughout their adult life. Even though these names were often absurd, Thais were so used to them that even the most ridiculous were never remarked upon.

"Yes, I'm returning a call from Nick Stokes?"

"Beer! Thanks for getting back to me . . ."

Nick gave him a quick rundown on what he needed: the arrest record, if any, of Khem Charong.

"Let me check," Sukaphat said. "Ah, here we go. Yes, he has been arrested before. Shall I send you his file? It's in Thai, of course."

"Can you just give me the highlights over the phone?"

Nick jotted them down as Sukaphat talked. By the time he thanked Sukaphat and hung up, his smile was gone.

Grissom closed the interview room door gently, then turned and smiled before taking his seat. "Hello, Lucas. My name's Gil Grissom. I understand you're interested in entomology."

Lucas swallowed, looked from Grissom to Riley and then to his mother beside him. She had her own gaze fixed on Grissom, as if she could control what questions he asked through sheer force of will.

"Uh, yeah," he said.

"So am I. In fact, I've studied insects for many years. Do you have a favorite?"

"I don't know. I like spiders, I guess. And scorpions. They're not insects, though, they're arachnids."

"That's true. I own a baboon spider, myself."

"Yeah? Those are pretty cool."

"I think so." Grissom smiled. "Don't be nervous. We just need to ask you a few questions. All right?"

"I guess."

Grissom glanced over at Riley, who took the cue.

"Where were you on the night Keenan Harribold died?"

"Uh—at home, I guess."

"I can confirm that," his mother said. "He spent the evening upstairs doing homework. If he'd gone out, I'd know about it."

Riley nodded. "Have you or your family traveled to the Pacific Northwest any time in the last year? Vacation, field trip, anything?"

"No."

"Vacation?" his mother said. "In this economy? Not for a while."

"Do you ever get insects by mail-order?" asked Grissom. "It can be hard to obtain certain specimens locally."

"No, I go to the Pet Cave for all my stuff. They know me down there."

Grissom made a note on the pad in front of him. "I'm familiar with the place myself. They have a nice selection, don't they?"

"I guess."

"Mrs. Yannick, do you or your husband keep any firearms in the house?"

"What? No. No, we don't."

"Thank you, Lucas, and thank you, Mrs. Yannick. I think we have all we need."

Riley looked less than satisfied but didn't say anything until after Mrs. Yannick and her son had left. "That was kind of brief, wasn't it? You didn't even ask about his relationship to Keenan Harribold."

"I didn't have to. While it's conceivable Lucas could have snuck out of the house without his parents being aware of it, he would still have had to obtain a gun to control Harribold and rent the motel room. Difficult for a teenager, even in Vegas."

"He could have an accomplice."

"Conceivable, but unlikely. If Lucas Yannick killed Keenan Harribold, he did it because he was an unpopular loner being bullied by a more popular athlete. Those kinds of kids rarely have accomplices."

"Maybe not in your day. In mine, they wear black trench coats and carry automatic weapons."

Grissom got up from the table. "Nobody wants to see a repeat of Columbine, Riley. But the circumstances in this case are very different. I suggest you concentrate on finding the man who rented that room rather than a fifteen-year-old who's interested in bugs." He left the room, closing the door behind him.

"Sixteen," said Riley to the empty room. "He's sixteen."

Khem Charong glanced nervously around the interview room. "I don't understand. Where is Dr.

Grissom? Why have I been kept waiting for so long?"

Brass smiled. "Patience, Doctor. It isn't Grissom who wants to talk to you—it's me. You don't have a problem with talking to a lowly police captain, do you?"

"No. No, of course not."

"Really? You seem a little jumpy."

Khem made a visible effort to control himself. "How may I be of assistance?"

"Let's see . . . I guess you can start with telling me where you were on the evening of the murder."

"I—I was in my hotel room."

"Alone?"

"Yes."

"Okay. The second thing you can help me with is, let's see . . . oh, I know. You can stop lying to me."

"What?"

"This is Vegas, Doctor, not the middle of the jungle. You sneak out of camp in the dead of night here, you get caught by security cameras. You left your room at around seven and didn't come back until midnight. Where'd you go?"

"I . . . I went for a walk."

"Sure. This is Vegas, after all. Things to do, places to go, twenty-four/seven. Get the urge to do a little gambling, maybe?"

"Yes. Yes, I did."

"Where?"

"I . . . I don't remember."

"What a shame. Convenient, too, what with all the casinos having round-the-clock video surveillance. How'd you do?"

"I broke even."

"Of course you did." Brass shook his head. "Well, you're about to lose big, Doctor. You may have managed to avoid a criminal record in Thailand, but that doesn't mean you're not in the system. This isn't the first time you've gone out for a little stroll, is it?"

Charong's face paled. "I don't know what you're talking about."

"Sure you do. When you hit the big city after being in-country, Bangkok is your destination of choice. Certain neighborhoods in Bangkok. In fact, very specific clubs in certain neighborhoods."

"You have the wrong man. Charong is a very common name—"

"I know exactly who I have, Doctor. You were arrested but not charged. Connections, or just a really good lawyer?" Brass held up a hand. "You know, don't bother answering that—I don't really care."

Charong was visibly sweating now. You didn't see that often in Vegas; it was too dry.

"Okay, you've told me your story," said Brass. "Now it's my turn to entertain you. Hope you don't mind if I switch styles on you, but I'm more of a nonfiction guy.

"It started online. Maybe you were trolling on high school sites when a picture of a star quarterback caught your eye. Unfortunately, his Facebook page didn't list middle-aged, male entomologists as one of his turn-ons, so you created a fake persona. You set up a rendezvous in a Vegas motel room to coincide with your visit—after all, what's a convention without a little illicit sex? Knowing that you'd be something of a disappointment in person, you came prepared for your own creepy-crawly party."

Charong swallowed. "That's crazy. I didn't bring any millipedes with me—ask the airline."

"Oh, you didn't bring them with you from Thailand—you got them here in the States. Wouldn't have been that hard for someone with your background; you probably had a colleague in the Northwest mail them."

"I didn't! I didn't do anything of the sort, and you can't prove that I did!"

"Maybe *I* can't," said Brass. "But I'm not the one you should be worried about . . ."

"Well, the cat's out of the bag now," Nick said to Grissom.

They were watching Brass question Charong through a two-way mirror. "This is the next logical step," said Grissom. "We had to treat them as suspects sooner or later. I'm just glad you found a viable reason to do so."

Nick looked uncomfortable. "Yeah," he said. "So . . . you think Charong's our guy?"

"We'll know more once we search his room. We're just waiting for the judge to sign off on a warrant."

"Right. Maybe we can close this one without putting your other colleagues through this."

Grissom frowned. "Actually, Nick, I was hoping you and Riley could conduct the interviews with Soames, Quadros, and Vanderhoff. I'm having them brought in now."

"Really? I mean, it might not even be necessary—"

"It's necessary, Nick. Just because I know them doesn't mean we treat them any differently. Brass suggested he conduct the interview with Doctor Charong because Charong seemed nervous around authority figures and Brass thought he could use that; I agreed."

"So that's why you want me and Riley to question the others? We're scarier than you are?"

Grissom smiled. " 'There can be no prestige without mystery, for familiarity breeds contempt.' "

"Sherlock Holmes?"

"Charles de Gaulle."

Nick sighed. "Okay, *mon generale*. We'll be your mystery men . . ."

"So, Nick," Jake Soames said, "what do you say we hit the town after this? As a local, you must know the best places."

Nick grinned despite himself. "Look, Mr. Soames—it really wouldn't be appropriate for us to socialize. We're both part of this investigation, but I'm afraid at the moment we're on opposite sides of it."

Soames chuckled. "I was wondering how long it would take . . . Guess you've got a few questions for me, eh? Want to know where I was and what I was doing on the night of, right?"

"You don't seem terribly surprised."

"Only thing I'm surprised at is how long it's taken you to ask. The others might be a little naïve, but I like to think I'm a man of the world—of course we're suspects! A boy gets killed with bugs while there's a bloody swarm of insectophiles in town? Come *on*!"

"So can you account for your whereabouts?"

"Well, let's see . . . I was in the hotel casino until half past eight; then I went to a club off the Strip called Bubble Bath. Amazing show they've got there . . . Feeling a bit peckish after that, got a steak dinner at this absolutely great diner, lots of chrome and neon—can't remember the name, but I think I have a receipt somewhere, the waitress'll remember me for sure . . . Met Grissom and Nathan for drinks, and then I felt the urge to play a little poker . . ."

The list went on for a while. Nick tried to keep a straight face, but it was fairly obvious Jake Soames not only had an alibi, it was one he was damned proud of.

Vegas, Nick thought. *It was made for some people . . .*

*　　*　　*

"So these photos are from Kanamu's place?" Greg asked. He had them spread out over the surface of the layout table and was scrutinizing one in particular.

"Yeah," said Catherine. "I've got Archie trying to decrypt his laptop right now. Didn't find a cell phone. His place was pretty bare, actually—I got the feeling he didn't spend a lot of time there."

"Except for these," said Greg, tapping a photo. It was a shot of the robot giraffe picture. "Clearly not part of the standard décor."

"No. I've been trying to figure out where they were taken—I thought at first they might be part of a Cirque du Soleil performance, but they all look like outdoor shots."

"That's because they were taken in the middle of a desert. This shot of the temple, here? That's not mist, it's dust."

"You recognize these?"

"Not these specifically, but the location? Absolutely. It's the Black Rock Desert, about four hundred miles north of here. Black Rock City to the locals."

"Black Rock City? Greg, there's nothing in that part of Nevada but alkali flats. It's where people go to break land-speed records—there's nothing to run into. It's like the surface of the moon, minus the craters."

"For most of the year, yes. But for one week,

there's a city of fifty thousand people, complete with streets, businesses—well, kind of—and lots and lots of *this*." He tapped the photo again.

"Robot giraffes?"

"*Fire-breathing* robot giraffes. Also fire-breathing dragons, aliens, tanks, and naked people. Okay, not all the naked people are fire breathing, but a lot more than you'd expect."

"Greg—"

He held up his hands, grinning. "I'm being straight with you, I swear. It's just that any accurate description of Burning Man very quickly turns surreal. It's a surreal place."

"Burning Man. Okay, I've heard of that. It's some kind of big party, right?"

Greg sighed. "That's like saying Woodstock was a few people listening to music. No, that's not right, either—Burners *hate* comparisons to Woodstock. Woodstock is to Burning Man like kindergarten is to college. That's a little closer."

"Burners?"

"It's what attendees call themselves. Okay, I'm going to try to distill this down to a short and reasonably rational description, but bear with me, all right? Constant interjections of "Yeah, right," and looks of disbelief won't make this go any faster." Greg stopped. His brow furrowed. He rubbed his chin.

"Greg?"

He held up one finger. "Hang on. I'm trying to

find the right approach . . . okay. Burning Man is about a lot of things, but first and foremost it's about *art*. It was started by an artist, it's run by artists, and it actively encourages every single attendee to *create* art."

"All fifty thousand?"

"Yes. Some people spend a year creating huge pieces and haul them out to the site. Some people create things on-site or drive around in bizarre vehicles they've built themselves—like fire-breathing giraffes. People wear costumes, or body paint, or nothing at all. And a lot of the art is based around fire."

"Is there an actual burning man, or is that just artistic license?"

"There is. The city is built in a semicircle, with a gigantic plaza in the middle. The plaza is where the large-scale art is, and at the very center they build a wooden figure on a base, outlined in neon. That's the man. He gets a little bigger every year—I think they actually hit a hundred feet last time."

"That's a pretty big structure to put up and take down in a week."

Greg chuckled. "Oh, it comes down pretty quick. They burn it on Saturday night."

"Must make one hell of a mess."

"It does—and it's all gone within a week or two. Burning Man's environmental record with the Bureau of Land Management is one of the best—volunteers stay on-site and go over every square inch afterward."

"I'm sensing a less-than-objective perspective, here."

Greg looked a little sheepish. "Sorry. I've never been, but I have a friend who goes every year and she's pretty evangelical about the place—especially when people seem to focus on nothing but the nudity and the drugs."

"My mistake. Now, let's focus on our vic—our dead, drug-using vic."

"Right. Well, I think it's pretty obvious he was a Burner. He probably took those pictures himself, though they might have been gifted to him."

"Gifted. You mean given?"

"Sorry. That's Burner-speak. There's no commerce allowed at the festival beyond a central café that sells coffee and a place to get ice. Everything works on a gift economy—people compete to see who can give away better stuff. Booze, art, food, services—whatever."

"Like a potlatch," said Catherine. "Native American tribes in the Northwest practice it. Whoever gives the most impressive gift attains the highest status."

"Pretty much. Done on a city-wide scale for a week, it's pretty amazing. You'd think there would be more people taking out than putting in, trying to take advantage of the system, but that's generally not what happens." Greg paused. "A good way to think of it is a bunch of people playing 'city' for a week. All the bars, the restaurants, the hair salons—don't ask—everybody's trying to have fun instead of turn a buck. After Vegas, it's . . . refreshing."

"Maybe so, but our vic still had to live in the real world the rest of the year. And he'd recently come into a lot of money."

Greg nodded. "And was spending some of it, at least, on drugs. There is a definite party element to the festival—drugs are pretty common, though it's mostly softer stuff. Could be that one of his Burner friends is also his dealer."

"So how do we investigate people from a city that only exists for a week a year?"

"Vegas has its own Burner community. I'll show Kanamu's picture around, see what I can find out."

"All right. Kanamu doesn't have a record in Nevada, but he may have one in Hawaii. I'm going to follow that up."

In the computer lab, Archie Johnson looked up from his workstation as Catherine walked in. "Catherine, great timing. I just cracked that laptop you gave me."

"Yeah? Find anything interesting?"

"Not as much as you might think. The usual gack—some games, music, downloaded movies. The oddest thing was probably all the files on vulcanology."

"You're talking about the study of volcanoes and not Mr. Spock, right?"

Archie grinned. "This guy had a serious jones for the subject. Not just the geological stuff, but the mythological, too. All kinds of Hawaiian folklore, especially about Pele—and no, I don't mean the soccer player. She's the Hawaiian volcano goddess."

"Let's skip the fairy tales, Archie. How about an address book?"

He handed her a flash drive. "Figured you'd ask. Dumped everything that looked interesting in there."

"Thanks." Catharine hesitated. "So, you read some of those files on the volcano goddess?"

"I skimmed them, yeah. Pretty interesting, actually."

"Anything in there about . . . virgin sacrifices?"

Archie studied her for a second before answering. "Not that I can recall. Why?"

Catherine shook her head. "Never mind. I should know better than to take everything Greg says seriously . . ."

Back at her own desk, Catherine checked through the data on the flash drive. Many of the names in the contacts list were just e-mail addys, but a few had brick-and-mortar addresses or phone numbers. She cross-referenced them with the information the Hawaiian PD had sent her, coming up with two names that matched both known associates and Kanamu's contact list: Lester Akiliano and Jill Leilani. Both had addresses in Vegas, and Akiliano had been arrested for possession of narcotics only two weeks ago, though he'd made bail and was out awaiting trial.

She made the necessary arrangements to see him, then found herself looking over the files on Hawaiian mythology. Archie was right; it *was* interesting.

The goddess Pele didn't seem to be interested in virgins. In fact, she seemed to go out of her way to seduce any young chief or god around. Most of her lovers met an unhappy end, though, one eerily reminiscent of Kanamu's fate; they were sealed inside the pillars of hardened lava that sprouted on a volcano's slopes. Hawaiian women used to tease their hair until it stood out, redden their eyes, then extort goods or services from fellow villagers by claiming to be Pele's *kahu*, or living incarnation. Anyone who didn't comply was threatened with fiery retribution.

"One hot-tempered mama," Catherine murmured.

Unlike that of many mythological figures, Pele's influence had survived to the present day; drivers on the islands told stories of picking up an old woman in Hawaii Volcanoes National Park, all dressed in white and accompanied by a small dog, both of whom vanished from the back seat. Catherine had heard that particular tale before, though she knew it as the Vanishing Hitchhiker—an urban legend almost as old as that of the escaped lunatic with a hook for a hand.

Interesting angle with the little dog, though, she thought. *Wonder what his name is—Lava? Rocky? Volcanine?*

She powered down her computer, then went out to find Jill Leilani.

5

RILEY EYED PROFESSOR VANDERHOFF, sitting on the other side of the interview table. "Professor Vanderhoff, can you tell me where you were on the day Keenan Harribold was killed?"

Vanderhoff studied her for a moment before answering. "I spent most of it at the conference, though I took a nap in the evening."

"Alone?"

"Yes. Jet lag."

"Not a very exciting way to spend time in Vegas."

Vanderhoff smiled. "I'm not really a very exciting person. But I did meet with Jake Soames and your boss later for drinks."

"Did you know Keenan Harribold?"

"No. Unless he posted anonymously on one of the entomology boards I frequent—which I doubt—I'd never heard of him until he was killed."

"Have you ever heard of anyone else being killed in this manner?"

"Never. I'm not a criminologist, but I have to admit it's a fascinating case."

"So you've never consulted on a criminal case before?"

"No. I'm afraid my exposure to this world has been strictly through film and novels. I will say I'm something of a mystery buff, though."

"Then you probably know why I'm asking you these questions."

"Of course. Someone with my expertise would naturally be considered a suspect."

"That doesn't bother you?"

"I haven't done anything wrong. Unless someone's trying to frame me, I don't think I'm in any trouble—and so far, the only inconvenience has been being forced to sit and talk to an attractive woman."

Riley didn't smile. "I don't think Keenan Harribold would agree."

"I'm sorry. Have I offended you? I may be an academic, but I grew up in the slums of Johannesburg; my childhood took place under apartheid. I have seen much brutality in my life, and sometimes I feel somewhat desensitized. But a young man's death is still a tragedy."

Riley glanced down at her notes. "No, it's fine. You didn't know him, after all . . ."

In Interview Room Two, Roberto Quadros was on his feet and pointing an accusing finger at Nick

Stokes. "This is an outrage!" Quadros exclaimed. "I am a respected researcher! Dr. Grissom will have your job when I tell him about this!"

Nick put his hands up in a slow-down-and-let's-talk-about-this gesture. "Dr. Quadros, I'm sorry if you feel singled out. But we're not targeting you; we're talking to everyone and gathering data. You're a man of science; you understand the principle of exclusion—this isn't an accusation. It's part of the process to eliminate you as a suspect."

Quadros simmered for a moment, then took a deep breath and retook his seat. "Very well. But at the very least Dr. Grissom could have talked to me *himself*."

I'm beginning to understand why he didn't, Nick thought. "Grissom's busy at the moment. Now, Dr. Quadros—you're not staying at the same hotel the others are, correct?"

"No. They charge absurd rates. I found a much more reasonable establishment a few blocks away."

You mean a run-down dump with no security cameras. "Right. And you were there all evening."

"Yes. There were some fascinating presentations at the conference the next day, and I wanted to be fresh."

"You know, some visitors to Vegas would take the opportunity to enjoy themselves. Go see the sights, take in a show—"

"I didn't come here for the *hedonism,* Mr. Stokes.

There's plenty of that in Brazil, believe me. I came for the intellectual stimulation provided by an exchange of ideas between men and women like myself. The last thing I wanted was to be drawn into some sort of sordid affair involving dead bodies in seedy motel rooms!"

Funny. You seemed a lot more eager when you thought you were going to help break a big case. "I understand that. So nobody saw you during the evening—the desk clerk, maybe?"

"No. I had dinner early and retired early. Would you like to know what I had for supper, as well?"

"No, that won't be necessary—"

"Perhaps you'd like a detailed itinerary of my trips to the bathroom? Or a list of the television channels I watched before turning in? I know—a record of my dreams! Perhaps I can persuade a talking dog or flying pig to provide me with an alibi!"

Nick sighed.

Jill Leilani worked at the Shoremont Hotel as a maid. Her supervisor pointed Catherine at floors nineteen through twenty-two; she found Leilani in the hall on the twentieth, trundling a cart loaded with laundry and cleaning supplies between rooms.

Leilani was a thin, sallow-faced woman with nervous eyes. She wasn't happy to see Catherine but didn't seem surprised, either.

"Jill Leilani? I'm Catherine Willows with the

Las Vegas Crime Lab. When was the last time you talked to Hal Kanamu?"

Leilani's eyes roamed everywhere but Catherine's line of sight. "I don't know. Couple weeks ago, maybe longer. I don't remember."

"You two have a falling out or something?"

"No, I—I just don't hang with him, is all. He don't have time for his old friends ever since he hit it rich."

"You've known him a long time, though, right? Back on the Big Island?"

"Yeah, I guess. We used to be tight." Even when she talked, she barely opened her mouth.

"And high, too. Drug buddies, right? You even got busted together."

"That was a long time ago. I'm clean."

"No, you're not. Your teeth are rotting out of your head, your skin's bad, and you've got the shakes. Know what I think happened? I think that when your pal Hal got his lucky break he threw one hell of a party, and you were one of the first people he invited. All the ice you could smoke, right? For a while, anyway. And by the time he decided the party was over and maybe he had better things to do than support his friends' habits, the monkey on your back had turned into a three-hundred-pound gorilla."

Leilani didn't even try to deny it; the bitterness in her voice told Catherine she'd been carrying her anger around for a long time: "He didn't even see what he was doing to me. He came here to get clean, you know? Get away from all his druggy friends in Honolulu. I thought, *If he can do it, so can I.* But when he got all that money . . . money's the worst thing, you know? Should be a law, you can't buy a lottery ticket if you're using."

"But he didn't win the lottery."

"Didn't he? Winning that crazy-ass bet . . . Everybody thought he must have cheated somehow, but he swore up and down he didn't. Said he had this dream, told him what to bet on. Even found a casino to take it—they weren't too happy when he won."

"And that's when the party started."

"Yeah. It was great, at first. Didn't have to worry about tomorrow, so we could party every day. And how much I was using, it kind of just crept up on me."

Catherine nodded. She'd seen case studies on drug use that showed that same pattern—that even with addictive drugs like heroin or cocaine, users didn't generally get into trouble until they had access to a large amount of the drug all at once, either from dealing or a sudden windfall of cash. Their drug intake climbed along with their tolerance, until the money was gone and they abruptly became aware of just how heavy—and expensive— their habit had become.

"So what happened?" asked Catherine. "Did he run out of cash?"

"No. I saw what was happening, knew it was gonna kill both of us sooner or later. Tried to talk him into quitting, but he didn't want to hear it. He thought—" She stopped, shook her head. "He was getting kind of crazy. Thought that winning the bet was some kind of sign, that he was supposed to do something special with the money."

"Like spend it all on meth?"

"No, but—the drugs were part of it. He thought they were making his thoughts more . . . I don't know, cosmic or something."

"Cosmic. What was he going to do, build a spaceship?"

"No, he was more interested in old gods and stuff. He was always talking about Pele and Kama-hua and Lono—Hawaiian gods, you know? I just used to tune him out. Sounded too much like my grandmother."

"Anybody else listen?"

"Sure. Lester and him would talk about that stuff for hours."

"Lester Akiliano?"

"Yeah. They've known each other forever, though I don't think Lester really cared about any of that mystical stuff—he was just there to get high. He woulda talked about senior citizens getting kinky if it meant a free hit."

"How'd Lester feel about you trying to convince Kanamu to quit?"

"What do you think? Went off on me. Told me

to stop being such a buzzkill—I didn't stick around long after that. Wasn't healthy, in too many ways."

Catherine sensed there was more to her words than what she was saying. "Did Lester threaten you?"

"Nah, I've known Lester a long time—longer than Hal, even. But the guys he was hanging around with? Bad news."

"What guys?"

"Oh, no. I don't wanna talk about them. Go talk to Lester, see for yourself. Just don't say I pointed you his way, okay? He needs to get to rehab, but he doesn't need to know I sent him there."

"You look like you could use some time there yourself."

Leilani gave her a wan smile. "Nah, kicking meth's easy. I do it every day, you know? Sometimes more than once. . ."

Lester Akiliano liked to drink in a bar called the Cross-Eyed Jack, a place that might have been glamorous when mobsters ruled the Strip but was now a dusty mausoleum of peeling chrome, scarred tables, and torn carpet. Lester himself was at the bar, nursing a longneck beer and watching women's basketball on the TV. The bartender squinted at Catherine warily when she came in, as if he were highly allergic to the natural light that spilled through the doorway behind her and was trying to remember where he put his epinephrine.

"Lester Akiliano?" she asked. "Catherine Willows, Las Vegas Crime Lab. I'd like to talk to you about Hal Kanamu."

Lester was a bulky Hawaiian with shoulder-length, straight black hair and a scraggly black goatee that looked like it was trying to escape his face. He wore a shirt of bright yellow silk missing the top two buttons, with irregular stains spreading from the armpits. He took a long swallow of his beer before responding. "What you want from me, huh? I don't know nothing except Hal's dead."

She took a seat next to him. "Well, that's the thing, Lester. Kind of my job to find out how that happened."

"Don't look at me. I wasn't there."

"And where would that be?"

"Out in the desert. That's where you found him, right? That's what I heard." He took another drink. "No place for a *kanaka* to die, I'll tell you that. Too far from the ocean. Too damn far from home."

Catherine studied him for a second. "You knew him a long time, right?"

"Forever. He was a good friend. Maybe a little crazy, but he always had your back."

"Liked to have a good time, right?"

"You better believe it. I can't remember how many times we couldn't remember."

"Got to catch up with you sometime."

"Maybe so. Maybe so." He finished his beer, signaled for another. The bartender ignored him. "But that's life, right? You have fun while you can."

"When was the last time you saw Hal?"

"Oh, must have been three, four days ago. We used to hang out every day, but—"

"Hey, Les. Who's your friend?"

Three men stalked out of the bar's gloomy recesses, two of them holding pool cues. The speaker was a muscular man in a sleeveless shirt, every visible inch of his arms covered in tattoos. His head was shaved, his face wide but uneven; the right side of his jaw bulged like he was storing nuts for the winter. His friends were taller than he was but not as wide, and despite the dimness of the bar they both wore sunglasses.

"Hey, Boz. She's no one," Lester muttered.

"I'm Catherine Willows," she said. "Las Vegas Police. And you are?"

"Didn't you hear Les? I'm Boz." He grinned, exposing receding gums. "You here for the wake? We're honoring our poor dead friend, Hal."

"So am I—I'm investigating his death." She eyed the three men coolly. "When was the last time you saw your good friend Hal?"

Boz shrugged. "I don't know—couple days ago, maybe. Hal was always on the go, you know? Lot of energy." He fished a cough drop out of his pocket and popped it into his mouth, wincing as he did so. His breath smelled like rotten fish in mint sauce.

"I'll bet."

"Anyway, we're just gonna go back to our wake, okay? Respect for the dead and all that."

"Uh-huh. I'm going to need to see some ID, Boz." She nodded at his two friends. "You too. Come on, guys, dig out those wallets."

Catherine kept her own hand near her gun. She knew tweakers when she saw them, and anyone high on crank was a dangerous and unpredictable commodity. An armed meth head was one bad impulse away from murder.

Nobody produced a gun, though—just identification and dirty looks. She took them, jotted down their names, and gave them back. "Thanks," she said. "I'll be in touch."

Boz's smile had been replaced by a look of wary confusion. "What for? Are you arresting us, or what?"

"Not yet, Boz." She smiled. "But I'd really like to get to know you—and your friends—better. Thing is, I'd prefer to do it at *my* place . . ."

Bosley "Boz" Melnyk, Catherine discovered, was no stranger to the system. In fact, she was pretty sure Boz and the system were about ready to pick out drapes together.

His earliest arrests had been for shoplifting. He'd graduated from that to B and Es, with the occasional car theft thrown in. He'd been busted several times for possession of narcotics, been to rehab twice, and barely skated on a dealing charge the last time he'd been arrested. It was a pretty typical career arc for a petty criminal, one she'd seen too many times before; start small, work your way up, learn just enough from your mistakes to avoid serious jail time. The type of crime escalated, not from any sense of ambition but through the same kind of process that told a shark to keep moving or die. Boz was still moving.

His friends were another matter. Diego Molinez was an unrepentant thug, one who'd spent nearly half his thirty-six years in custody; he'd done time for aggravated assault, possession of an unregistered firearm, and narcotics trafficking. Aaron Tyford had been arrested on both narcotics possession and conspiracy to commit murder, but the charges had been dropped due to insufficient evidence.

The file on the Tyford case told an interesting story. Tyford had apparently been a dealer for a local gang and during the course of his business had learned the location of the drug lab used to manufacture product for sale. Deciding that wholesale prices just weren't low enough, Tyford had tried to rob his own supplier; unfortunately for him, he'd learned the hard way that volatile chemicals and gunfire just don't mix. While the resulting explosion had destroyed his reason for the robbery, it had also wiped out any evidence tying him to the lab itself.

She could see why a small-timer like Boz would attach himself to Hal Kanamu; he was more remora than shark, hanging around in the hopes of feeding off any scraps. But Tyford and Molinez were another breed entirely, more predator than scavenger. The only reason they'd spend time with someone like Boz would be because they saw an opportunity waiting to be exploited.

An opportunity like a newly rich, just-fallen-off-the-wagon ex-busboy.

Grissom performed the search on Khem Charong's hotel room himself.

It wasn't out of a sense of guilt or because he didn't trust anyone else to do so. He was simply curious.

Charong's room was as neat as his person. Four well-tailored suits hung in the closet, clean and pressed. Toiletries were lined up in the bathroom, as orderly as soldiers waiting for inspection.

He found no stashes of pornography, no sex toys, no indications that Charong was anything but what he seemed: a scientist visiting another country for a conference. Grissom even used a gas sniffer to scan the room for traces of hydrogen cyanide, but nothing showed up.

Everything seemed normal—except Grissom couldn't find a laptop.

It was probably the most ubiquitous tool today's scientist owned, and Charong didn't seem to have one. After a moment, Grissom called down to the front desk, identified himself, and asked if Charong had left it with hotel staff for safekeeping. He had not.

He went over the room again. Nothing inside the mattress, the air vent, the back of the toilet. Grissom sat on the edge of the bed and thought.

After a moment, he called down to the front desk again. "Yes, I was wondering if you had a lost and found. You do? I'm looking for a laptop. Turned in within the last day, encrypted. There won't be anything on it to identify the owner. You do? I'd appreciate it if you could send it up— I'll be able to prove ownership when he shows it to me."

He didn't have long to wait. A few minutes later, there was a knock at the door; Grissom opened it to find a bellman standing there with a silver laptop under one arm.

"Please set it down on the desk," said Grissom.

The bellman did so. "I'm, uh, under instructions to have you enter the password," the bellman said. He looked like he was still in high school himself. He opened the laptop and hit the power button. "Just to, you know, confirm that it's yours."

"It's not," said Grissom. "But now that it's in the room, it's the property of the Las Vegas Police Department." He pulled out the search warrant and handed it over.

The bellman took the form and studied it. "Okay," he said. "Does this mean I don't get a tip?"

Nick strode into the AV lab. "That the laptop Grissom brought in?" asked Nick.

"Yeah," said Archie. "It's encrypted, but I think I can get in. Might take me a while, though."

"You hear how Charong hid it? Turned it in to the lost and found. All he had to do to get it back was prove it was his."

"Easy to do when you know the password. But how do you explain turning in a laptop and then asking for it back?"

"Easy—you never deal with the same person twice. Turn it in to someone at the front desk, get a bellman to bring it up to your room when you want it back. It's how Grissom recovered it."

Archie grinned. "That's pretty slick, actually. Long as nobody rips it off in the meantime, it's in limbo—hidden in plain sight. How'd Grissom figure it out?"

Nick gave him a look. "He's *Grissom*."

"Yeah, sorry. Dumb question."

"So, how long you think it'll take?"

Archie frowned. "I don't know—as long as it takes. Decrypting isn't straightforward science, you know. Every box is different. Might get lucky with a password cracker, might have to look a lot deeper. Why? Is this guy gonna disappear or something?"

Nick shook his head. "Hard to say. We've got him locked up but . . . I guess I just really want to put this one away."

"Not to worry, *kemo sabe*. I'm on it."

Normally, that would have been enough for

Nick; Archie was one of the best, and if it were possible to pull anything off the laptop Archie would. Nick was pretty sure what he'd find, too: the kind of pictures that would put Khem Charong away for a long, long time.

But that wouldn't necessarily prove he'd killed Keenan Harribold.

It was a strange case, and not just because of the millipedes. While Nick could accept that someone would be twisted enough to kill a high school boy with bugs, Harribold's body had shown no signs of sexual assault. Khem Charong, based on his past history, wouldn't have left the boy untouched. And why go to the trouble of implicating a rival school after killing someone in a distinctive way that practically screamed *Arrest me! I'm an entomologist!*

It didn't make any sense.

"Hey, Boz," said Catherine. "Nice to see you again."

Boz didn't seem quite as happy. He slouched in his chair on the other side of the interview table like a sullen adolescent in the principal's office. Catherine tried not to take it personally; maybe his sore tooth was just making him moody.

"So," she said. "Hal Kanamu. Tell me about you and him."

"I don't have to be here, you know. I came in as a favor."

"And we appreciate it. Of course, your friends Aaron and Diego might not."

"They're not friends. I was just shooting some pool with them."

"They were friends of Hal's, though, weren't they? That's what you told me."

He looked away. "I don't know. I mean, I guess they were."

"And you were the one who introduced them, right? Hal was handing out the party favors and you couldn't keep your mouth shut. Bad move, Boz. Guys like that aren't satisfied with a little free fun. They always want more."

"Is that what this is about? Look, those guys are into their own thing. I don't—I'm not down with that. If they had anything to do with Hal getting killed, I don't know anything about it."

And even if you did you wouldn't talk, right? she thought. *I mean, you may not be the brightest bulb on the tree, but you're not* that *stupid. One body dumped in the desert may be murder, but a second is just cleaning up loose ends.*

"Looks like you've got an infected tooth," said Catherine. "Must be painful."

"Taking antibiotics for it. Doc says I've got an abscess."

"That's not all you've got, Boz. You own a leaky pen or just eat a lot of blueberries?"

"What?"

"Your fingertips are stained blue. I noticed the last time I talked to you."

"So what? It was a leaky pen, like you said."

"I don't think so, Boz. Hey, you want to see something really cool?"

He watched her warily as she dug out a pocket mirror and handed it to him. "Here."

"What's this for?"

She got up from the table and walked over to the door. "I asked to use this room just for this," she said. She turned out the lights.

"What—what am I supposed to do now?"

"Just wait a second, let your eyes adjust."

Catherine could hear him breathing in the darkness. He sounded nervous.

"Okay," she said. "Now hold the mirror up to your mouth. And smile."

Catherine knew when he did so—because she could see the faint, greenish-white glow that came from his open mouth.

"Oh my God," said Boz. He sounded sick—but then, he was.

She turned the lights back on. He looked as bad as he sounded. "What's wrong with me? Do I . . . do I have radiation poisoning?"

"Nope. You have a condition known as phossy jaw. Pretty rare these days, but it used to be an occupational hazard for match makers. I don't mean people who play Cupid—I mean actual, honest-to-God people who made matches."

"I don't understand."

"Let me explain it to you. Those stains on your fingers are from iodine. The abscess in your mouth is from exposure to white phosphorous—it gets in the maxillary bone and basically causes it to rot, which is why your breath smells so bad. White phosphorous used to be used in the production of matches, until it was replaced by red phosphorous—it's a lot less toxic. Unfortunately, red phosphorous is a lot harder to obtain these days, isn't it? You found a source of iodine but had to settle for white phosphorous instead of red."

"I don't know what you're talking about."

"Sure you do, Boz. You work in a meth lab. Consider yourself lucky—phosphorous poisoning does more than make your teeth glow in the dark. Not only will it kill you through organ failure, it'll drive you insane."

"I want a lawyer."

"You'll get one. But you should see a doctor first."

Archie looked up from his keyboard when Nick walked in. "Okay," said Archie. "I've got good news and bad news."

Nick pulled up a stool and sat down. "Hit me."

Archie tapped a key on the laptop he'd been working on. "I've decrypted the files on the laptop. It's exactly what we suspected—kiddie porn, some of it starring Charong himself. He's definitely going away."

"And the bad news?"

"Keenan Harribold doesn't make an appearance.

There's no kinky stuff featuring bugs. And the latest opus I found was time-stamped—check it out." He tapped a few keys and pointed to the bottom of the screen.

Nick flinched and looked away. "How long is this file?"

"Two hours. I don't know where it was shot, but it falls right in the middle of the TOD for Harribold."

"Sick bastard," Nick said grimly. "But it gives him an alibi."

"Only for murder," said Archie. "He's still going to prison."

Nick shook his head. "No matter how much time he does, it won't be enough. Thanks, Archie. I guess."

"You're kidding," said Grissom, peering over the top of his glasses. "Phossy jaw?"

Catherine nodded. "Yeah. Everything old is new again—I'm expecting an outbreak of smallpox at any moment. Figured you'd get a kick out of it." She paused. "How's the Harribold case going?"

"Not so good. Archie just eliminated our prime suspect."

"One down, I guess."

"I suppose. Is your glow-in-the-dark suspect co-operating?"

She shrugged. "He lawyered up. One of the symptoms of phosphorous poisoning is mental instability, so I don't want to push him too hard—anything he says now might get thrown out later."

"Does he seem irrational?"

"No, but who knows what he'll be like after the lawyer finishes talking to him—he might start speaking in tongues and wearing his underpants on his head. I don't think he's my killer, anyway."

"You have a working hypothesis?"

"Still putting it together, but it looks like Kanamu's big gambling win threw him in the deep end of the drug pool. I think he just started hanging around with guys a lot heavier than he was used to and got in over his head."

"So how does a killing over drugs produce a vic with wax in his lungs?"

"You've been talking to the doc?"

"He mentioned a few details over tea."

"That would be the part I'm still putting together . . ."

The sign over the door read PET CAVE in large, friendly letters. An old-fashioned bell tinkled when Grissom pulled open the door and stepped inside.

The store was large and clean, one wall lined with large aquariums and terrariums on four rows of shelves stretching from the midpoint toward the back. Two big pens dominated either side of the cashier's island, right in the middle: one held puppies, the other kittens.

"Mr. Grissom!" The man who bustled up to him

was shaped like a pear, dressed in an old-fashioned white lab coat with SOUTHFORD stenciled over the breast pocket. He had a wide smile on his wide face and a comb-over of hair dyed so black it looked like strands of black thread. "Haven't seen you in a while. How's Hank?"

"He's fine. Putting on a little weight."

Southford grinned and patted his own belly. "Well, it happens to all of us as we age, doesn't it? I've got some good special diet stuff, perfect for a dog Hank's size and age. I'll throw in a sampler with your regular order of crickets, no charge—if he likes it, come back and I'll give you a ten percent discount. Fifteen if you buy in bulk."

"That's very generous. Thank you."

"How's Sara?"

"She's . . . away on a trip."

"Oh? Not gone for too long, I hope."

"No. No, I . . . I hope not."

"Well, at least you have Hank to keep you company."

"That's true." Grissom paused. "He misses her."

Southford's smile was gentle. "I'm sure she'll be very glad to see him again. You know, I still remember the very first time you brought her here . . ."

So did Grissom.

The bell over the door tinkled.

"So this is it," said Sara. "Not exactly what I imagined."

Grissom walked in behind her. "Oh? What did you expect?"

"Something more . . . cave-like. Something more like your office."

"My office is not a cave."

"Oh, please. You could have bats roosting on the ceiling and no one would even notice. Except maybe Hodges—and he'd probably just compliment you on your excellent guano-collection technique . . . Oh! Puppies!"

Grissom smiled. Sara was already kneeling by the pen, sticking her fingers through the mesh and letting them lick her fingers. "They're so adorable . . ."

"Yes," Grissom said softly. "Adorable."

"—that all, Mr. Grissom?" said Southford.

"Hmm? I'm sorry, Dale. Woolgathering . . . Actually, I was hoping to talk to you about one of your customers—a teenage boy named Lucas Yannick?"

"Oh, I don't know, Mr. Grissom." Southford frowned. "My customer records are highly confidential. I'm afraid you'll need a court order to get access to them."

There was a moment of silence.

Southford burst into a fit of giggles. Grissom sighed, but he did so with a smile on his face.

"Sorry," said Southford. "I couldn't resist—I miss working at the lab sometimes. Sure, I know the kid you're talking about—let me just pull up his file."

He went behind the cashier's counter and tapped

a few keys on the keyboard. "Here you go—Lucas Yannick. He's got a Chilean rose-haired tarantula, a striped scorpion, and a praying mantis. Comes in here to buy bug chow."

Grissom knew "bug chow" meant feeder crickets; spiders and scorpions preferred their food to still be kicking. "Did he ever order anything else? Millipedes, for instance?"

"No, nothing like that. Seemed interested in a snake the last time he was here, though—could be he's decided to move up, evolutionarily speaking."

"Thanks, Dale. I'll pick up that dog food later, if you don't mind."

"Sure. Say hello to Sara for me, will you? When she gets back."

Grissom glanced down at where two puppies were wrestling happily. "I'll do that," he said.

Diego Molinez stared levelly across the interview table at Catherine. There was no overt hostility in his face, just the blank hardness of someone used to prison.

"Consorting with known felons is a violation of your parole," said Catherine. "I could have you sent back to a cell right now."

Diego didn't respond. Then again, she hadn't really asked him a question.

"Tell me what I need to know and that doesn't have to happen," she continued. "Security footage at the Braun Suites shows you, Lester Akiliano, and Aaron Tyford visiting Hal Kanamu. Hal knew how to party, didn't he?"

"So?"

"So sometimes a party can get out of hand. Maybe somebody says the wrong thing. Things get out of control—"

"It wasn't like that."

"No? Tell me how it was, then."

"We respected each other. That's all."

Catherine studied him for a minute. If there was one principle Grissom had drilled into her, it was that the evidence never lied—but people did. Even so, people were always part of the equation, and Catherine's ability to read people was finely tuned. *Respect* was one of those key words in Diego's world, not one he used lightly. If he was going to lie to her, she didn't think he would do it using that particular term.

He was telling the truth. And she knew what that meant.

6

Clive Crabtree stood on the sidewalk, watching the artificial volcano in front of the Mirage erupt. He thought he knew how it felt.

Clive had never been to Vegas before. Gambling had never been his thing, or his wife's, and seeing big glitzy shows with topless showgirls didn't really appeal to him, either. But the shift in the 1990s toward a more family-friendly Vegas had changed his attitude; roller coasters and theme restaurants and acts like the Blue Man Group seemed more his speed. Plus, both Clive and his wife had been known to enjoy the occasional buffet, and there had never been any shortage of those in the city.

Fireballs shot into the air to the rumble of explosions—recordings of actual volcanic eruptions, Clive had heard. He could feel the heat of the flames on his face, though he doubted real volcanoes came with a drum soundtrack and smelled like a piña colada.

Their first mistake had been to book rooms in a resort they'd never heard of. The ad had claimed it was on the Strip, but that was only technically true; it was at the very end of Las Vegas Boulevard, about as far as you could get from the Strip and still be on the same street. The promised five-star accommodation had turned out to be more like one, and Clive suspected it was a star in danger of burning out. Construction next door had woken them up at six in the morning, and they'd been forced to park across the street because the resort's parking lot was full of heavy equipment and building supplies.

Smoke and fire belched into the air. Flames danced on red-tinted water intended to simulate lava. Clive wondered if the pirates next door at Treasure Island ever got a headache from all the noise. Probably not; a propensity toward migraines didn't tend to steer you down the buccaneer career path.

The biggest mistake Clive and Sheila had made was agreeing to the free breakfast. It turned out to be a meager offering of cheap Danishes and second-rate coffee, accompanied by a two-hour, mind-numbing presentation on time-share condos—located at this very resort, what a bargain, you just can't beat these prices. The only reason they hadn't walked out after the first ten minutes was the promise of half-price tickets to a show they'd really wanted to see.

But that hadn't been the worst of it. After the crappy breakfast and a tour of a show suite in far better condition than the one they were actually staying in came Brent.

Brent was deeply tanned, with large white teeth and blow-dried blond hair. Clive was pretty sure Brent was also a robot, because his single-minded dedication to selling them a time-share verged on the mechanical. No matter how many times they said they weren't interested, Brent would keep going. He showed them cost breakdowns that to Clive's eyes—he was a CPA—were laughable, even insulting. Even when Clive pointed out that for the amount of money they were expected to invest they could stay in an actual five-star hotel for a week every year, Brent would not be dissuaded. In fact, he became even more aggressive, his demeanor suggesting that only a complete bona fide idiot wouldn't grab the deal he was offering.

Clive was not a man easy to anger. It had taken an hour of being badgered, lied to, and treated as no more than a wallet with legs before he'd finally lost his temper. He hadn't actually punched Brent in the face, but he'd come close. He'd stormed out of the presentation, leaving Sheila to try to claim the promised tickets—which he *knew* would just turn out to be another con—and marched off down the street in the closest thing to a blind rage he'd experienced since high school.

That had been over an hour ago. He'd walked

off most of his anger, gotten to the point where he thought he could talk to another human being without shouting at them. Watching the volcano helped—for all its implied violence, it was strangely soothing. *Look at what human beings can do*, it seemed to be saying; *we can tame even the most destructive forces of nature*.

It was an illusion, of course. Just like the whole city. Sexy showgirls you could never sleep with, huge piles of money you could never win. The more Clive thought about it the more he felt that his encounter with Brent, with his empty eyes and his vacant good looks, was like a personification of Vegas itself. Clive had never met someone he'd felt less of a human connection to in his life; he was pretty sure that if he pumped Brent's arm up and down a few times, the salesman's eyes would spin around and then show a lemon and a horseshoe.

Clive sighed and resumed his walk. He shouldn't let one bad encounter with a soulless huckster ruin their trip. All he'd lost, after all, had been a few hours of his time—that was a lot better than some visitors to the city could claim. He could have been a real Vegas success story: arrive in a ten-thousand-dollar car and leave in a hundred-thousand-dollar bus.

He found himself turning off the Strip and onto the quieter streets that paralleled it. The glitter and flash of the big hotels were still visible, but they were less overpowering. The farther away they got the better he felt, so he just kept going.

Clive wasn't stupid. He knew the shadows that lay alongside the expensive glare of a place like the Strip held their own, much less civilized dangers— but his own less civilized self, the ape that lived at the back of every human's brain, was telling him that no one would dare mess with him right now. And even if they did, they'd be sorry. Hell, just let them try.

There was a man sprawled out on the sidewalk ahead.

At first, he thought the man was just drunk. A tourist like himself who'd had a few too many Bloody Marys with his eggs—Vegas was the only town Clive had ever been in that had a drinks section in the breakfast menu—and wandered off for some desert air to clear his head, who needed to just lie down for a moment . . .

Then he got closer and saw the blood.

Grissom stared down at the dead man as David examined the body. *Some break*, he thought. Grissom was supposed to be at a conference, exchanging ideas with fellow professionals, and had found himself dragged back by the Harribold case. Now he was answering another call, simply because they were so short-handed. *Maybe I was fooling myself by thinking I could get away at all. Maybe that's how it's always going to be.*

Maybe Sara was right.

David pulled the wallet from the dead man's back pocket and handed it to Grissom. "Tourist taking a walk found him. Can't have been dead more than an hour—almost no rigor, no postmortem lividity."

Grissom opened the wallet. "Paul Fairwick. Thirty-eight, has an address in Henderson. I've got an all-access pass to the Athena Jordanson show, too."

"Oh, she's great," said David. "I took my wife to see her Motown revue for her birthday. Amazing voice."

Grissom bagged the wallet, then knelt down beside the corpse. "Well, COD seems pretty obvious." There was a bullet hole in the center of the forehead. "Powder burns and a muzzle stamp—he was shot at close range."

David held up one of the man's arms. "Ligature marks on the wrists, too."

"But very little blood. He wasn't killed here, just dumped."

"Strange place to dump a body. It's awfully close to the Strip."

"Not if you're trying to send a message . . ."

Aaron Tyford did his best to fill the interview room with the hate radiating from his eyes. He was a tall, wiry man with a scar that ran along his jawline and a nose that had been broken more than once. His body language told her there was nothing he'd enjoy more than throwing her through the nearest window.

"You're lucky you don't glow in the dark," said Catherine. "Guess you left the chemistry to Boz, huh? Moving product is probably more your line."

"You're crazy, lady. Don't know what you're talking about."

"There are three things essential to any business, Aaron. You need someone to do the work, you need someone to sell what you're offering, and you need the capital to get started in the first place. Everything else is details."

"If you say so."

"You and Diego had the business plan. Boz had the skills, you had the contacts—all you needed was the cash to get started. Which is where Hal Kanamu came in."

"Hey, I barely knew the guy."

"But you wanted to know him better. You wanted to be more than just party buddies—you wanted his *respect*."

He leaned forward, his jaw clenching before he spoke. "Listen—*everybody* respects me. You know someone who doesn't, give me his number and I'll pay him a little visit."

"Sorry, I don't give my number out on a first interrogation. And what you're talking about isn't respect, it's fear—fine for intimidating business rivals, but not so good for someone you want as an investor. What happened, did Kanamu get cold feet, decide to back out at the last moment? Or did you just get impatient, decide to kill him and take the money?"

He studied her for a moment, and then a cold smile spread across his face. "You want to know what happened? Nothing. Maybe I did float a business idea his way, and maybe he was too stupid to see how sweet a deal it was. But since you seem to know so much about business, let me ask you this: how many investors do you think an entrepreneur is going to attract if he starts killing everyone that says no?"

He shifted in his seat, leaning back and throwing an arm over the back of the chair. "Maybe that's what a small-timer would do, grab the cash and run. But that's not my style."

"Sure it is. I've got a detailed review right here." She tapped the sheet on the table in front of her. "Not a very good one, either—most of the people involved gave you zero out of five stars. Or, more accurately, seven out of ten years."

He shrugged. "Live and learn. I'm still alive, so I guess I'm doing something right."

"Changing your approach?"

"Absolutely. Look, Kanamu was high most of the time and paranoid all the time. He knew who I was, what I've done. You really think he'd be alone in a room with me and Diego and a big pile of cash? Forget it. He was always talking about all this Hawaiian folklore crap and that big party out in the desert—that was what he was into. He had all the money he wanted; he didn't care about making more."

"Unlike you."

Aaron spread his arms wide. "Hey. It's the American dream."

Greg Sanders loved science, even as a kid. He loved it the way some kids love comic books or video games or TV shows; to him, it was a window into another world, one that seemed infinitely more interesting than the one he lived in. To him, science and imagination went hand in hand, one just as full of possibilities as the other. The Norwegian myths and legends his grandparents told him fed his imagination growing up, and he loved the show *The X-Files;* it combined science and fantasy in a way he found irresistible. It was too bad that mix wasn't available in real life . . .

And then he heard about Burning Man.

The festival attracted much more than the partying maniacs portrayed by the mass media. Engineers of every stripe were not only common but necessary: you didn't build a city of fifty thousand people in the course of a week without serious planning and execution, especially not in the middle of a desert. Structures in Black Rock City ranged from people sleeping in pup tents anchored to the playa with two-and-a-half-foot lengths of rebar to pyramids that towered five stories high.

And those were just the buildings; the art was the truly impressive part.

A fifteen-story-high tangle of yellow wooden beams, made of a hundred miles of wood and shaped like a distorted wave. Two full-size oil tankers bent around each other and stood on end like mechanical caterpillars swing dancing. Temples of intricately carved wooden filigree like the skeletons of cathedrals. The largest flame cannon ever built, shaped like an oil derrick and fueled by two thousand gallons of propane and nine hundred gallons of jet fuel . . .

Maybe this year he'd actually go, instead of just staring at pictures on the web. But despite his fondness for the place, Burning Man was a place of extremes; one of those extremes could easily be murder.

He got online, made a few inquiries. The electronic presence of the Burner community was huge; they were one of the first groups to embrace the Internet. Greg had heard one person describe the festival as a physical extrusion of cyberspace into the real world—all the theme camps were like live versions of websites. Free, interactive, and limited only by imagination.

There was a bar that hosted Burner events in Vegas, and one of those gatherings was happening tonight. The purpose of these events was usually twofold, the first being simply to try to re-create that sense of freedom and connection that the festival itself fostered.

The second was more pragmatic: fund-raising. Burning Man, despite its ban on commerce, wasn't cheap. Admission to the event was upward of three hundred dollars, and even though you might not spend a dime for a week you still had to invest in all the resources necessary to travel to and spend seven days in the desert.

That was only the bare minimum, though. Theme camps could spend tens of thousands of dollars bringing their vision to life, and that amount went up by a factor of ten when it came to some of the big art installations.

Greg had never actually made it out to the playa, but it was time to talk to a few people who had.

Doc Robbins was in the groove.

He was listening to the Doors on his new iPod— a birthday present from his youngest child—and nodding along as he got ready for the next autopsy. "Riders on the Storm," one of the great oldies, with Jim Morrison not so much singing as chanting a dire description of imminent doom and killers with toads in their brains. It was a dark piece to listen to in a morgue, but that just added to its power. Robbins was kind of sorry Morrison had died in Paris instead of Vegas; this town seemed far more suited to the singer's dramatic lifestyle and death than any place in France.

And Robbins would have loved to add Jim's picture to his collection.

Never mind that Robbins was only nineteen and still in medical school when Jim died. Robbins figured that if Vegas could keep Elvis alive until he was forty-two, it could have done the same for the Lizard King. Which meant Morrison would have survived until '85—still a number of years before Robbins hit town, but maybe he would have been here visiting, even here to catch Morrison performing at Caesars or the MGM Grand. Jim could have collapsed onstage, ODing right before everyone's eyes, and Robbins would have responded to the call of "Is there a doctor in the house?" by leaping to the rescue . . .

By the time the fantasy played itself out in his mind, the song was nearly over and he and Mr. Mojo Risin' were jamming together at the Copa. He smiled to himself, had Jim expire mid–poetic rant, and got down to work.

"Body is that of a young African-American male, approximately midthirties," he said, enunciating clearly for the recording. "Cause of death appears to be a single gunshot wound to the anterior portion of the skull."

And now for the interesting stuff. "There's a twelve-inch-long incision from the navel to the base of the breastbone that's been sewn up with green thread. Lack of a vital reaction along the edges of the wound indicates it was made postmortem. I'm cutting the thread and will send it to Trace for analysis."

He did so, using a scalpel to sever the crude

stitches and a forceps to pluck out the strands, placing them in an evidence bag. He'd seen bodies with these sorts of postmortem cuts before—usually on drug mules who had died when one of the heroin- or cocaine-stuffed balloons they'd swallowed had burst. Whoever had hired them to carry the drugs in the first place would simply extract their product from the body's intestinal tract, slicing open layers of flesh like a bubble-wrapped FedEx package.

He had to admit, though, this was the first one he'd seen that had been resealed.

"It appears that a small white plastic cylinder, three to four inches in diameter and approximately six inches in length, has been inserted in the abdominal cavity. One end of the cylinder has a much thinner, transparent tube feeding into another incision in the esophagus. Opening the mouth—no sign of the tube's end. It looks as if it's been fed all the way into the sinus.

"The other end of the cylinder appears to be open. Taking a closer look . . ."

Doc Robbins was not a squeamish man. Years of experience in dealing with corpses in states that ranged from dismembered to liquefied had given him a strong stomach; nevertheless, there were still certain things that unnerved him.

In particular, he hated rats.

He dealt with their leavings often—he could spot rat predation on a body with a glance, even tell you how big a specimen had been gnawing on the remains from the size of the tooth marks. He'd found rat droppings on and in corpses many times. But all that was simply physical evidence—it didn't affect him the way the sight of one of the filthy, evil rodents themselves did. Loathsome, disease-ridden, foul vermin, each and every one . . .

What leapt out of the cylinder and sank its fangs into Doc Robbins's hand wasn't a rat.

The Thunderbolt Lounge was old-school Vegas. Pictures on the wall behind the massive bar showed the celebrities who had frequented the bar in the past: the Rat Pack, Jerry Lewis, Rita Hayworth, Jimmy Durante. One framed picture hung in an odd spot, near the ceiling, and was no more than a clear pane of glass in a wooden frame; it was there to show off the two bullet holes in the wall behind it, put there during a dispute between Maximillian "Maxy" Fratoni and Joey "One Roll" Lido in 1956.

The dance floor was small and concrete, the lighting was dim, the fixtures old and badly in need of repair; but the place sprawled out over several rooms, built when land in Vegas was cheap, and featured three different stages. It was one of Greg's favorite spots in Vegas, and he wasn't the only one who felt that way.

Tonight the place was full of Burners. They dressed the same way they would out in the desert, in costumes that ranged from the practical to the bizarre: cargo shorts and mesh tops; leather chaps and chain-mail vests; Hawaiian shirts and grass skirts; *Star Wars* stormtrooper outfits; Santa suits. There were people dressed as winged fairies, as kung-fu monks, as zombie cheerleaders, as space pimps, robot gorillas, mad scientists, and evil clowns.

Greg paid the door fee to a large, hairy man wearing a torn wedding dress and foot-long glow-in-the-dark antennae. "Slow night, huh?"

The doorman shrugged. "What can you do?"

Greg strolled inside and glanced around. A DJ was spinning house music, something catchy and hypnotic with samples of an old Marx Brothers routine for lyrics. He grinned and looked around, then spotted a fire spinner he recognized as Glowbug.

He showed her the picture he'd brought along of Hal Kanamu. "Yeah, I know him," Glowbug said. She wore a short silver wig, a silver Mylar corset, bright orange fishnets, and five-inch platform boots. "That's Kahuna Man. Met him at the Burn last year."

"Yeah? What was he like?"

"He seemed okay. He was a first-timer, so he was really into it. Didn't see him that much at the festival, but that's how it is—you can spend the entire week camping with the same group of people and be so busy you never see them twice."

"How about since then?"

"Yeah, he came to the decompression party in October. He seemed a lot more intense then."

Greg nodded. Decompression parties were usually thrown a month or two after the event itself, functioning as the sociological equivalent of a hyperbaric chamber that gradually introduced a diver to increasing levels of pressure so he wouldn't suffer from the bends. The festival itself was such an intense and all-encompassing experience that the return to normal life—what some Burners called "the default world"—could be something of a shock. Decompression helped lessen that.

But Hal Kanamu had experienced another massive shock to his system by then—he was several million dollars richer. "Intense how?"

She shrugged. "Hey, I don't want to get the guy in trouble with the cops."

"You can't," said Greg. "He's dead. I'm trying to find out how it happened."

Her eyes got wider. "Oh, wow. Was he . . . was it drugs?"

"Why would you say that?"

"Because the last time I saw him he was using. Hey, I try not to judge, but meth will *kill* you, man. There are other ways to have fun, you know?"

"Sure. Was he hanging around with anyone in particular?"

She hesitated. "Look, I'm just trying to retrace his movements," he said. "I'm not here to bust anyone, I'm just collecting information."

"No, yeah, sure. He was hanging out with Doozer and his crew a lot."

"They're the guys who built the Fire Truck, right?" The Fire Truck had been exactly that, an old hook-and-ladder that had been retrofitted into a vehicle covered in gas jets and flamethrowers; the ladder itself became a mobile fire sculpture extending sixty feet into the air.

"Yeah, that's them. They're not here tonight, though. I think they're pretty busy working on next year's project. Oh, look, there's Neon Girl. I'll, uh, see you later, huh?"

And then she was gone.

"Great," Greg muttered. "Just great."

The paparazzi caught Grissom by surprise.

They ambushed him coming out of the police station with Jim Brass, snapping flash pictures and yelling questions. "Grissom! Do you have any suspects in the killing of Paul Fairwick?"

"Captain Brass! Is it true Athena Jordanson has been receiving death threats?"

"Gil! Gil! Is it true Fairwick died of an overdose?"

Grissom stopped. "The Fairwick case is still in the preliminary stages," he said. "I cannot comment on any details at this time." He knew it wouldn't stop the barrage, but it was like tossing a bone to a pack of wild dogs; it might slow them down enough to let him get away.

They followed him to the Artemis Hotel, of

course. It was where Athena Jordanson was currently headlining and had been for the past four years. What Brass had discovered was that Paul Fairwick wasn't just a guy with a backstage pass—he was Athena Jordanson's personal assistant.

The billboard at the front of the hotel made sure everyone knew who their star was, too: ATHENA JORDANSON, QUEEN OF SOUL glittered in electroluminescent letters twenty feet high and flashing every color of the rainbow.

Grissom parked and went inside, Brass meeting him in the lobby. Hotel security met them and took them to the diva's penthouse suite via private elevator, leaving the swarm of photojournalists behind.

"So if Athena's the queen of soul," asked Brass as they rode up, "what does that make Paul Fairwick? Earl? Duke? Baron-in-waiting?"

"Corpse," said Grissom. "In morgue."

The elevator doors opened onto a lobby that looked more like the entrance to a jungle. Palms, ferns, and tropical flowers reached from floor to ceiling, with springy green moss underfoot. Water trickled down the front of an abstract crystal sculpture and into a stone-lined pool. The two hotel security men who had ridden up with them rode back down again, leaving Grissom and Brass alone.

"After you, Bwana," said Brass.

They made their way along a mossy path that led to a huge living room, just as filled with greenery but with one curving glass wall that looked out over the Strip. It had been widely reported that Ms. Jordanson had asked for—and received—the penthouse suite, built to her specifications, as part of her contract.

The queen of soul herself was reclining on a moss-green couch that looked like it had grown out of the floor. She wore a bright pink tracksuit, her brown feet were bare, and her famous Afro looked like she'd been sleeping on her left side. She had a box of Kleenex in her lap, and used tissue littered the floor like crumpled white flowers.

"Ms. Jordanson?" said Brass. "I'm Captain Jim Brass, and this is Gil Grissom with the Las Vegas Crime Lab. We have a few questions for you, if you don't mind."

She shook her head. "No, I—of course. Please sit down."

Brass chose the other end of the couch, while Grissom settled into an armchair. Its legs seemed to branch out into polished roots.

"When was the last time you talked to Paul?" asked Brass.

"Last night, just before my ten o'clock performance. We talked backstage, I told him what I wanted to eat afterward—that was the last thing I said to him, you know? 'Make sure my steak is medium-rare.' I can't believe it." Tears welled up in her eyes. "What a stupid thing to say to my best friend. To be the last thing I said to him."

"Did Paul have any enemies?"

"It's my fault," she sobbed. "All my fault."

"Why do you think that?"

"Because I'm always getting threats. Nobody wanted to hurt Paul—he was a sweetheart, a saint. He put up with me and all my bullshit, and that's saying a lot. No, the only reason someone would hurt Paul would be to get at me."

Brass and Grissom had dealt with celebrities before. They tended to live in worlds that centered around them, and any significant event—like a death—was naturally assumed to be about them, not the actual victim. Sometimes they were even right.

"Do you have copies of these threats?" asked Grissom.

"You'd have to ask Paul—oh, God!" She started weeping again. "How am I going to cope without him? He handled that kind of thing . . ."

They waited until she got herself under control. "Do you have a chief of security?" Grissom asked gently.

"Yes. He's with the hotel. I don't remember the name, though."

"Don't worry, I'll find out and I'll talk to him," said Brass. "If his staff has intercepted notes or calls, there may be something we can use."

Grissom's phone vibrated. "Excuse me," he said. He rose from his seat, took a few steps away, and answered. "Grissom."

He listened intently, then frowned. "David, calm down. Where is he now? All right, good. I want you to meet me outside the morgue, all right? Don't let anyone else in."

He snapped the phone shut and headed for the elevator. "I have to go, Jim."

Brass had been a cop for a long time, and he recognized the tone in Grissom's voice instantly. "What's wrong?"

"It's Al," said Grissom. "He's in the hospital."

7

Groups that came to Black Rock City organized themselves as theme camps. A theme camp could be as small as one person operating out of the back of their vehicle or number a hundred people or more and involve a structure the size of a circus tent. Theme camps could be based on literally anything, though in recent years the festival had announced an overall art theme to lend some direction; people were free to embrace or ignore the theme as they chose. There were camps that gave away food, massages, costumes, alcohol, haircuts; camps that offered dating services, minigolf, tea, floggings, live music, swing dancing, trapeze lessons, or meditation circles. There were hundreds. Each had its own identity, was run entirely by volunteers, and was responsible for packing out every single scrap of material it brought in.

Doozer's crew was an art collective who called themselves the Phyre Brigade. They were hardcore pyromaniacs, building vehicles and sculptures that played with flame the way a fountain played with water. The group's base of operations was an old garage on the outskirts of town, its use donated by a fellow Burner who had no current plans for the property.

Greg pulled up next to the rusting spots where the gas pumps had once stood. He could see sparks and the ultraviolet glare of a welding rig inside, through the narrow glass panes of the rolling panel doors. It was late, but Glowbug had told him Doozer preferred working late.

The front entrance was unlocked; a stuffed deer head gazed at the ceiling from the spot on the counter where the cash register had once stood. A door beside that stood open, leading to the garage; Greg stood in the doorway and called out, "Hello?"

A man in blue coveralls turned off his welding torch and turned around, flipping up the smoked glass visor. His face was as greasy as his clothes, and a cinder smoldered in his heavy black beard.

"Hi," said Greg. "You're, uh, on fire." He pointed.

The man reached up and snuffed out the cinder by pinching it with two fingers. He didn't say thanks, and he didn't flinch. "Yeah?"

"I'm Greg Sanders, Las Vegas Crime Lab. Doozer, right? I'd like to talk to you about Hal Kanamu—Kahuna Man."

Doozer snorted. "Let me guess. He ODed."

"Not a surprise, huh?"

"No. He was headed there in a hurry—only a matter of time."

"You don't seem real upset by that."

Doozer glared at him. "Hey, it pisses me off, okay? Every time some sponge brain with no sense of judgment and a death wish kills himself through sheer stupidity, it makes everyone else look bad. And by everyone else, I mean anyone who might like to indulge in a little chemical recreation now and then."

"Okay, I get it. He was irresponsible. But if so, why let him be part of your camp?"

Doozer studied him for a second before responding. "That's just it—we didn't. Turfed him a few weeks ago. He'd show up to planning meetings so wired you could have hooked him up to a klieg light. Rambling on and on about all this Hawaiian stuff he was into. Don't get me wrong, I like a good rolling tiki bar as much as the next guy, but he was trying to convince us to change our plans for next year. We're already halfway done—no way we're gonna suddenly shift to some half-baked tweaker idea."

Greg had to admit the vehicle Doozer had been working on was impressive: a gigantic metal scorpion on wheels, the articulated tail ending in a flame-thrower. It looked skeletal at the moment, the metal segments that would make up its armor leaning against the wall like a knight's inventory of shields.

"So this is it, huh? Pretty damn cool."

"Thanks. Gonna outline the whole thing in elec-troluminescent wire—either blue or red, not sure. Thing'll kick some serious ass after nightfall."

"So what did Kanamu want to build instead?"

"Ah, he kept changing it. Some kind of giant volcano goddess one week, then a fire-breathing shark the next. He was all over the place."

"You hear about his gambling win?"

"Yeah, everybody knew about it. Only reason we didn't tell him to take a hike sooner—kept say-ing he'd finance the whole trip, you know? But there was just no way. Black Rock's not about money, anyway—it's about self-suffiency. Find yourself relying on a junkie, that's a recipe for di-saster."

"Anyone try to get him to straighten out?"

Doozer shook his head. "Yeah, a couple people talked to him. But he was just as high on the money as the meth, you know? Didn't *want* to come down."

"When was the last time you talked to him?"

"Couple weeks ago. Heard he hooked up with another artist, was gonna pay him to build some-thing and take it to the playa himself."

"You have the artist's name?"

"Sorry, no. And Kahuna Man kind of dropped off the radar after that."

"Okay, thanks." Greg took one final, admiring glance at the scorpionmobile. "Have fun."

"Always do."

* * *

"Slow down, David," said Grissom. "Take a deep breath. Now let it out."

They were in the hall outside the autopsy room. Grissom had rushed over after a panicked, nearly incoherent phone call from David. "Good. Now tell me again what happened."

David swallowed. "I was just outside. I heard Doc yell—not like he'd dropped something and was angry, more like something had scared him. I ran in there."

"What did you see?"

"I saw . . . I saw the biggest spider I've ever seen in my life."

"Can you be more specific?"

"It was as big as my hand. Tan colored. It was sitting on the thigh of the body and waving its front legs in the air. Doctor Robbins was on the ground, not moving. I didn't know what to do, so I grabbed a chair and sort of waved it at the spider. It jumped off the table and ran away, I think under one of the shelves. I grabbed Doctor Robbins and pulled him outside, then called the paramedics. He was in a lot of pain—"

"Were its fangs red?"

David frowned. "I—yes. Yes, I think so."

"All right. Call the hospital and tell them he's likely been bitten by a Brazilian wandering spider. Its venom is neurotoxic, not necrotic. Got it?"

"I—yes, yes, I've got it. Is he going to be all right?"

Grissom hesitated. "Less than one percent of those bitten by this spider die. I'm sure he'll be fine—just make the call."

Grissom left David guarding the door while he made a quick trip to the supply closet, returning with a pair of heavy gloves and a large plastic jar.

"I told them," said David. "They said they had the antivenin."

"Hopefully they won't need it. Don't let anyone else in, all right? This species is highly aggressive— it's one of the few spiders in the world that will pursue and attack animals much larger than itself."

"You're—you're going in there?"

Grissom slipped on the gloves. They were made of industrial rubber, more suited to chemical spills than inch-long fangs, but they should provide some protection. "I'll be fine."

He opened the door cautiously, slipped inside, and closed it behind him.

The body of Paul Fairwick lay on the autopsy table. Robbins must have grabbed at the overhead light as he fell, because it was tilted up at a crazy angle, throwing odd shadows across the room.

What Grissom hadn't told David was that the Brazilian wandering spider was listed in the *Guinness World Records Book* as the most venomous spider on the planet. Its venom contained a neurotoxin known as Tx2-9, an ion-channel inhibitor that caused profuse sweating, vomiting, and tachycardia. The venom also contained a high amount of serotonin, producing intense pain that could range from local to radiating throughout the body. The spider itself didn't weave a web and wait for its prey to come to it; it was a nocturnal hunter, moving through the jungle night in search of something to kill and eat. It was incredibly fast and agile and wouldn't hesitate to attack if it felt threatened.

Grissom scanned the base of the room first. The spider would most likely have found refuge under something low, but it would be attracted to anyplace warm. He got down on his hands and knees, putting the jar down beside him, and peered under the row of shelves along one wall.

He hoped Robbins would be all right. While most victims of the genus *Phoneutria* survived, two types were most at risk: children and the elderly. While Al Robbins was only fifty-seven, he had a pacemaker—and when the spider's venom did kill, it was through pulmonary edema. More worrisome was the fact that Doc Robbins had two prosthetic legs, meaning a much lower body mass for the venom to be distributed through; that was thought to be the factor that killed children who had been bitten.

He took a flashlight out of his pocket and shone it under the shelf. The Brazilian wandering spider had eight eyes, two of them quite large; Grissom knew they would reflect light well

No spider. He stood up and turned in a slow circle, looking for movement. Nothing.

It would look for a heat source, but the autopsy

room was kept cold. Perhaps he should just wait and let the chill slow it down?

No. Better to trap it now, before it hid itself away in some unreachable nook or cranny.

And then he saw Doc Robbins's laptop sitting on the stainless steel counter. It would be radiating heat, but the spider would have no way to get up there; the stainless steel legs would be too smooth for it to climb, as would the tiled wall it was attached to. The laptop, though, had a power cord trailing down the side . . . and the transformer in the power adapter would be just as warm and a lot more accessible.

He put the flashlight in his mouth, held the open jar in one hand and the lid in the other. He crouched down, peering around the edge of the counter at the plug near the floor. There was no spider . . . but a thin line of web glinted in the beam of the light. A strand that led upward, paralleling the power cord itself.

Grissom turned his head. Eight eyes gleamed from behind the open laptop, on the same level as his own—and no more than two feet away.

The spider leapt at his face—but Grissom was quicker.

He brought the open jar up just in time and the arachnid landed inside. He slapped the lid on a split second later, the spider already frantically trying to get out.

He examined it critically as it tried to strike at

him through the transparent plastic. "Lovely," he murmured.

"Grissom?" David called from the other side of the door. "Are you all right?"

"I'm fine, David. You can come in now."

The door cracked open. "I just got off the phone with the hospital. Doc's in a lot of pain, but they think he's going to be all right."

"Where did this come from?" asked Grissom.

"I have no idea."

Grissom put the jar down and approached the body on the autopsy table. He noticed the cylinder with the tube attached to it immediately. "I don't believe it . . ."

"It came from in there?"

"It appears so. This tube was inserted up and into the sinus cavity to provide air, while the body itself would have kept the spider warm. Once discovered, its natural inclination would be to attack."

David blinked. "That's insane."

"No, it makes perfect sense." Grissom paused. "To an entomologist . . ."

Neither Aaron Tyford nor Diego Molinez would admit to any involvement in Hal Kanamu's death, dealing methamphetamine, or manufacturing it— and Catherine hadn't expected them to. The evidence seemed to point to some kind of drug deal gone wrong, and she thought if she could locate the drugs she'd be one step closer to solving the riddle of Kanamu's death.

They had to be making the meth somewhere. The problem was that there was no shortage of places to do so in and around Vegas. Trailers or rural properties were often used because of their isolation, but meth labs had also been found in up-scale condos and suburban homes. Even hotel and motel rooms were being used, the "cooks" leaving behind all sorts of toxic chemicals once they were done. One of the biggest tip-offs of a meth lab was the foul smell it tended to exude, but Catherine hadn't noticed any such odor on Tyford or Moli-nez; that suggested they had extremely good ven-tilation, but maybe they'd just been careful about showering and changing their clothes.

She went through their records carefully. Nei-ther owned any property, at least not under his own name. Molinez had spent a lot of time incar-cerated and still had to report to a parole officer on a regular basis.

The proof of Boz Melnyk's exposure to a meth precursor was enough to get a search warrant for his residence, anyway. Maybe it would lead to something more incriminating.

Boz Melnyk lived in a run-down house in north Vegas. It clearly wasn't where he cooked meth—no burn pits in the yard, no oxidation on the alumi-num window frames—but it was still a sty. Catherine shook her head as she picked her way through the trash-strewn living room, the floor littered with fast food wrappers, old newspapers, stacks of porn magazines, and empty beer cans. The bedroom was just as bad and the kitchen was worse; roaches skittered away from the beam of her flashlight, hiding under overturned dirty dishes with a film of mold growing on them.

There was an attached garage but no car. Instead, she found plastic crates of two-liter soda bottles stacked three high along one wall, many with mismatched caps. Each was full of a yellow liquid, and she knew even before she opened one and took a whiff what she would find.

"Well, well," she murmured to herself. "Mr. Melnyk's a tinkle tweaker."

Catherine was never amazed at just how far an addict was willing to go to get a hit of their favorite drug. This particular method, while more high-tech, wasn't new; desperate alcoholics sometimes saved their own urine and drank it the morning after, essentially running it through the same system twice to strain out any remaining alcohol. Tweakers did much the same thing, saving their own urine and then adding acetone, lye, or paint thinner to filter and separate out the chemicals they were after. A gallon of urine produced around half a gram of meth—of noticeably poorer quality, but still enough to get the user high.

She looked around but didn't find any of the filtering agents. *He must take it to the lab for that; this is just for collection and storage. Which means these crates have presumably been to the lab and back.*

She replaced the bottle, then knelt down and examined the crates themselves. There were bits of brownish matter stuck to the underside of several; they had their own distinctive odor, one she recognized. *That narrows it down, but I'm going to need more information than my nose can give me.*

She scraped a sample into an evidence vial. The next step was up to Hodges.

Robbins blinked at Grissom blearily from his bed in the ICU unit of Vegas General. He was propped in a sitting position, a swiveling tray over his lap. His prosthetic legs had been removed, creating the disturbing illusion that he wasn't so much lying in bed as part of it, a sort of mattress centaur.

"How are you, Al?" asked Grissom.

"I feel like I was thrown in an industrial washing machine with a dozen baseball bats. What the *hell*, Gil?"

"You were bitten by a poisonous spider indigenous to South America. They sometimes show up in shipments of bananas."

"I hate to tell you this, Grissom, but if there were any bananas around this spider, they were in the process of being digested." He winced and held up his hand, which was beet red and extremely swollen. "Little bastard got me good."

"The venom contains a high degree of serotonin—

that's what makes it so painful. In fact, once the serotonin wears off you may experience a downturn in mood—like coming off antidepressants."

"Oh, good, something to look forward to."

"Don't worry, I captured it."

"Don't suppose you'd leave me and it alone in a room with my crutch, would you?"

Grissom smiled. "A rematch? I think you need to get back in shape first."

"I don't know if I already said this, but—*what the hell*, Gil?"

"I think this is related to the Harribold case."

"First millipedes, now a spider. Both used as weapons."

"That's how it appears, yes."

"So we've got a psycho on our hands?"

Grissom raised his eyebrows. "I think that judgment's a little premature. We have someone with a knowledge of entomology, that's undeniable. What's more troubling is his choice of victims."

"I'd have to agree with you on that one."

Grissom shook his head. "The first victim was stalked online, with a great deal of preparation. The second attack was an elaborate trap, but its target was one of circumstance—the spider could have bitten anyone who was present at the autopsy. It could have been me."

"Maybe it's just the drugs they gave me, but I'm not sure I follow. Are these random killings or carefully orchestrated?"

"Both. It isn't the identity of the victim that's important," said Grissom. "It's how they die."

"I hate to disappoint you, but I'm not planning on dying just yet."

"Good. I'd hate to have to train another coroner."

"You're going to keep the damn spider, aren't you?"

"It's evidence. But they only live a year or two, anyway."

"That's a real consolation."

"Is there anything I can bring you? Reading material, something to eat?"

Robbins shook his head. "I don't think so. I ache too much to concentrate, and I'm too nauseous to eat."

"Let me get that tray out of the way, then."

Robbins stopped him by grabbing the tray with his good hand. "You can leave that, actually."

Grissom frowned—and then a look of understanding crossed his face. "Oh. I don't know if you know this about the *Phoneutria* species, but one of the side effects of the venom is priapism. It's actually being studied as an anti-impotence drug."

"I wondered. It's temporary, right?"

Grissom smiled. "Let's just say that when it comes time for you to testify, it won't stand up in court."

"You can go now."

Hodges looked up from his microscope. "The sample you brought me," he told Catherine, "was crap."

Catherine refused to rise to the bait. "I know that. What I need from you is what *kind* of crap it is."

"Oh. Bovine. But what may be of more interest is what said moo-cow was eating that *became* the crap."

"Which would be?"

"*Eustoma exaltatum,* or as it's more commonly known, catchfly prairie gentian. A pretty purple flower, to be prosaic."

"And what sort of distribution would the pretty purple flower have?"

"Sadly, widespread—at least in California. In Nevada, though, it's made it onto the at-risk botanical list; there's only one place it's known to grow, out at Red Rock Springs."

She nodded. "So I'm looking for a rural property near Red Rock. Thanks."

"I live to please."

"Okay," said Greg. He and Catherine were in the layout room, comparing notes on the light table. "Here's what I've got. Kanamu *was* hanging around the Burner community, but they weren't comfortable with his drug use. He tried to convince an art collective that calls itself the Phyre Brigade to change gears on the art project they were already half-finished with to work on his, but they turned him down and turfed him because of the drugs."

"What did he want them to build?"

Greg shrugged. "It changed depending on how high he was, but a volcano goddess *was* mentioned. And a fire-breathing shark."

"What happened after they cut him loose?"

"Apparently he hooked up with another artist, but I haven't been able to track him down. Still working on it."

"All right. Lester Akiliano led me to three meth heads named Boz Melnyk, Aaron Tyford, and Diego Molinez. They didn't have any problem with Kanamu's using; in fact, I think they planned on going into business with him. According to them, he wasn't interested."

"You think they killed him over it?"

"Maybe—but the funds had to be for expansion, not start-up. They're already in business." She told him about the phossy jaw.

"Glow-in-the-dark grin, huh?" He shook his head. "Either of the other two have alibis?"

"Each other. Claim to have been up late watching movies at Melnyk's place, which I've been to. A palace it isn't. And I found something interesting—though disgusting—while I was there." She described the garage, the crates of urine, and the manure sample that Hodges had analyzed.

"Red Rock Springs," said Greg. "Can't be that many properties within grazing range. Let's do a title search and see what we come up with."

"My turn to be one step ahead." She handed

him a printout. "Ready to go hang out with some livestock?"

"Okay, but this time I'm wearing boots."

They knew they'd found it by the smell.

It was an abandoned barn, turned a faded gray by the elements, half its roof gone. Where a farmhouse once stood was only the crumbling remains of a stone chimney. A narrow dirt track led up to it, but there was no vehicle visible.

Catherine parked the Denali a good distance away and rolled down her window. The prevailing wind carried a chemical stink both she and Greg recognized immediately.

"Think anyone's in there right now?" asked Greg.

"If they are," she said, pulling out her cell phone, "they're gonna wish they weren't."

The Las Vegas Police Department didn't screw around when it came to meth labs. Even though the number of operations had dropped drastically in the last few years, largely supplanted by Mexican "superlabs" that smuggled their product across the border, there was always a local chemical entrepreneur willing to start his own enterprise—and the LVPD had learned not to take any chances with the smaller variety. The smaller the lab, the more likely it was run by addicts; that increased the danger on several levels.

Methamphetamine produced a wide variety of

effects, both physical and psychological. Of the latter, paranoia and a compulsion to tinker—sometimes manifesting as dismantling and reassembling electronics—often led to a lethal tendency to build booby traps to protect the lab itself. Tweakers could be endlessly inventive: pit bulls, venomous snakes, even alligators were used as watchdogs; automatic weapons were trained on doors, triggers attached to doorknobs with fishing line; canisters of homemade poisonous gas or large amounts of high explosive were wired to light switches.

Those were the immediate threats. More indirect but no less dangerous were the large number of hazardous chemicals that could be present: solvents like acetone, ether, methanol, benzene, toluene, isopropanol; acetic, sulfuric, or hydriodic acid; ammonia, phosphine, or Freon gas; and metals like mercuric chloride, lithium, red phosphorous, metallic sodium, or potassium. The last two were especially dangerous—usually stored in kerosene, either one would react explosively when exposed to air or water.

Because of this, police responding to reports of a meth lab approached it with extreme caution. The large van trundling up the dirt track toward Catherine and Greg didn't stop when it reached their position, but instead kept going to within fifty yards of the barn itself, where it opened and disgorged a team of six officers in hazmat suits, body armor, and full-face respirators. There was nothing but gentle rolling hills on either side of the structure and no trees at all. If the people inside tried to run, there was no place to run to.

The men quickly took positions around the building. Once they were in place, the officer in charge raised a bullhorn to his mouth: "ATTENTION! THIS IS THE LAS VEGAS POLICE DEPARTMENT. YOU HAVE ONE MINUTE TO EXIT THE BUILDING. COME OUTSIDE WITH YOUR HANDS CLEARLY VISIBLE AND LAY FACEDOWN ON THE GROUND."

"Think they'll put up a fight?" Greg asked.

"Depends on how stupid they are," said Catherine.

The minute ticked by. There was no response.

"Might not be anyone home," Greg murmured.

"Lot of cooks do leave during the last forty-eight hours of the process."

"Yeah, 'cause that's when the whole thing is most likely to go boom."

The officer in charge gave the signal, and his men started to move in, very slowly, with weapons drawn. They looked like futuristic storm troopers advancing on the site of a concealed UFO.

"I hate this part," said Catherine.

"I know. No telling what's in there. . . ."

8

RILEY AND NICK LOOKED at Grissom expectantly. Grissom, on the other side of the light table, pinched the bridge of his nose and closed his eyes.

"You okay, boss?" asked Nick.

"Fine. Just waiting for the migraine medication to kick in."

"Hey, if you've got a migraine—" Nick began, but Grissom cut him off with a wave of his hand.

"No, Nick, really. Migraines are always worse if you delay too long before treatment; I think I caught this one in time." He picked up a sheaf of papers from the light table and flipped through them. "Anyway, this can't wait."

"I heard about Doctor Robbins," said Riley. "Is he going to be okay?"

"Yes. He's still in considerable pain, but his heart rate's stabilized. However, we can't ignore the consequences of his being attacked."

"What are we going to do, fumigate the morgue?" asked Riley.

"The morgue isn't the problem. This is the second insect-themed homicide within days; the planning, execution, and choice of victims suggest someone who's more interested in the act itself than who he kills."

Nick frowned. "Wait. You think our guy's a serial? One whose weapon of choice has six legs?"

"Eight in the case of the spider. Sixty to sixty-two for the millipedes—depending on sex."

Riley nodded. "Are we still looking at the ento-mologists as our prime suspects?"

"They would seem to be the most likely, yes. Neither Roberto Quadros nor Nathan Vanderhoff has an alibi for the Harribold murder."

"Serial killers usually escalate," said Nick. "Two murders in less than a week? He's already off and running."

"True," said Grissom. "And both killings—while different in circumstance and execution—required a fair bit of preparation. Anyone who goes to that much trouble isn't going to be satisfied with only two; it's likely he has several more scenarios ready and awaiting implementation."

"This guy doesn't sound like any serial I've ever heard of," said Riley. "He doesn't seem to be get-ting any sexual satisfaction out of it, and the targets don't seem to have anything in common. One he did up close and personal, the other at a distance and almost at random."

"I don't think the victim matters to him at all,"

said Grissom. "Paul Fairwick was killed by a gunshot and had an insect planted in his corpse—similar to the way certain wasps will paralyze spiders and lay eggs in their bodies. Keenan Harribold was lured to a rendezvous by an online imposter posing as a romantic interest—not so different from the way the *Photuris* insect lures fireflies to their doom by duplicating the flashing light of a receptive female."

"Pixels and text instead of pheromones and mating displays," murmured Riley. "But with the same eventual effect."

"Professor Vanderhoff already pointed out the similarity between one high school attacking another and anthills waging war. Even the graffiti left at the scene was reminiscent of chemical traces used by colony insects to mark property. I think our killer is more fascinated by the process and the resulting consequences than the immediate result."

Nick crossed his arms. "So the riot at Plain Ridge High was what he was actually after, and killing Harribold was just a means to that end?"

"All serial killers express a desire for control, Nick—even Jack the Ripper's letters to the press were a way for him to influence the behavior of the entire citizenry of London. Our . . . 'Bug Killer' is simply demonstrating a more advanced knowledge of sociology."

"In that case," said Riley, "why was Paul Fairwick targeted? What kind of effect was the killer trying to create?"

"Perhaps we should ask Fairwick's employer," said Grissom. "The queen . . ."

It was several long minutes before an officer walked out of the barn and waved an all-clear to them.

"Let's suit up," said Catherine.

Both of them slipped into hazmat suits with respirators—though they skipped the body armor—then drove up to the barn and got out.

"Nobody home," said Sergeant Loyola. He kept his mask on, though, and so did they. "Nothing cooking, either."

"That's a relief. No traps?"

"Couple tripwires, nothing fancy. Give my guys a minute to finish up and you can go in."

Greg hefted his CSI case in one hand. "Anything we should know?"

"Yeah," said Loyola. "If your air conditioner ever gets sick and vanishes, I think I know where it crawled off to die."

They saw what he meant when they entered the barn. A double-wide trailer was parked along one wall, beneath what was left of the roof; the rest of the floor space was taken up by a rusting pyramid of metal and plastic that reached to the rafters.

"Wow," said Greg. "He wasn't kidding. There must be hundreds here—maybe even a thousand. It's like a temple to climate control."

"Climate catastrophe, more like. Freon's one of

the chemicals used to make meth; they must have cracked open every one of these units to get at the leftovers."

"Tweakers plus a gazillion AC-cooled rooms equals appliance graveyard," said Greg. "It's kinda cool, in a nonenvironmental, highly illegal way."

They entered the double-wide. Most of the meth labs Catherine had seen were filthy: garbage strewn on the floor, every available surface crammed with dirty or broken glassware, open containers of chemicals everywhere.

This place was different.

A bulging plastic garbage bag sat in one corner, tied shut. It was the only evidence of trash in the place; every surface was clean, from countertops to tables to floor. Containers of chemicals had been lined up in cupboards like exotic spices. The sink was freshly scrubbed.

"Damn," said Greg. "This is the best-kept illegal drug facility I've ever seen."

"Yeah. I think I'm starting to understand why Boz Melnyk stored his urine at home; someone thought it was too unhygienic to keep around."

"So which one do you think is the clean freak?"

Catherine shrugged. "I wouldn't apply that description to any of them. Let's see if we can find out."

They found a bedroom in the back, with nothing in it but a mattress on the floor. Greg pulled out his UV light and shone it over the bedding. "I've got definite evidence of sexual activity."

"So someone liked to party as well as cook. If we can match DNA samples to Tyford or Molinez we can tie them to the whole operation."

The bathroom was next. It was as clean as the rest of the place, but one particular detail caught Catherine's eye. "Greg. Take a look at this."

"Oh, ho. That *is* above and beyond," he said.

"Not really. But it is the mark of a professional. . . ."

Henry Stancroft was a wide, bullet-headed black man in a dark suit. He could have been mistaken for an ex-prizefighter, except for the spidery, almost delicate eyeglasses that perched halfway down his flat nose. The impassive, evaluating look he gave Grissom from behind his desk was that of a small-town sheriff staring down a rival from another county intruding on his turf.

"Yeah, no, it's a real shame what happened to Paul," he said. "You like anyone for it?"

"The investigation is ongoing," said Grissom. "I was hoping maybe you might have some ideas."

"Of someone who'd want to kill Paul?" He shook his head. "Honestly, that's a tough one. Paul's job was to grease the wheels, make sure everything ran smoothly for Her Highness. And he was real good at his job—had the gift of gab, know what I mean? Everybody liked him. Guy should have been a diplomat instead of a glorified gofer."

"How about his employer? I understand Ms.

Jordanson recently received some disturbing mail from a fan."

Stancroft snorted. "Yeah, she gets some pretty weird stuff sent to her. You think Paul was killed by some wacko? Because he was close to her?"

"It's a possibility. Do you still have the letters?"

"Of course. We keep a file on guys like that, just in case." He got up, moved over to a filing cabinet against the wall, and pulled open a drawer. Stancroft's office reminded Grissom of the lab; it had the same kind of open layout and lots of glass so the head of security could keep an eye on everything in his domain. But instead of white-coated lab technicians strolling past outside, it was burly pit bosses with earpieces and dark blue blazers.

"Here," said Stancroft. He handed Grissom a manila folder. "Everything he sent her. You need exemplars for fingerprints, I can provide them—nobody's touched those but me, Fairwick, and whoever sent them."

"Thank you."

Stancroft hesitated. "You used to work with Warrick Brown, right?"

Grissom blinked. "For a number of years, yes. Did you know him?"

"Yeah—a long time ago. We grew up in the same neighborhood. Got into some of the same trouble, even dated some of the same girls. We were never that close, but—I don't know, I kind of kept track of him. We were sort of on parallel paths, you know? When I heard what happened—"

Stancroft broke off. Warrick Brown had died in the line of duty, shot by a rogue cop; he'd died in Grissom's arms. "Wish I'd made more of an effort to get to know him, that's all."

"He was a good man."

"Yeah. Too damn few of those around. I'm sorry."

"So am I," said Grissom.

A radio car found Paul Fairwick's car, parked two blocks away from where he lived. Nick and Riley took the call.

"Driver's-side window is smashed," said Nick as they walked up.

"More glass in than out," said Riley. "No blood spatter in the car, though. He wasn't shot here."

"No, but I'll bet this is where he was grabbed. Smash the window for maximum shock value, then stick a gun in his face."

Nick opened the driver's door and shone a flashlight into the interior. "Keys are still in the ignition. We're lucky somebody didn't grab it for a joyride."

"Whoever took him would have had to put him into another vehicle—probably in the trunk."

Nick checked the pavement close by. "No tire marks. He didn't lay down any rubber when he left."

"Kidnapping someone like that, in a relatively

open area, then calmly driving away? Cool customer."

"Yeah. Ligature marks on the body indicated he was bound—so he must have driven Fairwick to another location and tied him up before killing him."

"And adding a little surprise to his box of Cracker Jacks," Riley murmured. "Let's get this back to the lab—maybe it can tell us why Fairwick parked two blocks away instead of in the lot of his own building."

Nick stood back and studied the car while Riley called for the tow vehicle. It was a different color, a different year, but the make of the car was the same as Warrick's.

Nick had helped process that vehicle. It was the car that Warrrick had been shot in, the car that he would have died in if Grissom hadn't been at the scene. Instead, he'd died cradled in Grissom's arms.

They'd caught the killer. Nick had pointed a loaded gun at the man's face while the killer shouted at him to shoot—and he had, into the ground. It hadn't been an act of kindness—the killer was an undersheriff, and Nick knew that his existence in prison would be one of isolation and constant fear.

Nick wasn't going to help Warrick's murderer commit suicide. Not unless it took a long, long time.

"Truck'll be here in ten," said Riley. She noticed the look on his face and added, "You okay?"

"Fine." Nick shook his head, forced a smile. "Just thinking about another case."

"Bad one?"

"Yeah," said Nick. "About as bad as it gets."

Grissom studied the twelve letters laid out before him on the light table. According to Stancroft, they had arrived over the last two months, one a week at first and then two.

The envelopes and the stationery the letters were printed on were all identical. Each had been mailed from within Las Vegas itself. Each letter was a single page, double-spaced and printed by an inkjet. The content was an almost mathematical progression of obsession, the first only hinting at it and the last practically raving. Despite that, there was a uniformity to them that was chilling—each was almost exactly the same length, each was folded at exactly the same place.

He had lifted numerous fingerprints from the envelopes, several of which were unknown—most likely those of postal employees. Fingerprints on the letters themselves were those of Henry Stancroft and Paul Fairwick, the only two people to have read them; it was Fairwick's job to read the mail, and he apparently passed the letters directly to Stancroft.

The letters made frequent disparaging remarks about the hotel itself and how Athena Jordanson deserved better. The writer insinuated that her safety was at risk and directed blame, again, at the hotel. The logic was faulty, but the intention was clear: if anything bad were to befall Athena Jordanson, it would ultimately be the hotel that was at fault.

One passage in particular, from the very latest letter, Grissom found especially disturbing: *I pity you, in your glass castle in the sky. You think yourself immune to all the ills that befall us ordinary drones, toiling in our endless busywork while you play and sing. I used to think that you were a goddess, that the divinity of your voice was there to lift us up; but now it only serves to remind me of everything we'll never have, of just how special you are and how unremarkable the rest of us will always be. Living in that penthouse, looking down upon all of us, we must seem no more than scurrying insects to you . . ."*

Scurrying insects was underlined. It was the only phrase in any of the letters that was.

When they got Paul Fairwick's car back to the lab, Nick processed the inside of the car, while Riley did the outside.

The first thing he found was a crumpled piece of paper on the floor. He flattened it out and read it: it was a single photocopied sheet informing the residents of 4359 Carleton that due to the parking lot being resurfaced, they would have to find alternate arrangements for the next forty-eight hours. A hand-drawn map suggested spots along the same block the car had been found in.

"I didn't notice any roadwork equipment when we drove past Fairwick's apartment building, did you?" asked Nick.

"No—but I did notice a security camera over the front door. Could be the killer was redirecting his target to a more suitable stalking ground, one where he wouldn't be observed."

"Like the spot where he was attacked. That suggests he was actually lying in wait."

"There were no obvious hiding places on that block, which confirms he was in a vehicle," said Riley. "So far, that's about all we've got."

The tiny white dog cradled in Jill Leilani's arms stared at Catherine with wide brown eyes. It seemed perfectly happy to stay where it was, though the same couldn't be said about its owner. Leilani shifted in her seat uncomfortably, glancing around the interview room as if she might bolt at any moment. Her eyes were bloodshot, her hair a wild, scraggly mess. She was dressed in club clothes: a short skirt, tiny top, and high-heeled shoes.

"So, Jill," said Catherine, "how's that plan to kick meth going?"

"Yeah, okay, maybe not so good," she mumbled. "But that's my problem, right? I mean, I don't have any or anything."

"Not now. But you've got a nice deal lined up for a steady supply, right? Straight from the source."

Her hands stroked the dog compulsively. "No. No, that's not true."

"Sure it is. Hanging around with Hal Kanamu got you a heavy habit, but then you and Hal had a falling out. You needed a new supplier, and you found it in Aaron Tyford and Diego Molinez. Didn't you?"

"No, no, no. I score on the street, same as anyone else, it's not hard to find, so much stuff moves through Vegas it's a hub it all comes up the interstate from Mexico and—"

Catherine cut her off. "No, Jill. The economy's bad, and you only work part-time at the Shoremont. Not enough to pay for what you need. So you decided to do a little moonlighting, right? Even a meth cook can use a maid."

"I—I don't—"

"It was the little folds you put in the end of the toilet paper that tipped me off. Habit, right? And probably more than a touch of meth-induced obsessive-compulsive behavior. We found towels from the Shoremont in the trash, too."

"That—that doesn't prove anything, so what, so what—"

"Maybe not. But we found traces of sexual fluid from three different people on a mattress at the meth lab—DNA from two males and a woman. Aaron Tyford and Diego Molinez are already in jail." She paused. "As for the female DNA—I'm pretty sure it's going to be a match to yours. Isn't it?"

Her bravado broke. Tears began to spill silently

down her face. "Yeah. Not enough they made me clean up their damn lab. They wanted other things, too."

"And how did Hal feel about all this?"

"He didn't know. I was ashamed to tell him, so I kept it a secret. That's the real reason we stopped hanging around together—I mean, at first it was because I was trying to get clean, and then it was because I didn't want him to know what I was doing. Lester knew, but I made him promise not to tell."

Catherine nodded. Jill had pointed her at Lester Akiliano but hadn't counted on Catherine finding out about Boz, Molinez, and Tyford. "So what happened, Jill? Did Hal find out? Did Lester tell him? Did Hal confront Molinez and Tyford about what they were doing to his old friend?"

"I don't know what happened, I swear to God," she sobbed. "Diego wanted me to convince Hal to go into business with them. Lester couldn't change his mind, but Diego thought I could. He was wrong, though—Hal was tweaking big-time on this art project he was into, didn't want to talk about anything else."

"I'll bet Diego didn't take that well."

"He was starting to get impatient. I told him I'd keep trying. But then—then Hal turned up dead."

"You think Diego was responsible?"

"I don't know." She stopped, wiped her eyes with the back of her hand. "Thing is, Diego didn't know where to find Hal. He'd been to his place, but Hal was spending most of his time at this warehouse, where him and this artist were working together. I knew where it was, but I never told Diego."

Catherine thought back to what she'd learned about Hawaiian women who used to dress up as Pele and extort favors from superstitious villagers. "Did you do that to keep him safe?" she asked. "Or because it gave you a bargaining chip with your dealer?"

Jill Leilani looked down and stroked her dog, who looked back with trusting eyes. She didn't answer.

She didn't have to.

Nick and Riley were supposed to interview Athena Jordanson—but the diva declined an invitation to come down to the police station, and so they went to talk to her at her hotel.

"Can you believe this?" Riley said as they walked through the lobby. "I don't care how many gold records she has, she isn't above the law."

Nick grinned. "This is Vegas, not Saint Louis. Town's kind of like an archeological dig: lots of different layers. You've got old Vegas, built by mobsters; high-roller Vegas, where the rich and famous come to throw away money and get quickie weddings; family Vegas, with kid-friendly hotels and roller coasters; and post-crash Vegas, where everyone's scrambling to make a buck and real estate values are dropping into the basement."

"Guess it's obvious which one Jordanson is."

Nick nodded at the security guards—he played golf with one of them now and then—and they punched in the code for Jordanson's private elevator. "Yeah, she's Vegas royalty. That doesn't mean she's above the law, but it does mean she gets a certain level of respect. The mob may have built this town, but it was people like her who filled it. These days, anyone who can put butts in seats has clout, and in Vegas that doesn't just trickle down— it gushes."

The doors opened and they got in. "So she gets special treatment?"

"Hey, would you rather talk to her in a luxury apartment or a windowless interview room? I'll bet her place smells better."

Riley smiled. "Okay, you got me there."

When the doors opened, Riley took two steps, stopped, and blinked. "This isn't an apartment," she said. "It's a theme park."

Nick chuckled. "Come on, Alice. Time to step through the looking glass."

He led the way down the path, calling out, "Hello? Las Vegas Crime Lab."

"Over here," called a voice.

Athena Jordanson was in a sunken hot tub, the edges lined with foam rubber that had been molded to resemble rocks. A steaming waterfall at one end of the irregular pool provided a steady trickle of white noise and hot water.

Jordanson herself was at the other end, her hair tied back with a length of scarlet cloth. There was an empty wine bottle at the edge of the tub, and she had a half-full one clutched in one hand.

"Ms. Jordanson," said Nick, "we were hoping we could talk to you about Paul Fairwick."

"All right," she said. She sniffed back tears and gestured with the bottle. "Please, have a seat."

Nick grabbed a wicker chair, while Riley stayed on her feet. "Can you tell us if anything strange happened involving Paul in the last few weeks?" asked Nick.

"All kinds of things. Paul was my man Friday; he handled all the strange little details of my life. I used to say his job description was 'weirdness wrangler.'" She smiled, a full-on face-stretching beam that only emphasized the pain in her eyes. "People don't understand what it's like, living my kind of life. They think, *Oh, she's rich and famous—what does she have to complain about?* But like a wise man once said, there's trouble at every level of life."

"Elvis Presley," said Nick.

She nodded at him, her smile fading into sadness. "Yeah. People get sick, or die, or break your heart—all the money in the world doesn't change that. And sometimes what you think is your strength turns out to be your greatest weakness. See, I counted on Paul for so many things. All the little necessary things, the food and the getting from place to place, getting stuff from the drugstore or going to the bank or—just the day-to-day things everyone does and takes for granted. And I haven't done any of them for over twenty years . . . I was thinking about grilled cheese sandwiches today. I hardly eat them anymore, but I used to love them when I was a teenager. You know, I couldn't remember how to make one. Isn't that stupid? Simplest thing in the world, but I couldn't remember it. If I lost all my money tomorrow, I'd probably starve to death."

"I doubt that," said Riley.

Jordanson leaned back, resting the base of her skull against the padded rim of the tub. "I know, I know. Someone who has as much as I do has no right to complain. One of the things money buys is freedom, freedom from all those little jobs— poor me, now I'll have to hire someone else to do them." She closed her eyes. Tears leaked through them, sliding down her face to join the water she was immersed in. "But I'll never be able to replace Paul. Losing him doesn't feel like losing someone I loved—it feels like an amputation."

Nick nodded. "I understand. He can't be replaced—but we can bring the person who did this to justice. If you depended on Paul that much, I'm sure you would have noticed anything out of the ordinary."

Jordanson took a long swig from the bottle of

wine without opening her eyes. "I've always gotten threats; it's just part of the business. But after your colleagues Captain Brass and Mr. Grissom came to see me, I talked to the hotel's head of security, Stancroft, myself." Her tone got angrier. "He told me that the number of crank letters I'd been getting had jumped in the last couple of weeks. I demanded to see them and he told me he'd given them to the police. I asked if Paul knew about them and he told me that wasn't Paul's job, it was his."

"We're studying those letters now," said Riley. "While they do mention you, they seem more directed against the hotel itself. They also make a reference to 'scurrying insects.' Does that mean anything to you?"

Jordanson opened her eyes and glared at Riley. "Scurrying insects? No. That's crazy." She shook her head. "But it doesn't matter. I've just about had it with this place. Stancroft should have done a better job; he should have told me what was going on. The Embassy Gold has been trying to lure me over there for years, and I'm seriously thinking about going. And if I do, I'll make damn sure their security is better than this place's."

Riley frowned. "Forgive me for asking, but—how exactly are you going to do that?"

Jordanson sighed. "The only way I know how, honey. With lawyers, and lots and lots of money."

*   *   *

"Okay," said Brass. "So we bring in Vanderhoff and Quadros and sweat them. It's got to be one or the other, right?"

Grissom shook his head. They were in Brass's office, discussing the case and their next move. "It's not that simple, Jim. Both of them are only here for the next few days; we can't hold them long unless we charge them, and we simply don't have the evidence to do that yet."

"And if we don't charge them soon, they'll just go back to their respective countries."

"Where the guilty party could simply disappear into the jungle, South Africa, or South America. Both men have years of field experience."

Brass sighed. "So we've got what, seventy-two hours? To either come up with better cards or fold."

"More or less."

"Wonderful. Anything else?"

"I'm afraid so. It's fairly likely that the killer has more attacks planned. The murders seemed to be planned to showcase his ingenuity—but the more complex the scheme, the greater the chance he'll make a mistake."

"Any idea who he'll go after next? So far, his victims haven't had anything in common."

Grissom rubbed his temples. "The victims are linked by the conceptual nature of the attacks, especially the secondary results. The Harribold case caused a riot, mimicking one anthill waging war against another. I believe Paul Fairwick was targeted because of his promixity to Athena Jordan-son, the 'queen' of soul."

"Why? What's his death supposed to accomplish?"

"Athena Jordanson's contract is almost up, and she's been considering moving to another hotel; one of the reasons she's cited has been lax security at her current venue. When the queen of a termite colony is threatened, her workers move her to another site."

"Or in this case, another penthouse suite. You think our killer's trying to accelerate the process?"

"It's possible. But I don't know why." Grissom paused. "You said the victims didn't have anything in common. But—conceptual link aside—there is one element both cases share."

"What?"

Grissom got to his feet. "Me."

"Is this a confession?"

"The killer is clearly trying to impress someone. I don't think it's any accident that he chose Vegas to stage his crimes."

"You think he'll come after you?"

Grissom shrugged as he headed out the door. "I'll be careful."

As soon as he'd left, Brass picked up the phone. "Dispatch. Yeah, I'm gonna need a couple of uniforms to set up on Grissom's place. Twenty-four-hour surveillance. I'll authorize the overtime."

With Doc Robbins in the hospital, the day-shift cor-oner had to finish the autopsy. He sent the spider cylinder and tube to the lab, along with the bullet he retrieved from the vic's skull and the thread Robbins had collected.

Nick examined the thread, Riley the bullet. Grissom took the cylinder.

There were no fingerprints on the cylinder or the tube, outside or in. Grissom examined the edges of the cylinder on the open end. They were rough, the cylinder itself being nothing more than a narrow plastic bottle sawed in half. The tubing was surgical grade, inserted into a small hole punched in the lid of the bottle at one end. He took high-resolution pictures of the tool marks on both.

Nick found that the thread used to sew shut the wound was a thirty-braided filament with a diameter of 0.3 millimeters. He took pictures of the cut ends, then checked the fiber database.

The bullet was .22 caliber Remington ammo, fired from a gun with six grooves, or "lands," in a right-hand twist of 1:14; that meant the bullet had to travel one turn in fourteen inches. Riley thought the gun was most likely a Ruger revolver.

"Okay," said Grissom. "What do we have?"

"The thread's surgical grade," said Nick. "Looked a little funky under the microscope, so I had Hodges run a chemical analysis. It's a homopolymer of N-acetyl-D-glucosamine."

"Chitin," said Grissom. "Used in self-dissolving sutures because of its antimicrobial properties—

that and the fact that it's the second-most common carbon compound on the planet."

"Cellulose being first," said Riley. "Chitin's derived from the outer shells of crustaceans, right?"

"And insects," said Grissom. "He's showing off. Common thread would have worked just as well."

"Good," said Riley. "Arrogance works for us in the long run. Got an IBIS hit on the bullet—matches one recovered at the scene of a liquor store robbery, though the gun was never found. The clerk identified a suspect later in a lineup, but without the gun the county prosecutor decided not to go to trial and the charges were dropped. Suspect's name was Richard Waltham."

"Any firearms registered in his name?" asked Grissom.

"No. But he does have a history of minor crimes ranging from possession of stolen property to burglary."

Grissom nodded. "The cylinder was made from a plastic bottle, cut down to size. The tool used had a serrated edge—it might be a handsaw, but I'd guess a kitchen knife. The cut's jagged and uneven, suggesting an implement that was handled in a start-and-stop fashion. There's no label, but the shape of the neck is distinctive."

"Nick, see if you can track down the source of that thread. Riley, I'd like you to concentrate on the bottle."

"I—all right," she said. "What about Richard Waltham?"

"I think I'll go see him," said Grissom.

Grissom talked to the manager of the motel Richard Waltham lived at; the manager described Waltham and told Grissom that Waltham could usually be found at the Tuxedo Casino, where he played cards when he had the cash.

The Tuxedo was brand-new, a hundred-million-dollar updating of an older Vegas property. It was heavy on classic style, lots of brass and oak and crystal chandeliers, HD plasma screens running clips of movies featuring Gene Kelly singing in the rain or Bogey and Bacall in a passionate exchange. All the black-and-white charm was somewhat offset by the crowds of tourists, many of them clutching drinks in gigantic novelty cups made of neon-bright plastic: three-foot-high replicas of the Eiffel Tower or stretched-hourglass shapes called yards, filled with daquiris or margaritas or piña coladas.

Waltham was sitting alone at a table, playing twenty-one. The dealer was a young blond woman dressed in a tuxedo-style top, fishnets, and heels. Waltham himself wore a faded chambray shirt, dark blue jeans, and grimy white sneakers; his hair was entirely gray and pulled back in a ponytail beneath a battered straw cowboy hat. He had a cigarette tucked behind one ear.

Grissom sat next to him. "Richard Waltham?"

Waltham gave him a wary glance. "Why?"

"Mr. Waltham, my name is Gil Grissom. I hate to interrupt your game, but I need to ask you a few questions."

Waltham signaled for another card and snorted when he busted. "What about?"

"Your gun."

"Don't own a gun."

"Maybe not now, but you did. You used it to rob a liquor store, remember?"

"That case was thrown out."

"Because nobody could find the gun. I assume you got rid of it?"

"I told you—"

"That would have been the smart thing to do. Thing is, a gun is a valuable commodity; I doubt if you just threw it away. I think you sold it, and I want to know who you sold it to."

Waltham pushed another chip from his dwindling pile at the dealer. "Everybody wants something, Mr. Grissom. I want to double down on a pair of aces, myself. You can see how that's going."

"Maybe I can change your luck. Your gun was used in a murder."

Waltham paused. "Not my problem."

"Not yet. But that gun is evidence in two different crimes, and I *will* find it. At that point, whomever you sold it to will probably accuse you of both crimes. At the very least, you'll be charged as an accessory to murder."

"If you find it."

"On the other hand, if you were to direct me to that person, you'd be assisting in the investigation. If that led me to locating the weapon, it's unlikely any further charges against you would be pursued."

Waltham thought about it for a moment and signaled for another card. Twenty-two. He shook his head. "So you're offering me a gamble, huh? Take a chance that you won't find it and risk getting dragged into a murder investigation—or fold my cards, give it up, and hope you'll honor your word."

"That's it."

Waltham sighed. He had a two-day growth of beard and a fifty-year growth of wrinkles, maybe sixty around the eyes. He sized Grissom up with the weary experience of a hundred wins and a thousand losses, then gave a rueful little laugh. "Tell you what, partner. Sit down and have a drink with me. You convince me you're an honorable man, I'll give you the hand. But if I'm gonna throw down my cards, I need to know the fella across the table from me; that's fair, don't you think?"

"Fine by me."

They left the table, Waltham scooping up the few chips he had left, and walked across the casino to the bar. Waltham greeted the bartender by name and asked for the usual; Grissom had a beer.

"You're not the kind of cop I'm used to," said Waltham. He pulled out a crumpled pack of cigarettes and lit one with a silver Zippo embossed with a pair of dice.

"I'm a scientist, actually."

"Yeah? That's a strange thing to be in this city."

"Is it?"

"Sure. Vegas is probably the most antiscientific place on the planet. This place feeds on hope, blind faith, and a complete denial of consequences. Don't matter if you're talking about sex, gambling, or entertainment; it's all about how you feel in the moment, not about how you'll feel later or what you should be thinking about right now. Even the shows—they'll make you laugh or gasp, or turn you on. But none of 'em will make you *think*."

"I know what you're saying. But Vegas isn't completely about feeling as opposed to thought; any good poker player will tell you that."

"Any good poker player tends to wind up with my money in his pocket, so maybe you're right." Waltham took a long swig of his drink, something clear over ice with a slice of lime. "But that's the exception to the rule. You can walk down the Strip, cut through a casino, wander through a few miles of mall, and you know the one constant you're gonna find? Music. The whole place is wired, speakers hidden in lampposts and fake rocks outside, everywhere inside. It's like one big nightclub, and the tunes they're pumping out are all about one thing: winning." Waltham shook his head. "Old sixties standards, seventies disco, eighties hair-band anthems, nineties-and-up pop; it's all put together to make you feel like you're in the last twenty minutes of a movie, just about to kick the ass of the bad guy. Don't stop believin', 'cause the kid is hot tonight."

Grissom drank some of his beer. He recognized when someone just needed to vent.

"Vegas has a special kind of despair built into it," Waltham continued. "When you've lost it all, when you're alone and broke and out of options . . . that's when all those bright lights, all that upbeat music, all that glitter and promise just make you realize how far you've fallen."

He was quiet for a moment then. Grissom realized that somewhere—not in the bar, but not far away—he could hear music. Something with a cheerful, danceable beat.

"Know what I like to do when I feel like that?" asked Waltham. "I find myself a fountain down on Las Vegas Boulevard. One of the big ones is best, outside Paris or Bellagio or Caesars. The water's always nice and clear, with lots of coins sparkling down at the bottom. But that's not all that's down there." Waltham stubbed out the remains of his cigarette. "You know those guys who line parts of the Strip? Wear T-shirts that tell the tourists they can get a girl to their hotel room in twenty minutes? They've all got these stacks of business cards in their hands, with pictures of pretty girls wearing nothing but smiles and Photoshopped stars over their nipples. These guys offer them to everyone who walks by, and they snap a finger against the cards to get your attention. *Snap. Snap. Snap.* That's the real soundtrack of Vegas. And after strolling past a line of these gentlemen—women, too, sometimes—I like to stop and stare down into one of those big, elaborate fountains that Vegas is so proud of. Because down there, among the coins, there's always some of those cards. I stare down at them and the pretty women stare back. To me they look like drowned strippers, or maybe mermaids that have decided to turn tricks . . ."

Waltham turned on his bar stool to look at Grissom. "You have any idea what I'm talking about?"

Grissom considered the question carefully before answering. "In my job, I see death almost every night. I don't just see pictures of those women—all too often, I see the women themselves. If you're talking about the feeling you get when you see the consequences of death—not just the end of a life, but the end of all the potential of that life—then yes. I know exactly how that feels."

Waltham finished his drink. "I'll tell you who I sold the gun to," he said. "What the hell. It's a gamble either way, and I've been making bets my whole life. Little late to stop now."

9

THE ADDRESS THAT Jill Leilani gave Catherine was for an old warehouse in a seedy industrial area west of the Strip. It was surrounded by chain-link fence with old newspapers and trash woven through it by the wind, illuminated by sodium-vapor lights that cast razor-edged shadows. The rolling steel doors at the loading dock were covered in graffiti, gang tags in neon-bright green and pink and yellow. A wheelless, overturned shopping cart guarded the front door like the skeleton of a robot turtle.

Catherine and Greg parked their Denali and got out. Music with heavy bass thumped from inside. "Sounds like someone's home," said Greg.

"Hope the door's open," said Catherine. "They'll never hear us knocking over that."

They tried anyway. After a moment of pounding, the music abruptly died. Footsteps slapped against concrete and the door swung open, revealing a chunky man with purple dreadlocks, dressed in paint-spattered coveralls and plastic flip-flops.

"Hey, about time—oh. You guys don't have a pizza with you, do you?"

"Sorry," said Catherine. "Las Vegas Crime Lab. And you are?"

"Monkeyboy."

Catherine's eyebrows rose. "Try again."

"Bill. Bill Wornow."

"I'm Catherine Willows and this is Greg Sanders. Can we come in?"

"Sure, sure. What's this all about?"

They stepped inside. "It's about Hal Kanamu," said Catherine. "We're—"

She stopped. The warehouse was maybe half the size of a football field, and almost all of it was dominated by a single structure that rose from the middle of the floor to a good twenty feet high.

A volcano.

It was half-finished, its angled steel supports visible through a skin of heavy-gauge steel mesh, but the steam rising from the top and the red rivulets trickling over the edge of the cone left no doubt about what it would ultimately represent. About a third of the structure was covered in red and black roofing shingles, the kind with sediment embedded in tar.

"—investigating his death," she finished.

"Oh, yeah, I heard about that," said Wornow. "Tragic, really tragic. He was so pumped about Mount Pele, too."

"Mount Pele?" asked Greg. "That's what we're looking at, right?"

"Well, it will be when she's finished," said Wornow. He picked up a dirty rag from a table and started wiping his hands. "This was Hal's dream. A fully functioning volcano out on the playa, complete with magma. Anybody can do fire and smoke; that's easy. Getting the lava right, that's the hard part."

"Looks like you're using wax," said Greg.

"Yeah, that seems to work best. Adding paper ash to it to make it look more rock-like, but still tweaking the mix."

One wall of the warehouse was lined with stacks and stacks of newspapers, tied in bundles with twine. "That's a lot of dead trees," said Catherine.

"Yeah, but I didn't kill 'em. Just recycling the corpses, right? Hal was actually buying these from a recycler—I said we could probably dig up our own sources, get it for free, but he didn't care about the cost. Just wanted to make sure we were up and running before August."

"For Burning Man," said Greg. "You were actually going to take this whole thing out to Black Rock?"

Wornow tossed the rag back on the table. "Still am. Totally modular, you know? Heavy-duty pumps to move the wax, built-in subsurface generator to power the pumps and lighting system, propane jets for heat and flame—and the whole structure will come apart and go back together in a day. Mount Pele is going to *kick ass.* I'm just sorry Kahuna Man isn't going to be there to see it."

"You're not worried about paying for all this?"

asked Catherine. "August is still a long way away, and, well . . ."

"Hal's dead? Don't worry about it. Most of the stuff's already paid for, and I'm seeing about getting a grant from the Black Rock Arts Council for the rest. We'll get her there one way or another."

A metal gantry stood beside the volcano, topped by a metal platform that extended out to the edge of the cone. The platform was large enough for a folding chair, a card table, and several pieces of equipment—a welding torch with tanks, a grinder, a mobile tool cabinet on wheels chained to the railing. There was no railing on the side next to the cone, presumably to give better access to the volcano itself.

"Quite the project," said Catherine. "You build this yourself, or did Hal help?"

"Oh, he liked to be involved. It was his vision, after all. But he wasn't an artist or an engineer, so he mainly stuck to helping out with grunt work."

"Grunt worker and financier," said Greg. "Kind of a strange combination."

Wornow walked over to a beat-up fridge against the wall and pulled it open. "I guess. You guys want a beer?"

"We're working, thanks," said Greg. "When was the last time you saw Hal?"

"Not for a couple days. I was out of town, picking up some supplies in Portland. Got back the day after Hal turned up dead."

"Can you prove that?" asked Greg.

"I don't know. Do I have to?"

"You might," said Catherine. "What kind of vehicle do you drive?"

"I don't. I borrowed an old friend's truck."

"Would that be a '94 Ford F150?" asked Greg.

"I don't know. It's a Ford; I don't know the year or model."

"What's your friend's name?"

"I just know him by his Burner name—Cricket. He just left on a road trip—Seattle, I think, I'm not sure."

"With his truck, of course," said Greg. "You mind if we take a sample of this wax?"

Wornow didn't say anything for a moment.

"We can get a search warrant if we have to," said Catherine.

"No, that's—I don't understand. I mean, you don't think I had anything to do with Hal's death, right?"

"Should we?" asked Greg.

"No! Jesus, I just assumed he ODed. I mean, everyone knew he was using, that stuff'll kill you sooner or later—"

"Didn't stop you from hanging out with him," said Greg.

"Hey, it wasn't like he was dangerous or anything."

"But he *was* rich," said Catherine.

"Okay, yeah, he was paying for the volcano. Making art costs money, you know? He wants to spend his cash on supporting creativity, what's wrong with that?"

Catherine put down her CSI kit on a table and opened it. "Nothing. But any time two or more people come together to build something, there are always creative differences. That happen here?"

Wornow shook his head vehemently. "No. I mean, yeah, we didn't agree on everything, but that's natural, right? It never turned into any kind of serious disagreement. We kicked around a bunch of different ideas before we came up with Mount Pele, and then we were *totally* committed. Same artistic vision, I'm telling you. Hal was always coming up with crazy ideas and stuff, trying to make it better, but I kept him reined in. He listened to me, he trusted my judgment."

Catherine gazed up at the metal gantry. "I don't know. Riding herd on a guy smoking ice all day long? Sounds pretty close to impossible to me."

"Frustrating, too," said Greg. "I mean, *you're* the artist, right? You do this for a living. If Pele here is the star, you're the director. Hal would have been more like a producer—he controlled the purse strings, which meant you had to spend half your time listening to every crazy, stoned idea he had and the other half explaining why they wouldn't work. Doesn't leave a lot of time to create."

"Okay, okay. You're right about the drugs. He was waaaay out of control. That was one of the reasons I drove up to Portland, just to get away from him for a while. But if you're looking for someone responsible for his death, you don't have to go any farther than the guys he was getting his drugs from. I only met them once, but they were hard-core, man. Put a bullet in your head for just looking at 'em wrong."

"One of these guys named Boz?" asked Catherine. "Or maybe Diego and Aaron?"

"Yeah, that's them. Me, I'm just a welder with delusions of grandeur, man. I make stuff, I don't kill people."

Catherine picked up an evidence vial from her kit. "Then you won't mind if we take a sample of this wax?"

He hesitated, then shrugged. "Sure. Go ahead."

"I sold the gun to a guy named Gus," Richard Waltham told Grissom. "Don't ask me what his last name is, 'cause I don't know. Gus is a pretty sketchy guy—got himself a pretty bad cocaine habit, and he prefers needles to smoking it or putting it up his nose. Used to hang around this place, but I haven't seen him in here in a while; I got the impression the phrase 'no fixed address' could be used to describe his usual living situation."

"How long ago was this?" asked Grissom.

"Six weeks or so, I guess. He'd acquired a little spending cash and a little more paranoia; since I was short on both, we worked out a trade."

Grissom nodded. "Any idea where his windfall came from?"

Waltham thought about it for a moment. "Couldn't say for sure, but I got the feeling it had something to do with drugs. Could be he was working as a mule, taking stuff across from Mexico—whatever he was doing, it was making him nervous. With good reason, maybe; like I said, I haven't seen him around in a while."

"Can you tell me anything else about this Gus—height, weight, approximate age?"

"'Bout five-ten, I suppose. Kinda thin. Long, greasy brown hair, scruffy beard the same color. Kinda Eastern European looking, if you know what I mean. I'd say he was in his fifties, but who knows? The street can add twenty years to your face, and not the easy kind."

"Distinguishing marks, tattoos?"

"Nothing I noticed, but I never took a steam bath with the guy."

There was no database for plastic bottles, so Riley was forced to do her research in a more roundabout way. She started by searching online for any kind of link to insects and found plenty to look through; spiders and scorpions were a popular theme for brands of hot sauce, energy drinks, and various types of alcohol.

She finally got a match with an energy drink called Parading Mantis, produced in Illinois. She printed a list of distributors in Vegas, mostly mom-and-pop corner stores, and hit the street.

Riley had no problem with legwork. She'd been a street cop before moving to Vegas, and she didn't think she'd ever want to completely give up the field for the lab; as much as she enjoyed the intellectual challenge of solving a case by analyzing data, there was still a certain charge she got from being out in the world, collecting that data.

She did, however, have a problem with being sidelined.

She hoped that wasn't happening. She hadn't worked with Grissom for long, but he didn't seem like the type to play favorites; she thought she'd been given the grunt work because she was the new kid, not because Grissom didn't like her—and that was a pattern that probably went all the way back to the Stone Age and the first rookie to be picked to clean up the cave and throw out the old mastodon bones.

Regardless, she would do what she always did—her best. Approval from authority figures had never mattered much to Riley, but getting the job done did.

Grissom returned to the lab and pondered what he'd learned from Richard Waltham—and then pulled all the autopsy reports on apparent OD cases for the last two months.

Tox screens were done on all of them as a matter of course, but the process wasn't foolproof; many poisons didn't show up unless you were looking for them specifically, and there was no reason to keep looking once you found a toxin that matched the physical evidence.

Not unless the toxin you found didn't kill your subject.

Grissom studied the reports carefully. He thought he found what he was searching for in the case of Gustav Janikov, a fifty-six-year-old man with no fixed address. Janikov had been found in an alley at the northeastern edge of Vegas three weeks ago, dead of an apparent cocaine overdose. A needle was found nearby containing a mixture of cocaine and water, with traces of blood that were a match to Janikov. The condition of the body and surrounding area suggested violent convulsions had taken place before death, and the mouth had been filled with saliva.

But the concentration of drugs in the bloodstream was wrong.

It was high, but not high enough to be lethal—not in a long-term addict who had developed a tolerance, and the number of old needle tracks on the body confirmed that Janikov was exactly that. While it was possible that Janikov's body had simply given up the ghost after years of abuse, Grissom didn't think so. There was something else at work.

Nick traced the thread back to a medical supply company called Willifer Surgical Providers, the only company in Nevada that carried it. They dealt mainly with hospitals but had a few clients who were dental surgeons; the chitin-based thread was infection resistant, which was important in a high-microbe environment like the human mouth.

Hospitals tended to have pretty good security. If the thread had been stolen, Nick was willing to bet it had probably been lifted from one of the dental surgeons. He did some checking and discovered that one, McKay Oral Health, had reported a burglary five weeks ago. Very little was taken, but suture supplies were one of the things listed as missing on the police report.

"Time for a trip to the dentist," Nick murmured.

Gustav Janikov's body had been disposed of, but his personal effects had remained unclaimed. They were spread out over the surface of the light table in front of Grissom now, the last pathetic remains of a life that had crashed and burned. A pair of stained and worn pants, a dirty T-shirt, a ripped jacket held together with duct tape and safety pins.

The boots, though, were in surprisingly good condition. They were leather, ex-military, the heels and soles hardly worn, the laces practically new. Grissom looked inside, found the remains of a price tag still stuck near the top; they were from an army and navy surplus store in Vegas, one Grissom was familiar with. The stains on the clothes were many, and Grissom used surgical scissors to cut a small swatch from every one. He wasn't sure what he was looking for, but it was possible that one of the stains held a higher concentration of whatever killed Gustav Janikov.

The samples went to Trace. Grissom went to the mall.

McKay Oral Health Offices was flanked on one side by an all-night convenience store and the other by a pawnshop. In another city this might have looked seedy, but in Vegas pawnshops and late-night stores were almost as common as casinos and wedding chapels.

The front door was locked, but there was a buzzer. Nick pressed it and was rewarded a minute later with the door opening.

And was greeted by a puppet.

"Hi there!" the puppet said. It was dressed like a dentist, in an old-fashioned white smock that buttoned up the front to one side. It had frizzy blue hair and gleaming white teeth, and peeked around the corner of the door. "Welcome to McKay Oral Health!"

"Uh, thanks. Is Doctor McKay in?"

A middle-aged man in white shirtsleeves and suspenders stepped out from behind the door, the puppet cradled in one arm. "Sorry," he said with a wide smile. "Can't resist doing that from time to time. I once had a five-minute conversation with a guy who was selling aluminum siding."

"I'm Nick Stokes, with the Vegas Crime Lab."

Nick smiled back. "I'm following up on the break-in you had five weeks ago."

McKay stepped back. "Come in, come in. I was just doing a little rehearsing."

Nick stepped inside and glanced around. The waiting room was tiny, only a single chair and a small desk with a computer on it. The standard diplomas and certificates hung on the wall, but the largest space was given over to a framed, glassed-in poster that showed a beaming Dr. McKay in a red tuxedo, with the puppet perched on his lap. DOC AND CHOMPERS, LIVE AT THE MIRADO ROOM! the lettering underneath read.

"Chompers, huh?" said Nick.

Chompers nodded. "I'm a star!" he said. McKay's lips hardly moved at all. "This guy's just my assistant. When I get a decent entourage he's H-I-S-T-O . . . R . . ." He stopped.

"Y?" said Nick.

"Because he always forgets my damn coffee!" the puppet snapped.

Nick laughed. "I'm a little confused. I thought you were a surgeon, not a performer."

McKay shrugged. "Who says I can't be both? Dental surgery pays well enough that I don't have to do it full-time, and I always got a kick out of ventriloquism. I made the puppet to calm down kids who were worried about having their teeth worked on, to show them exactly what I was going to do, and—well, things kinda snowballed. I'm not exactly a superstar, but I do a few shows here and there and enjoy myself."

"Well, this is the town for that. So you're not here all the time?"

"No, only a couple of days a week. I have a part-time receptionist, but she's not in today." McKay took the puppet off, set it down on the chair. "So, what brings you here today? You catch the guys?"

"I'm afraid not. I'm actually investigating another case, one I think might be related to the burglary at your office. I've read the police report, but would you mind going over it with me?"

"No, not at all. Let's see . . . I was here by myself. I wasn't operating that day, I was just doing a little office work. I heard the buzzer and went to the door. No Chompers, though."

"And that's when you first saw the suspect?"

"Yes. Older gentleman, in his fifties or sixties, quite thin. He said he wanted to talk to me about his granddaughter and possibly doing some sort of presentation for her school—it was a little vague, but I didn't have any reason to be suspicious. He asked if he could come in out of the heat and maybe have a glass of water. I said sure."

"Okay. What happened then?"

"There was this big commotion outside—lots of swearing and threats, and then this body smacks into my door. Cracked the glass but didn't break it. I rush out to see what's going on, and I see these two—street people, I guess, going at it right outside.

I didn't want to get involved, but I also didn't want to be calling an ambulance when one of them went through a plate-glass window. I try to get them to calm down, and they just keep yelling at each other—something about how one of them stole the other one's shoes. I forget all about the old guy in the office, until I hear the alarm on the fire door inside go off. I rush back in, but the old guy's gone. I put two and two together, and sure enough the two that were fighting have disappeared, too."

"Doesn't sound like they took much, though."

McKay shook his head. "Wasn't much to take. Some painkillers, a topical anaesthetic I use for sensitive gums, and some surgical thread. I have no idea why they would even bother with the thread."

"I might. You gave a pretty good description to the responding officer, but I was wondering if there were any details you might have remembered, anything unusual you might have noticed or realized since then."

McKay paused, then said, "Actually, there is. I want to show you something."

He led Nick halfway down a short hall to a room marked SUPPLIES and used a key to open the door. "I never used to keep this locked, but now I do," he said. Inside, two walls were stocked floor-to-ceiling with supplies that ranged from boxes of gauze to needles. "The suture supplies are kept on the top shelf. I didn't even notice some were gone until I did a complete inventory after the robbery. The thing is,

I usually have to use a step stool to reach them, and it wasn't in the supply room that day—I was using it in the surgery, down the hall. The thief would have had a hard time reaching it—and why would he go to all that trouble for sutures, anyway?"

"I'm thinking that's what he actually came here to get," said Nick. "But you're right, he wouldn't have been able to reach. Unless . . ."

Nick took out his flashlight. The supply room was dimly lit by a single low-wattage bulb, and the far corners were hard to see. He shone the light on the surface of a back shelf, right next to the wall and about three feet off the floor. There, barely visible, was a dusty footprint.

". . . he gave himself a little boost," said Nick. "Looks like a military boot to me."

The army and navy surplus store was painted almost entirely in camouflage colors, which wasn't really that wise a choice; half their stock simply disappeared into the background, giving the odd feeling that you were in a store crammed with nothing. That was far from true, though: locked glass cases displayed weaponry ranging from jackknives to bayonets, while World War II–era gasmasks goggled at customers from behind the counter. Racks of clothing ran in rows to the back of the store, everything from heavy-duty peacoats to lightweight jungle fatigues.

"Excuse me," said Grissom to the clerk behind the counter.

He was young, probably still in his teens, with a shaved head and a shadow of a mustache. He wore a faded combat jacket that was too big for him and was reading an old copy of *Soldier of Fortune* magazine.

"Help you?"

"Yes, I was wondering if you remember this man." Grissom showed him a picture of Gustav Janikov. "I believe he bought a pair of boots here."

"Yeah, I know him—that's Gus. He lives on the street, but I guess this is his neighborhood because I always see him around. Came in a few weeks ago, said he'd come into a little extra cash. Wanted something to keep his feet warm and dry, something that would last."

"I see. Would you happen to know anything else about him—where he slept, other people he talked to?"

The clerk frowned. "I don't really follow what those guys do. Gave him a good deal, though—guy who pounds the pavement as much as he does needs some decent footwear. Haven't seen him around lately."

"You won't," said Grissom.

"Grissom, you never fail to impress me," said Hodges. "I followed your instructions and ran the samples, checking specifically for any type of insect-related poison. I was thinking maybe a pesticide, an organophosphate or neonicotinoid—but no. So I moved on to actual bugs, venom from black widow or brown recluse spiders—that came up dry, too. But—like you—I never disappoint." He produced a printout with a flourish and a triumphant smile.

Grissom took it without comment and quickly scanned its contents. "Homobatrachotoxin?" he said.

"Indeed. A steroidal alkaloid that's ten times more powerful than puffer fish poison and usually found in the skin of poison dart frogs. But what, you say, does a poison from a Costa Rican amphibian have to do with insects—"

"*Phyllobates* doesn't produce the poison itself," said Grissom. "Members of the genus aren't poisonous when raised in captivity. It's thought that they process the toxin out of the environment—probably something they eat."

Hodges's smile faded a little. "Well, of course you'd know that. The most likely contender is the Melyrid beetle, which is loaded with the stuff."

"True, but they probably don't manufacture it either—the likely culprit is thought to be even farther down the food chain. And a little farther up from the frogs are the Ifrita and the hooded Pitohui—both birds that eat Melyrid beetles and process the poison into their feathers."

"Making them the, uh, only poisonous birds in the world," said Hodges, clearly derailed. "But it looks like you're already well aware of that."

Grissom gave Hodges a small smile. "Good work, Hodges.

10

GRISSOM COMPARED THE boot print Nick had lifted from McKay's supply-room shelf to the one he'd taken from Gustav Janikov's boots, then placed it back on the light table. "We have a match. Good work, Nick."

"Thanks. But with Janikov dead and buried, he can't tell us who told him to steal that thread."

"The same person who gave him enough money to buy Richard Waltham's gun and obtained it either before or after Janikov overdosed."

Riley strode in. "Sorry I'm late. I've been all over town trying to source that bottle, but there are just too many places that carry it. The stamp that would have told us the batch number and expiration date was on the part of the bottle that was cut off—I narrowed it down to brand, but that was it."

"It was a long shot," Grissom admitted. "But you can never tell when you might get lucky."

They brought hcr up to speed. "So Janikov got the gun from Waltham but was dead before it was used on Paul Fairwick," she said. "The killer could have gotten it from his body."

"Possible," said Grissom. "Janikov was clearly being paid to work for the killer—he was sent specifically to obtain the surgical thread."

Nick nodded. "He might have been killed for refusing to follow orders. Maybe he was supposed to shoot Fairwick himself but wouldn't."

"I don't think so," said Grissom. "The killer's plans are intricate; I don't think he'd leave such an important element to someone else. In fact, Janikov's involvement doesn't really fit with the pattern the killer's established thus far."

"Maybe it does," said Riley. "Janikov wasn't the only person involved in the robbery. There were the two transients who staged the fight."

"Easy enough to do," said Nick. "Janikov probably paid them off with drugs or booze."

"Unless our killer has more than one person on his payroll," said Riley. "He's imitating insect behaviors, right? Well, colony insects send out workers to obtain supplies."

Grissom looked thoughtful. "True. Which would imply a nest or hive location—as well as a larger scale of operations. Even given his obsession with insects, he wouldn't acquire his own drones unless he needed them. But what for?"

"Bees go out and collect pollen," said Nick. "Maybe he's got his people doing something similar."

"No," said Riley. Both Grissom and Nick turned

to look at her. "I know what this reminds me of. Large-scale cocaine processing labs need a significant workforce. They're sealed in a building and guarded by soldiers."

"Not collecting pollen," said Grissom. "Making honey. Ants do much the same thing, but with slave labor—drones kidnapped from other colonies are imprinted chemically and put to work."

"So our serial is a drug lord, too?" said Nick.

"Whatever he's producing," said Grissom, "I don't think profit's his motive. In fact, if he *is* processing large amounts of a particular chemical, I very much doubt it's one anyone would take willingly." He paused. "In fact, it might be the very same thing that killed Gustav Janikov." He told them about the homobatrachotoxin.

"Dangerous stuff," said Nick. "What's the lethal dose, five hundred micrograms?"

"One hundred," said Grissom. "Around the equivalent of two grains of table salt. If our Bug Killer is attempting to produce this poison in quantity, we have an extremely serious problem."

"Hey, Monkeyboy," said Catherine, taking a seat across the table in the interview room. "Guess what? The sample of wax we took from your warehouse was just full of stuff: industrial effluents, food-grade shellac, perfume, metals . . ."

Monkeyboy, aka William Wornow, looked distinctly uneasy. "Well, that's because of where I get it. All over the place. I mean, I scavenge from Dumpsters, industrial waste sites, wherever I can get access. None of it's stolen, I swear."

"Oh, I believe you. The thing is, you've mixed up a particularly distinctive batch for your fake volcano, and it just happens to be an exact match for the wax we found hardening in Hal Kanamu's lungs."

"What?"

She smiled. "Yeah. And since that's what actually killed him, your whole art project is now officially a murder weapon. Afraid you're going to be skipping your trip to Black Rock City this year."

"Whoa!" He held up both hands, clearly frightened. "Maybe Hal did die in that volcano, but I had nothing to do with it. I was out of town!"

"Maybe. You better hope you can prove that, because until you do you're our prime suspect. And we're going to be taking a very, *very* close look at Mount Pele . . ."

Dale Southford looked up from his newspaper when Grissom walked into the Pet Cave. "Hello, Mr. Grissom. Back to pick up your order?"

"Afraid not, Dale. I've got another question for you. Ever have someone ask you about Melyrid beetles?"

The chubby man looked surprised. To one side of the counter, a cocker spaniel puppy gave a mournful little howl that ended in a much more upbeat yip. "Funny you should ask. Had a guy call a couple months back asking about the very same thing. Said he was a researcher, needed a large representative sample. I got in touch with a guy I know in New Guinea."

"Did he want live samples or dead ones?"

"Both. I asked him how many he wanted, and he said at least a hundred had to be alive."

"And dead?"

Southford shrugged. "He said he'd take as many as I could get. Turned out to be around a thousand."

A thousand beetles. Grissom knew they could produce about ten micrograms of HBTX each, which meant ten beetles' worth could kill a human being. A thousand was enough for a hundred fatalities.

But it was the live ones that bothered him the most. If the Bug Killer established a successful breeding program, he could process a hundred times that.

"What was his name?" asked Grissom.

"Just a sec." Southford turned to his computer. "Ah, here it is. L. W. Smith. No address, just a contact number. Paid in cash."

"What did he look like?"

"Well, I don't think he picked them up himself— pretty sure the guy that dropped off the cash and took the beetles was homeless. He told me he was just running an errand for a friend."

*   *   *

"Thanks for coming in again," said Nick, shaking McKay's hand.

"Glad to help," said the oral surgeon. "I don't know how much use I'll be this time, either, though. None of the faces in all those mug shots jumped out at me a month ago, and I doubt if my memory's gotten any better."

"We'll see," said Nick. "You might surprise yourself."

He led the surgeon from the front counter to the AV lab. Archie nodded at both of them. "Hey, Nick. This our witness?"

Nick introduced the two. "Doc, Archie here is gonna take you through a new program we just got. Hopefully, it'll help us ID the two guys you saw fighting."

"So he's an artist?"

Archie grinned. "Yes, I am—but my area of expertise is software as opposed to pen and ink. I'm going to be using a program called EvoFIT to come up with a facial composite of our suspects."

He had McKay sit down in front of a workstation. "Okay, here's how this works. Some studies have shown that regular sketches done by police artists only have a success rate of around ten percent. That has nothing to do with the skill of the artist; it's just how our brains work. In the process of trying to remember the features of someone, we wind up changing them—the image that's finally produced is something the subject has actually been building as opposed to recalling. Going feature by feature, the way the old Identi-Kit worked, just reinforced that."

Nick nodded. "This program works on a different principle. Caricature."

"What, like those sidewalk artists do?"

"Not exactly," said Archie. "It starts with seventy-two images. You pick the six that you think have the closest resemblance to the person you saw, and it uses those six to generate another seventy-two. We do that a third time, and you pick a final six. Those are blended into one, which we fine-tune."

"The cool thing," said Nick, "is that these aren't static images. They gradually morph from one face to another, exaggerating features as they go. This concentrates attention, which is supposed to trigger flashes of memory—you don't so much remember the face as recognize it. The inventor claims it bumps up the success rate by up to twenty percent."

"Caricature police sketches," said McKay with a smile. "Well, considering that I'm a ventriloquist dentist, I can't really criticize. Only in Vegas, huh?"

"Now this," said Greg, "is a crime scene."

He and Catherine stood at the foot of Mount Pele. It was glowing a brilliant crimson from the cone, the wax-based lava releasing the occasional *blorp* of heated air.

"Yeah, but we still don't have a suspect," said Catherine. "Not since security footage from that gas station in Oregon cleared Wornow. No way he could have gotten to Vegas in time to kill Kanamu."

"Maybe not. But the truck he was driving—you know, the one his mysterious friend lent him and then drove off into the sunset with?—looked a lot like a 1994 Ford F150 Supercab."

"True," Catherine admitted. "Since we can't find the truck, we can't compare the treads to what we found in the desert—but we can take a close look at where Kanamu probably died. Right here."

"Mind if I take the volcano?"

"It's all yours, lava boy. I'll tackle the rest of the warehouse."

There was a small bathroom in the corner; Catherine started there. She found cleaning supplies under the sink, but the dust on them told her they hadn't been used in some time. She lifted prints from the sink and the toilet.

There was a lounging area next to the loading dock, with a couch, a few ratty armchairs, a microwave, and a refrigerator. The fridge contained nothing but beer, soda, and a few frostbitten TV dinners in the freezer. She located a few good hairs on the couch with root tags, and a number of fibers. The depths of the couch turned up nothing but lint.

Bits of wax spatter were on almost every surface; she guessed they must have had more than one uncontrolled eruption. That worked in her favor, because wax was notoriously hard to remove—and held a fingerprint incredibly well. It looked as if someone had even turned it into a game at one point, pressing a digit into every wax droplet before it fully hardened to leave a perfect print behind. She carefully photographed each one before lifting it.

Catherine remembered a term from her research into Hawaiian mythology: Pele's tears. They were elongated bits of hardened lava, spatter from the lifeblood of a volcano. She was looking at a man-made approximation of the same thing—but not all the spatter was random.

There was a large, roughly circular pattern at the base of the volcano. Streaks of wax led from there to the loading dock door. "I've got a drag trail," she called out. "Looks like the body was moved, fake magma and all, from here to the loading bay."

Greg had scaled the gantry and was crouched on top. "Yeah, it's pretty visible from up here." He reached out and grabbed a thick chain dangling from a pulley. "I've got transfer on this chain—it's probably how the body was moved from up here to down there."

"There was an awful lot of wax around the body," said Catherine. "It must have at least semi-hardened before the body was yanked out."

"And it would have cooled from the top down. Since we found the vic's body with his head exposed, that means he was upside down in the volcano's cone, with his head in the wax that was still hot."

"Greg, what shape is the wax reservoir up there? Can you tell?"

"Just a sec." He ducked his head into an uncovered section of the volcano like a mechanic disappearing under the hood of a car, then popped back up an instant later. "It's an inverted cone, wider at the top than the base. So when our vic was pulled loose, he would have had a roughly volcano-shaped wax plug around his body, with his head exposed."

"Just how we found him." She sighed. "Now all we have to do is figure out how he got there."

"So these are the composites the EvoFIT program produced?" asked Riley. She and Nick talked as they walked across the parking lot. The sheet Nick had just handed her showed a man with long, scraggly blond hair, a wide nose and chin, and blue eyes.

"Yeah, here's the other one." She took the second paper and studied it; it showed an olive-skinned man with a short, dark beard and wavy black hair.

"How accurate do you think these are?" she asked him. "I mean, this is unproven technology."

"Better than nothing. We showed him mug shots first—anyone busted in the last year who listed no fixed address on the arrest report—but came up dry. Just because someone's on the street doesn't mean they're in the system."

"You do know there are over eleven thousand homeless people in the city, right?"

Nick unlocked the Denali and climbed into the driver's seat. "I know. So the sooner we get going, the better."

They started at Huntridge Circle Park, sandwiched between the north and south lanes of Maryland Parkway. Though technically closed, it still attracted many of those with no other place to go, and most of the park's benches were being used as makeshift beds.

They made the rounds, showing the pictures to anyone who would talk to them, trying for a positive ID. A one-legged man in a long, tattered coat and a baseball cap told them he thought one of them lived on the banks of the Flamingo Wash, one of the creeks that drained the city's runoff into Lake Mead. His name, the man said, pointing to the picture, was Buffet Bob—so called because of his habit of sneaking into buffets and cramming as much food as he could into his pockets.

At the wash, they had less luck. Camping overnight was prohibited, and the encampment had recently been cleared out. They tried Molasky Family Park next, another spot where the homeless congregated; there, several of the people they talked to agreed that the picture looked a lot like

Buffet Bob. The other one, several of them said, resembled a Latino man named Zippo who often drank with Bob.

"Yeah, that's them," said a black man in his sixties without a tooth in his mouth. "Bob and Zippo, you always see 'em around together. Not for a while, though."

"When was the last time you saw them?" asked Riley.

The toothless man shook his head. "Musta been at least a month ago. Mebbe more. They ain't the only ones, either."

Nick frowned. "Hold on. You say they disappeared a month ago—and so did some others? Who?"

"Lessee. Big Johnny, ain't seen him around since then. Old Gus—"

"Gus Janikov?" asked Riley.

"Don't know his last name," the man said testily. "Don't interrupt. Who else . . . oh, and I guess I ain't seen Paintcan in a while, neither. Course, he could just be in jail."

Riley gave Nick a skeptical glance. "So could any of them."

"Don't think so," said the old man. "Ain't nobody seen 'em or heard nothing. Ask around."

"We will," said Nick. "Thanks."

The contact number L.W. Smith had left with the Pet Cave turned out to be a dead end; it was for a throwaway cell phone that had been used exactly once.

So Grissom went for a walk.

Las Vegas Boulevard, more commonly known as the Strip, was the backbone of Vegas. It stretched from the southern extremes of the city to the northern edge of downtown, and every block held its own character and history. Grissom was familiar with each one.

As he walked, he tried to see the city through the killer's eyes.

This was not LW's home. He was a tourist, just like the hundreds of thousands who flocked here every year. But how did he view Vegas? Was it a modern Xanadu, a high-tech playground that everyone could share, or a twenty-first-century Sodom or Gomorrah, an artificial abomination in the middle of a desert?

The killer was here because Grissom was here. Grissom was well-known in the relatively small overlap between entomology and law enforcement circles; if Grissom could be said to be famous for anything, it was using his scientific knowledge—of insects, among other things—to give the Vegas Crime Lab one of the highest case-clearance rates in the nation. As an embarrassing story in the *Las Vegas Globe* had said about him some years ago, he "used bugs to put bad guys behind bars."

The Bug Killer had obviously seen that as a challenge, but Grissom didn't think his life was in danger—not yet. The killer wanted to beat Grissom at his own game, on an intellectual level; even the spider trap had been more of a test than an assassination attempt.

But as Grissom knew from personal experience, Vegas was impossible to ignore. The sensuality, the spectacle, the timeless siren environment of the casinos; it had an effect on people, even those who tried to resist. Sometimes, the resistance affected you just as strongly as the place itself.

He thought about Richard Waltham and his take on Vegas. Waltham was a Vegas survivor, someone who'd been around the block a few times and managed to hang on. If he kept going the way he was, the city would eventually kill him, but so far it hadn't.

So far, he'd been lucky.

Grissom didn't think the Bug Killer viewed Vegas as either Xanadu or Sodom. He thought he saw it in insect terms—a cluster of termite columns, perhaps. Termites were the skyscraper architects of the insect world, some species constructing mounds that could reach as high as thirty feet; they boasted an elaborate cooling system that regulated their temperature as efficiently as any hotel air-conditioning system. Mounds could contain millions of individuals and more than one queen; some even provided their own buffet by cultivating and feeding on a certain type of fungus.

Grissom stopped to watch an extremely drunk

college-age boy throwing up in a parking lot. He appeared to have bypassed the buffet in favor of tacos.

What bothered Grissom more than anything was the homobatrachotoxin. A chemical fifteen times more lethal than cyanide, in a town where the most popular form of dining was essentially a shared trough. If the Bug Killer decided he wanted to graduate from single homicides to mass murder, he could do so with nothing more than an eyedropper and a little careful sleight of hand.

Termites had something else in common with Vegas: just like the Strip that ran north/south, a species known as the compass termite always built its wedge-shaped mounds with the long axis oriented north/south.

But maybe termites were the wrong analogy. Ants, bees, and wasps were colony insects, too, and displayed a bewildering variety of adaptations and social behaviors. It wasn't just a question of whom the Bug Killer would target next; it was what sort of point he was trying to make.

Nick and Riley canvassed several more spots, and though the information they gathered was thin and somewhat contradictory, a pattern did begin to emerge. Around a half-dozen homeless people—including the two they were looking for and Gustav Janikov—had disappeared off the street around a month ago. Only Janikov had been seen since, and only briefly.

Rumors abounded: that they'd been kidnapped by a cult, that they'd been rounded up as part of a secret government plan, that they'd been killed and buried in the desert by a gang.

Nick and Riley retired to the diner where the CSIs sometimes ate breakfast to discuss the case over coffee. Riley slid into the booth, pulled off her baseball cap, and tossed it next to her with a sigh.

"Two coffees, please," Nick told the waitress. "Thanks."

"Well, what do you think?" asked Riley. "Are we chasing ghosts?"

"I don't think so. I mean, yeah, the two guys we're looking for could be dead, but the homeless population might actually be down half a dozen. What's your gut say?"

She frowned. "Despite the high number of crazies, junkies, and thieves, people on the street tend to look out for one another. I can't say much for the theories I've heard, but I'm starting to believe those people are actually missing."

"Would fit with your theory about a labor force. Once you've lured them into working for you, it probably makes more sense to keep them locked up than risk one of them talking."

"Yeah, which doesn't say much for their chance of drawing unemployment once the job's finished."

The coffee arrived. Nick changed his mind and ordered a Danish as well.

"Janikov was probably his right-hand man," said

Riley. "He had enough freedom to spend a little of his hard-earned cash. The killer trusted him to come back, gave him the job of obtaining the surgical thread."

"True. If we had a residence to toss, we might be able to come up with where the hypothetical factory is—but that's kinda hard to do when the people we're chasing are homeless."

"Maybe not. Even homeless people need to sleep somewhere—and some places are less transient than others."

Nick took a long sip of his coffee. "You're thinking Silver Hills?"

"If any of our missing subjects were crashing there, could be their stuff is still around."

"After a month? Doubtful—but I guess we don't have anything to lose."

They finished their coffee, paid up, and left.

Silver Hills was downtown, just off Main Street and alongside Woodlawn Cemetery. An iron fence marked the boundary of the graveyard; the sidewalk that ran parallel to it held around two dozen dome-shaped nylon tents in a single row. Men sat cross-legged in the doorways or stood around at the edge of the street, some drinking beer from cans.

Nick and Riley approached the first person they saw, a woman offloading flats of bottled water from the bed of a truck to the sidewalk.

"Excuse me," said Riley. "I was wondering—"

The woman whirled around. She was short, Latino, and wearing a T-shirt that read COMMUNITY OUTREACH. "You want to arrest me? Go ahead!"

Nick gave her what he hoped was a disarming smile. "No, no, we're not going to arrest you—"

"I see—you'll just give me a ticket then, eh? Some more money the mayor can flush down the toilet while these people suffer from dehydration!"

"Calm down, ma'am," said Riley. "We don't care if you're giving the homeless water—"

"Really? Did someone repeal that damn law and forget to tell me?"

Riley gave Nick a puzzled frown, and he gave her a look of embarrassed admission in return.

"No, ma'am," he said, "I'm afraid that law's still in effect. But while it's technically still illegal to distribute food or water to the indigent, I personally don't see any such infraction going on. And neither does my partner. Right?"

Riley blinked. "Uh, no, of course not. We're more interested in trying to locate certain individuals who have gone missing."

She glared at them, but her voice was slightly less hostile. "Why? You going to throw them in jail because you caught them sleeping in a park?"

"No, ma'am," said Nick. "We're actually worried that they may have come to harm."

That appeared to mollify her. "You have a picture?"

Riley handed her the composites. "We understand these two go by the names Buffet Bob and Zippo."

The woman nodded as soon as she saw the picture. "Mmm-hmm. That's Bob, all right. I've seen this other one hanging around with him, but I don't know him by name. Some of them, they're leery about giving you any personal information at all, even when you're trying to help them." Her glare returned. "I can't imagine why."

Riley nodded. "We're also looking for Paintcan and Big Johnny."

"There're a couple Big Johnnys. Paintcan was a regular. Haven't seen him around in over a month—same for Bob and his friend."

"Did any of them camp here?" asked Nick.

"Bob did. That's his tent, the blue one second from the end. Or it used to be, anyway; someone else might be living there now."

They thanked her and moved on. The tent she'd pointed out was zipped up, but a young man sat in front of it on the remains of a torn sofa cushion. A brindled pit bull lazed beside him, tongue lolling in the heat.

"Hi," said Nick. "I'm Nick Stokes, Vegas Crime Lab. You staying in this tent?"

The young man looked up, his eyes hidden by cheap plastic sunglasses. A tattooed skull wept inky tears down his right cheek. "No, man. This is Buffet Bob's crib. I'm just looking after it, you know?"

"That a full-time job?" asked Riley.

"Nah, we take turns. Figure he'll turn up sooner or later, you know?"

"I'm sure he'll appreciate it," said Nick.

"Hey, Bob's a good guy. Any time he had food, he'd share. Long as you're not picky—this one time, he had a plastic bag full of hot shrimp stuffed in his pants. Sure were tasty, though."

"I'll bet," said Riley. "Look, nobody's seen Bob in over a month. We're trying to find him—not because he's in trouble, but because we think something may have happened to him. So we're going to have to look through his things."

"I don't know. Don't you, like, need a warrant or something?"

"This is a sidewalk, not an apartment building," said Riley. "Public property."

The pit bull seemed to notice them for the first time. It raised its blocky, muscular head and growled.

"Take it easy," said Nick. "I understand you're just looking out for Bob's best interests. I get that. But like I said, we're not here to bust him for anything—we're just trying to find out what happened to him. Whatever's in that tent could help. What do you think is more important—guarding Bob's stuff or making sure he's okay?"

The tattooed man thought about it, stroking the pit bull's head. "I guess," he said at last. "But if you find anything illegal, it's not mine, right?"

"How could it be?" asked Riley. "You're going to

be sitting way over there." She pointed at the opposite end of the row of tents.

After the man and his dog had left, Nick crouched down and unzipped the tent. The smell that wafted out was musty and unclean, but the aroma of a little dirty laundry ranked way below decomp on a CSI scale of stink.

The tent held a sleeping bag, an overturned cardboard box used as a makeshift table, and several bulging garbage bags stuffed with clothes and personal items.

"What do you think?" said Riley. "Take it all back to the lab, sort through it there?"

"If we have to. I'd rather take a quick look now, see what we come up with. This place may not be much, but it's where someone lives; how would you feel if the police stopped by and confiscated your home and everything in it?"

Riley shook her head. "Like my life was broken and I'd better fix it. What was that about it being illegal to give food or water to the homeless?"

"Yeah, I know. Law passed in 2006. Some people thought it was 'encouraging' the homeless as opposed to helping them."

"Wow. Pretty hard-line."

"Yeah, well, it's a hard town."

11

GRISSOM KEPT WALKING. The thing about colony insects, he thought, was that their behavior mimicked intelligence.

Ants, for instance, displayed behaviors that were truly astonishing. They grew food, they kept "herds" of aphids that they milked for nectar, they formed symbiotic partnerships with other species. But a single colony ant was no more intelligent than a single cell in a complex organism; it was just following a set of simple behaviors that, when viewed in the context of the entire anthill, suggested the operation of a single mind.

But that was an illusion.

He'd wandered past the big theme hotels, the 5/8 scale replica of the Eiffel Tower, the artificial volcano, the pirate ships. He'd reached the part of the Strip that was still being developed—though that was true, in a way, of the whole thing all the time—and to his left he could see a huge lot with the angular structure of a half-built hotel sitting far back on the property. Next to the sidewalk, fully grown trees sprouted from huge wooden crates like the world's biggest bonsai, waiting to be artistically placed. They might have to wait a long time; Grissom had read that the development was stalled, victim of the economic downturn. No laborers scaled the iron girders, no dirt-encrusted yellow vehicles powered their way around the lot.

Mimicry was one of the things insects excelled at. There were bugs that looked like twigs, bugs that looked like leaves, bugs that looked like other bugs. Sometimes mimicry was employed to hide in plain sight, providing cover for a predator or potential prey; sometimes it was used to imitate a creature who occupied a much more successful biological niche.

A double-decker bus drove past, an Elvis impersonator on the open upper level belting out "Viva Las Vegas" for the passengers and passersby. Grissom thought he was pretty good.

After the hotels came the chapels, several blocks offering various flavors of fast-food matrimony. You could pay a flat fee any time before midnight and get married within minutes—at a church, at a hotel, even at a golf course. For those in a real hurry, there was always the drive-through option—or, if you wanted something a little more elaborate, you could choose from almost as many themes as there were casinos themselves: *Star Trek,* gothic, fairy tale, pirate. Those who still worshipped Elvis could have their union blessed by an imitation of the real thing.

Industry, illusion, imitation; common threads that ran through the world of insects and that of Vegas. But were they ideals the Bug Killer aspired to or elements he despised?

After the chapels came the pawnshops and then downtown. Grissom had thought, more than once, that the progression said more about human nature than anything else Vegas had to offer. And while downtown was gritty—especially the homeless corridor around Main Street and Owens Avenue—downtown was also home to the Fremont Street Experience, five blocks of older casinos and hotels that had reinvented themselves by roofing over the entire stretch and using it as a screen for a high-tech projection system. To Grissom, it seemed like an example of the possibility of rebirth and renewal in the midst of decay.

But then, the same could be said for fly larvae in a corpse.

A person's possessions always told a story. Nick had read his share; the first page was usually a search warrant. But if combing the contents of a house was like leafing through a novel, looking through Buffet Bob's meager possessions was more like a short, disjointed poem about loss and failure. There was an old driver's license, now long expired, that showed a grinning man in his twenties with the

name Robert Ermine; an empty bottle of painkillers with the name ripped off the label; an application for social assistance from Albuquerque, New
Mexico, that hadn't been filled in.

A few tattered paperbacks seem to indicate an
interest in science fiction, while a battered miniature chess set with three pieces made of cardboard
showed a mind that had once been sharp. Nick
didn't know what to make of the mug, wrapped
carefully in several layers of socks, that bore the
motto ROOFERS DO IT ON TOP; it was immaculately
clean, no coffee stains on the interior or exterior.
There were no pictures of family or a partner, only
a single photo of a black-and-white cat, once ripped
in half and then carefully mended with Scotch tape.

They sorted through everything, but there was
nothing to indicate where Robert Ermine had disappeared to. In the end, Nick agreed that the best
thing to do was to confiscate it all; maybe a closer
examination in the lab could tell them more.

Grissom stopped to rest on a public bench. There
was a newspaper lying there, folded open to the
crossword puzzle. Someone had abandoned it halfway done . . .

"An eleven-letter word for openhearted."

*"Mmm." Sara paused, spreading jam on her last piece
of toast. "Ventricular?"*

*"Ah. How about a nine-letter word for cosmically iso-
lated, fifth letter's a P?"*

"*Solipsist. Give me a hard one.*" He put down the newspaper and raised his eyebrows. She grinned at him. "*You know—one you couldn't get on your own.*"

"*Are you suggesting I'm only asking you the easy ones?*"

"*I'm suggesting you don't really need my help.*"

"It depends," he said, "on your definition of *need.*"

A car drove by, its windows down, bass-heavy music thumping out like the heartbeat of a Godzilloid monster. It jarred Grissom out of his reverie but not his mood; in fact, it reminded him of something else. Warrick had loved to listen to his music that loud.

Grissom wondered what either Warrick or Sara would have made of the current case. They would have worried about him, probably.

He sat for another few minutes, thinking. Then he got up and walked away.

He took the crossword with him.

The prints that Catherine lifted from the spatters of wax in the warehouse all came back a match to one person: Hal Kanamu, the vic. The hairs from the couch were a mix, but none of them were a match for Diego Molinez, Aaron Tyford, or Boz Melnyk.

"Okay," said Catherine. She and Greg stood on top of the metal gantry next to the volcano. "Coroner puts TOD at around three A.M. We know Kanamu was a night owl and that he liked to tinker with his pet project."

Greg nodded. "So he's here, he's high, he's messing around with the volcano. His partner—the guy who's actually building the thing—isn't here to stop him, so he can do whatever he wants."

"Right. Now, though it was immersion in the wax that killed him, he was knocked unconscious first."

"By a chunk of rock that came from Hawaii. Weapon of opportunity?"

Catherine frowned. "It's possible they were planning on introducing obsidian to the exhibit to add to the realism—but why use obsidian from Hawaii when there's a whole desert full of it practically next door?"

"I know. And if they were going to use obsidian, where is it? We've been all over this warehouse and haven't found any."

"Not in any large amounts, no. Maybe we need to focus on something smaller."

"I see where you're going. Obsidian's basically a glass—you're thinking maybe we can find a shard that broke off."

She shrugged. "Worth a try. This is a big space with a lot of nooks and crannies—plenty of space for a piece of black glass to hide."

"A piece of *hot* black glass, according to the doc. Which means whoever smacked Kanamu in the forehead was wearing gloves or has some nasty burns on his hands."

"The wax system has built-in heaters, but that's

only to keep it warm enough to stay liquid—around a hundred and twelve degrees. Not nearly hot enough to burn flesh."

"Meth addicts often use miniature butane torch lighters—they produce a hotter flame, burn the drug more efficiently." Greg glanced around. "There's a couple of handheld bottle torches here, as well as a welding rig. And the volcano is designed to shoot jets of flame from nozzles at the rim—any of them could have been used to heat the obsidian."

"Let's see what kind of prints we can get off them first. Then we go rock hunting."

"Hey, Grissom," said Brass. He put the remains of the sub sandwich he was eating on his desk and wiped his mouth with his other hand. "Where've you been?"

"Field research. I think I may have some insights into our killer's methodology."

"Yeah? Well, I've got news, too. Athena Jordanson just announced that she's breaking her contract and moving to the Embassy Gold. They're already planning her opening night—the publicity machine is shifting into high gear."

"The Embassy Gold. Isn't that the one that just opened a new restaurant?"

"Yeah, the Mile of Gourmet something or other. More like the Mile of Heartburn, if you ask me—"

"That's his next target," said Grissom. "Jim, we have to shut that restaurant down. Now."

Brass stopped with his sandwich halfway to his mouth. He put it back down and sighed. "Great. You sure about this, Gil? Because the stink this will cause would make even Doc Robbins upchuck."

"All of the killings so far have been intended to manipulate other events. Paul Fairwick's killing was intended to make Athena Jordanson move to another location—just like a termite nest moving their queen when the colony is threatened. The Harribold killing sparked a school riot—I think he has something much larger planned this time." Grissom shook his head. "This guy's extremely organized. If he's pushing Jordanson to switch to this hotel, it's because he already has something set up and ready to go. We have evidence he's producing an extremely powerful poison, possibly in large quantities."

Grissom paused. "We have to shut down that hotel and search it."

Like all cities, Vegas's lifeblood was money. Casinos were the beating heart that kept that lifeblood flowing, and hotels were like lungs; they inhaled and exhaled tourists while separating them from their earnings like alveoli straining oxygen from air. And like lungs, they operated twenty-four hours a day—to stop was to die.

Grissom's proposal to shut down the Embassy Gold was not met with enthusiasm.

The manager of the hotel talked to the mayor.

The mayor talked to the police chief. The police chief talked to Brass—though, by that point, the term *talked* wasn't really accurate.

Grissom refused to back down. If a disaster of the magnitude he feared did happen, he wouldn't keep his mouth shut, either—and the political fallout once the public discovered the authorities knew of the threat but hadn't acted would destroy the political career of everybody involved. Everybody but the one who had tried to blow the whistle.

In the end, a compromise was reached. All food and beverage facilities—restaurants, bars, room service—would be suspended while Grissom's team conducted their search. The hotel would continue to operate otherwise; neither room rental nor casino operations would be affected. It was far from an ideal solution, but it was the only one on the table.

And if the attack occurred anyway, fingers could now be pointed in Grissom's direction. Even with his hands tied, it was still his responsibility to stop the Bug Killer. If Grissom failed, no one would care about technicalities—only about the body count.

The hotel had three restaurants—including the Mile of Gourmet Grand—two nightclubs, and a poolside bar, in addition to the full-service bar in the casino itself. All of them closed down; the hotel's official excuse was that a court-ordered inventory was being conducted as part of an ongoing fraud investigation. Everyone was very careful to not use the word *contaminated* in the same sentence as *food* or *beverage*.

Nick spearheaded the group checking the restaurants, while Riley oversaw those checking the bars. They pulled in the lab's day shift to help with the workload, and Grissom gathered them all together in the main kitchen before they started.

"All right," he said. "What we're looking for is a very concentrated poison called homobatrachotoxin. Exposure to even tiny amounts can result in numbness of the extremities or sneezing, so be aware of any symptoms. It could be in any form— liquid, solid, possibly even aerosolized. Take samples of anything that the public is going to come into contact with or consume."

And then they went to work.

Samples were taken from every open container. Unopened containers were inspected for tampering. Public common areas were searched top to bottom. Equipment for the preparation and handling of food or drink was dismantled and scrutinized—from the pressurized system that delivered carbonated soda to the ice machines on every floor. Walk-in freezers were emptied and examined; industrial meat slicers were disassembled and swabbed.

They found nothing.

Catherine lifted prints from the butane bottles and the welding rig, while Greg crawled underneath the superstructure of the volcano to do the same for the propane tanks and surrounding hardware used to power Mount Pele's flame effects.

After that, they began to look for possible shards of obsidian, starting from each possible heat source and spiraling outward in a gridded search pattern. They used flashlights to highlight any possible glint of reflection, though both were aware the rock wouldn't reflect at all unless the surface exposed to the beam was polished instead of rough.

It was time-consuming, painstaking work, much of it spent on hands and knees. "Hey," said Greg. He was on the upper gantry, looking underneath a worktable. "You ever been to Hawaii?"

"Can't say I have. You?"

"Nah. Seems a long way to go to get the same kind of heat we get in Vegas. It's just . . . moister, I guess."

"How about Burning Man? Ever been?"

"Not yet. I've done a lot of research online, been to a few local events, but I haven't made it out to the festival itself yet."

"So—what's the attraction? I have a hard time thinking of you running around naked in the desert."

"It's kind of hard to explain. I think the social engineering is the part I like the best."

"You mean the gift economy?"

"That's part of it. The festival's been around since 1986—though they didn't start going to the desert until 1990—and it's always evolving. They put a lot of thought into changing people's perceptions and behaviors; the gift economy is a good example of that, but they also emphasize environmentalism, community, and what they call 'radical self-reliance.' Basically, it means you need to come prepared to survive in a harsh desert climate for a week without counting on all the trappings of civilization we take for granted."

"Like indoor plumbing?"

"Well, they do provide porta-potties. But there's no garbage collection—everything you pack in you have to pack out. They encourage interactive art as much as possible. It's not the kind of event where you go to just passively observe; you go to become part of it, to join in."

Catherine picked up a small chunk of dark matter and examined it critically. "Sounds—kind of exhausting, actually."

"It can be. Challenging, definitely. But hey— when's the last time you went to a party with fifty thousand people and didn't feel like they were all strangers?"

"I can't remember the last time I went to one with fifty—"

"Hey. I think I've got something."

Catherine got to her feet. "Obsidian?"

"No, something else. I can see something inside the volcano superstructure—it looks like some kind of tool, stuck between the outer skin and a support strut. Must have fallen inside from up here."

"Hang on—I'll see if I can reach it from underneath."

Catherine crawled under the raised base of the volcano. The interior was a maze of thick plastic and metal tubing, electric pumps and exposed wiring. She shone her flashlight upward until she saw Greg's gloved hand waving through an opening, then followed where it pointed to. Something was wedged between a strut and the exterior wall.

"It's too high to reach," she said. "We're going to need a ladder."

"I think I saw one next to the loading dock."

A few minutes later she was twenty feet above the ground, while Greg steadied the ladder from below. "Got it," she said. "Looks like a pair of metal-cutting shears."

She climbed down, handing it to Greg when she was on the bottom rung. "Looks like we might have blood," she said.

Greg grinned. "I'll get the luminol."

Conrad Ecklie hadn't been undersheriff for long, but he already had a firm grasp of the job's internal politics. He leaned back in his chair, bright sunlight shining through the window behind him, and considered his former CSI colleague sitting in the chair in front of him.

"Gil, I really don't know what to say," he began. "It's not like you to jump at ghosts."

Grissom met his boss's gaze squarely. Even

when Ecklie had been day-shift supervisor of the lab, he'd always had his eye on bigger things; as undersheriff, he was on his way. Grissom didn't care about Ecklie's ambition one way or the other, but he knew just how bright that flame burned—Ecklie wouldn't hesitate to sacrifice one of his own if it meant saving his own career.

"I'm not," said Grissom. "I still believe our suspect is planning an attack on the Embassy Gold."

"The evidence says otherwise, Gil. You didn't find anything at the hotel, and I know how thorough you are."

"Not thorough enough. If I could conduct a room-by-room search—"

"Gil, the GCG has over seven hundred rooms. Even if the hotel agreed to evicting their paying customers, it would take forever; there's no guarantee we could even stop any alleged attack in time."

"We could try."

Ecklie sighed. "Look, I'm on the same page with you about preventing loss of life. I just don't see the same potential threat—so far, all you have is two isolated victims. Hardly the kind of massacre you seem to be expecting."

"Plus the students injured in the riot and Gustav Janikov. This killer isn't about one-on-one homicides, Conrad; he's more interested in the butterfly effect. Kill a single target to trigger a much larger chaotic event."

"So you say. What I see is something more along the lines of professional jealousy."

"What?"

"The killer obviously shares some of your expertise in the field of entomology. He wants to make you look bad while making himself look good—the spider thing was clearly meant for you." He paused. "How's Al doing?"

"Fine. The hospital's releasing him tomorrow."

"Good. Gil, I think you're off base on this. I agree that the Fairwick murder had a secondary reason, but it was to target you, not the Embassy Gold. It's made you jumpy—hell, it's made all of us jumpy. But let's focus on specifics here, not wild theories."

Grissom frowned. "Jumpy?"

"Nobody's disputing your evidence, just your interpretation. If this Bug Killer does strike again, it'll either be directly at you or possibly at someone close to you. I'm sorry, Gil, but you're a hazard to be around right now. I'm assigning you round-the-clock protection for the next few days. If you're right about the killer being either of your two fellow professionals, they'll both be out of the country by then."

"And out of our reach." Grissom got to his feet. "Someone may be getting jumpy," he said quietly, "but it isn't me."

"Mr. Wornow," said Catherine. She smiled at the artist on the other side of the interview table, who didn't smile back. "Or would you prefer Monkeyboy?"

"Bill is fine. Are you almost done with Mount Pele? 'Cause I really need to get back to work, and if you've shut down the pumps it'll take forever to clear all the hardened wax out—"

Greg placed the clear evidence bag containing the shears on the table. Wornow stopped talking.

"A good craftsman always takes care of his tools," said Greg. "But even a good craftsman drops one now and then. Especially if he's doing something as nerve-wracking as cutting off his partner's fingers."

Bill swallowed. "That's—that could belong to anybody—"

"Maybe so," said Catherine. "But it's got Hal Kanamu's blood on it and your fingerprints. Plus, tool marks on the finger bones are a match to exemplars made with this particular pair of shears. So—whether it's yours or not—you were the one who used it to de-digitize the body."

Wornow stared dully at the bag. "I didn't kill him. I swear. I got back from Portland really early, and I went to the warehouse to drop off some stuff I bought. I found Hal in the wax. The heaters were shut down, so it had cooled off and semi-hardened. I . . . I didn't know what to do." Wornow put his head in his hands. "We worked *so hard* on that thing. We'd stay up all night, coming up with new ideas, trying all kinds of stuff . . . Yeah, Hal could be a pain, but he was *committed*, you know? He wasn't going to give up on this, he was going to make it happen. And then we got into an argument over whether or not we should add color to the flames, and I took off. I should have known better . . ."

"We know you didn't kill him," said Greg. "But you did move the body."

"What else could I do? If the cops found a dead drug addict inside the actual cone, I knew they'd confiscate it and take it apart. And without Hal's money, how was I supposed to rebuild? I can't even pay the rent on the damn warehouse."

Catherine nodded. "So why remove the fingers of one hand?"

"I wasn't thinking straight. I didn't even notice until after I'd dropped the tin snips that the other hand was totally encased. I could have dug it out, but that would have made a huge mess . . . I just wrapped the whole thing in a tarp, dumped it in the back of my truck, and ran. Then when I went to look for the snips later, I couldn't find them. It's not like I do this every day, you know?"

"Well, you're not going to be doing it again soon," said Catherine. "Tampering with a body— while not as serious as murder—*is* still a crime. I don't think you or Mount Pele are making a pilgrimage to the desert this year."

12

EDVIN BONIFAK HAD RUN the Valentino Motel for twenty-seven years. He had seen a lot of people come and go; newlywed couples, newly divorced singles, prostitutes, alcoholics, salesmen, wiseguys, drug dealers, professional poker players, amateur magicians, lounge singers, tourists from everywhere from Japan to Jamaica. The only question he was ever interested in asking any of them was how they were going to pay, and sometimes when. Other than that, he didn't care what they did in the privacy of their own rooms—more than once, he'd wished someone would be careless enough to burn the place down. So far, nobody had.

But hey, it was a new day. Maybe he'd get lucky.

The man in room 217 was no odder or stranger than the rest. He'd paid for a week in advance, and that week was now up. Edvin, who at sixty-four was getting around with the help of a cane, was on his way to remind Mr. Lance Wheeler that it was now after two P.M., and if he planned on staying any longer he was going to have to pony up for another day.

It was hot, and most of the air conditioners in the rooms he passed were cranked up and running, heated metallic breath on his skin as he hobbled past, like caged dragons imploring their keeper for their freedom. He noted that the unit in 215 was drooling far too much water again and resolved to take a closer look at it later.

The door to room 217 was locked, the curtains drawn. Maybe Mr. Wheeler had simply left without checking out; that was hardly unusual at the Valentino. Edvin knocked. "Hello? Mr. Wheeler?"

No answer—but now there was a loud buzzing from the AC unit. When one of them kicked up like that, it was usually about to die. Edvin passed his hand over the vent and was disgusted to discover no air was blowing out at all. The damn thing must be in really bad shape.

He knocked again. Strangely, the buzzing got louder, as if the air conditioner was trying to get his attention—maybe it wanted him to summon emergency assistance, call the appliance paramedics to swoop in and save its failing life.

Fat chance. If Edvin couldn't fix it himself, it was going on the junk heap.

He pulled out his passkey. Wheeler was either gone, unconscious, or dead—none of which would surprise Edvin terribly much. He unlocked the door and opened it.

And was greeted by hell.

The buzzing became a chainsaw roaring. His vision swirled with black dots, but they weren't the precursor to a fainting spell; they were alive, they filled the air of the room, and they were angry.

The first sting was just below his left eye. It was followed within seconds by dozens more, on his face, his arms, his neck and hands. By that time he had bolted, stumbling along as fast as he could, but only as far as the next room. He fumbled for the passkey, trying to ignore the burning jabs of pain on every inch of his exposed flesh, and got the door open. He leapt inside and slammed it shut behind him.

"Wha?" said a sleepy voice from the bed. A fat, hairy man sat up in bed, blinking in confusion. "What's ow!"

And then he joined Edvin in what the motel manager later called the bee-slapping dance—swinging your arms wildly, trying to swat away or kill as many as you could, either against your own body or in midair. It didn't last long, Edvin would say when telling the story, but it sure was energetic.

The fifteen-year-old boy in the parking lot wasn't as lucky.

"Grissom, glad you're here." Nick had just arrived at the motel and was talking to one of the uniforms on-site when his boss walked up.

"Are the bees still active?"

"Honestly, we haven't gotten close enough to check. Everybody in the motel is locked down in their rooms. We've—" Nick stopped and shook his head. "We've got a body in the swimming pool, looks like a teenage boy. Haven't been able to retrieve it yet. Looks like he jumped in there to get away and either drowned or had an allergic reaction to being stung."

Grissom was already opening the rear of his Denali. He pulled out two hazmat suits, complete with respirators. "We'll use these—they're thick enough to prevent stings. I've called a beekeeper I know in Henderson—he'll capture and remove the swarm. We should try to keep them contained in the room, though; they may abscond otherwise."

"Abscond?"

"It's what happens when a bee colony feels threatened." Grissom stepped into the hazmat suit, then shrugged on the sleeves. "Essentially, they flee the hive and relocate."

"And the last thing we want is a swarm of killer bees descending on the Strip. You think this is the big attack the Bug Killer was planning?"

Grissom secured the hood before replying. "I don't know. It could even be a natural event; Africanized honeybees have been present in Nevada for almost a decade. We need to see what's in that room."

Nick started to pull on his own suit. "You're the boss."

Grissom stopped him with a hand on his shoulder. "Nick—it's okay if you sit this one out."

"Thanks, but I'm more of a get-back-on-the-horse kind of guy. Can't avoid bugs in this line of work, right?"

Grissom smiled. "No, I suppose you can't."

They ducked under the yellow tape sealing off the motel grounds and headed for the pool first. Immediately, the white of their suits was crawling with black bodies trying to sting them.

Grissom plucked one carefully from his arm and held it up to the transparent plastic of his face mask. "Africanized bees have five times as many defensive guards around their hives as European species. They're no more poisonous but much more aggressive—up to half the entire colony will respond to an intrusion, and they'll deliver eight to ten times as many stings as a normal hive. They've been known to chase intruders up to a mile and to remain agitated for as long as several days afterward."

The body was floating near the edge, facedown, the exposed skin puffy and red. Small black bodies circled above it, buzzing angrily. Nick knelt and pulled the body out of the water and onto the concrete. "Poor kid. Looks like he was stung hundreds of times."

"Africanized bees are much more tenacious. They would have circled above the water and attacked every time he surfaced . . . Nick, this isn't a natural incursion."

"How do you know?"

"Because this isn't *Apis mellifera scutellata,* which is actually a hybrid of African and European bees. It's *Apis mellifera intermissa,* a distinct species from North Africa. They're entirely black in color."

"But just as dangerous?"

"Oh, yes."

They climbed the stairs to the second floor. Bees flew in and out of the doorway of room 217. As they walked toward it, there was a loud tapping at the window of the adjoining room; two men, faces bumpy with stings, waved at them. One of them asked, "How long are we going to be stuck here?"

"Not long," Grissom said, speaking loudly to be heard. "We have an expert coming to remove them soon."

Grissom pushed the door to 217 open a little wider and stepped inside.

The first thing he noticed was the body. It lay sprawled at the foot of the bed, a man dressed only in a pair of boxers. His face was so swollen it was almost unrecognizable, but the distinctive white beard was enough for Grissom.

Nick was right behind Grissom. "Is that—"

"Yes. It's Roberto Quadros."

Grissom knelt and checked for vital signs but found none. "It looks as though he died from envenomation—he was stung thousands of times, more than enough to kill him." Nick was already taking pictures. "Looks like this is what the bees were transported in." A large wooden crate stood on the room's single dresser, its top open. A lamp lay on its side beside the bed.

Grissom stood and moved to the bathroom, where the bees covered the shower curtain like a heavy tapestry, threatening to tear it off its rings. Grissom quickly shut the door. "I think I have the majority trapped," he said. "Bees need moisture to survive—they've congregated in the dampest area available."

"Well, that should make cleanup easier." Nick shook his head. "What are we looking at, Grissom? This doesn't seem like the others."

"No. There're no signs of restraint—in fact, it looks as if he knocked the lamp over when he was attacked."

"Yeah. And why was he in his underwear?"

"He was an experienced entomologist—presumably he knew what was in the case and didn't feel threatened by it. Maybe he was napping and the bees got loose while he was asleep."

"And he gets woken up by being stung and panics?"

"An attack could have happened regardless of his reaction. Bees release an alarm pheromone when one of them is agitated; it's sort of the equivalent of a carny yelling, 'Hey, rube!' And African bees not only produce more of this pheromone, they respond more aggressively to it, too—three times as many bees will take flight to defend the hive."

"So one nervous bug and they all pile on . . . I've got luggage." Nick checked the suitcase he'd found. "Tag says it belongs to Quadros. Looks like he was staying here."

"There's a laptop on the bedside table." Grissom brushed bees off the keyboard and tapped the space bar. "It doesn't seem to be encrypted."

"Think we just got lucky?" said Nick. "I mean, it looks like either Quadros was the Bug Killer, or the real thing decided to thin out the competition—meaning it has to be Vanderhoff."

"Maybe," said Grissom. "We'll know more once we take a closer look at this laptop."

"Congratulations," said Ecklie. He smiled at Grissom as if he'd just won an award. Grissom didn't smile back. "It looks like our killer got so overconfident he solved our problem for us."

"I'm not so sure that's the case. In fact, I'm not sure the case has been solved."

"How can you say that? Your own report lists what you found on that laptop—the text of the letters sent to Athena Jordanson, the e-mails used to lure the Harribold vic—even how he planned to poison the buffet at the Embassy Gold." Ecklie shook his head. "I have to hand it to you, Gil—you were right on target about that. You saved a lot of lives."

"Did I? I didn't have anything to do with stopping Quadros—he did that to himself. And that's what bothers me." Grissom leaned forward, frowning. "I'm finding it hard to believe that someone who's demonstrated nothing but careful planning until now would slip up in such an obvious way."

"They all make a mistake sooner or later, Gil. You know that. Just be glad we caught this guy before it was too late."

"We only found a small amount of homobatrachotoxin in the room. The evidence points to his manufacturing it in quantity."

"Homeless people being recruited to process mass amounts of an esoteric poison? Come on, Gil—there's no proof of that, only a few missing indigents. And you know as well as I do that they could have just as easily moved on. People living on the street don't usually leave a forwarding address."

"And experienced entomologists don't usually die of bee stings."

"Well, this one did. Unless you have some doubt that the body you found is actually that of Roberto Quadros?"

Grissom shook his head. "The thought had occurred to me—but we got in touch with the Brazilian university he worked for, and they supplied an exemplar of his fingerprints. It's Quadros."

"Then the case is closed, Gil. Stop worrying about it."

*   *   *

"Good to have you back, Al," said Grissom, standing in the doorway to the autopsy room.

Doc Robbins turned around and said, "Hello, Grissom. Good to be back. Can't wait to get back to work."

"Here. A little welcome-back present." He walked forward and handed Robbins a small cardboard box.

Robbins leaned on his crutch with one hand, took the box with the other. He let the crutch dangle off his forearm by the support as he opened the box.

It was a large tarantula, encased in Lucite. Robbins grinned as he hefted it. "Nice weight," he said. "Should come in handy the next time I need to squash a pest."

" 'It is difficult to say who do you the most mischief; enemies with the worst intentions or friends with the best.' "

"Benjamin Franklin?

"Edward Bulwer-Lytton."

"Isn't he the guy who wrote 'It was a dark and stormy night'?"

"Very good. Most people attribute that line to Snoopy."

Robbins set the paperweight down on the very same counter the Brazilian wandering spider had leapt from. "Snoopy had a better agent. Is this strictly a social call, or was there something else?"

Grissom walked over to the autopsy table, where the body of Roberto Quadros lay. His skin was still red and grossly swollen, dotted with approximately three and a half thousand stingers; the Y-shaped suture on his chest told him that Robbins had finished his autopsy. "Is the tox screen back yet?"

"Just came in. It was definitely the envenomation that killed him, though we did find small amounts of the homobatrachotoxin you told us to look out for."

"How much?"

Robbins limped over to his desk and picked up a piece of paper. "Point-zero-four micrograms," he said.

"Not a lethal dose," said Grissom, "but more than you'd expect from simple environmental exposure."

"And definitely enough to have an effect."

"One of the initial symptoms of homobatrachotoxin poisoning is paralysis. I think the amount in Quadros's bloodstream was enough to produce that."

"It would explain why he didn't try to get away from the bees—he couldn't move."

Grissom studied the corpse's face; it was so swollen as to be unrecognizable. "Al, can you send a sample of Quadros's hair to tox? It's possible these levels built up over time—if so, I'd like to know how long."

"Sure. You think he was exposed repeatedly?"

"Maybe." Grissom shook his head. "But something doesn't add up here."

Grissom found Nathan Vanderhoff beside the pool.

Vanderhoff sat up on his lounger when he saw Grissom approaching. He was in one of the shaded cabanas, dressed in shorts and sunglasses and with a laptop beside him.

"Nathan," said Grissom, "mind if we talk?"

"Not at all. I heard about Roberto—terrible, just terrible."

"Yes." Grissom took out his own sunglasses and slipped them on. "Excuse me. The glare off the pool—bright light is one of the things that can trigger a migraine."

"Not to mention stress. I imagine you've been under a great deal of that lately."

Grissom shrugged and pulled up a deck chair. "Part of the job. I'm just sorry I missed so much of the conference."

"Yes, there were some good presentations this year—though I'm afraid I missed quite a few myself."

"I apologize if the investigation inconvenienced you."

"Not at all. You were simply being professional. I'm afraid I haven't been—Vegas simply offers too many opportunities to indulge."

"That it does. What's been occupying your time?"

Vanderhoff smiled. "Oh, this and that. I'm a bit of a foodie—the restaurant selection is quite impressive." He paused. "Afraid I'm not much of one for the buffets, though. They remind me too much of repletes."

Grissom knew what he referred to: a replete was a specialized class of worker ant, one that essentially functioned as a living food dispenser. It hung upside down from the roof of a storeroom, its distended belly holding so much liquid that if it were to fall it would burst. Its sole purpose was to regurgitate stored nectar when other sources of food weren't available.

"Better selection, though," said Grissom. "Nathan, did Roberto ever talk to you?"

"About the case? Of course. All four of us discussed it, even after it became obvious we were suspects. Then Khem was arrested, and we assumed you had your man. But now that Quadros is dead . . . well, I have to say I'm a bit nervous."

Grissom glanced around. Two women in extremely brief swimsuits had just climbed out of the pool, sunlight gleaming off their perfect tans. "You don't seem nervous," he said.

Vanderhoff chuckled, eyeing the women. "I thought I'd make a poorer target if I stayed in public. Of course, there are some fringe benefits . . ."

"Did Quadros ever say anything that seemed . . . odd?"

"It's hard to say what would qualify, Gil.

Roberto, as you know, was more than a little out-spoken—and had quite a temper, as well. I would have classified any discussion with him that *wasn't* punctuated by an outburst or two as odd."

"Did he ever say anything about Athena Jordanson?"

"The singer? No, not that I can recall. But really, I didn't know the man well; I only met him in person for the first time here."

"So did I," said Grissom. He got to his feet. "Enjoy the rest of your stay, Nathan. I don't think you have anything to worry about."

Jake Soames was harder to find. He wasn't at the conference, and he wasn't at his hotel; Grissom had his cell phone number, but Soames wasn't answering. Grissom left a message for Soames to call him back.

He did, no more than twenty minutes later. "What's up, Gilly?"

"Jake. I was wondering if we could get together and talk."

There was a brief pause. Grissom heard coughing in the background. "Uh, yeah, that'd be fine. Look, I just got out of a show—why don't we meet in the hotel bar for a drink? It's called—let's see—Glimmer."

"I know where that is. Half an hour?"

"I'll be waiting."

As he drove, Grissom reflected on his friendship

with Jake Soames. It seemed to prove the adage that opposites attract; where Grissom was quiet and thoughtful, Jake was brash and impulsive. Where Grissom took most of his pleasure from the cerebral, Jake was more interested in the visceral— though they had found common ground in an appreciation of roller coasters.

But that was how some relationships worked. Traits Grissom might have found irritating in others he tolerated, even appreciated, in Jake; his friend, in return, seemed to enjoy the counterbalance of Grissom's calm.

But he really didn't know Jake Soames at all.

He'd never been to his house or even his hometown. He'd never met any of his other friends, other than professional colleagues they both shared. They had probably exchanged more words via e-mail than they ever had in person. His overall view of the person named Jake Soames, if he were to try to quantify it, was based largely on less than a hundred hours of face-to-face time and a great deal of written correspondence. And if there was one thing Grissom knew, it was that people— unlike evidence—were always capable of lying.

Face-to-face or in writing.

Glimmer was one of the trendy nightspots where there was always a line at the door, the only white light was in the bathroom, and the constant pulse of music made it almost impossible to talk. He used his CSI ID to bypass the line, then found

Soames in a back booth. Miraculously, the music was slightly less obtrusive there.

The booth was circular, with a high padded back. Grissom slid in, close enough to Soames so they could talk without shouting. Soames had a beer in front of him, but he'd hardly touched it.

"Good to see you, Gilly. One of the main reasons I came on this junket was so's we could catch each other up."

"It's good to see you, too, Jake. Sorry I've been so busy."

"No worries. Though I'm a little surprised you didn't interrogate me yourself."

Grissom started to reply, then stopped himself.

"I mean, if you go to all the trouble of hauling an old friend off the street, the least you could do was show up for the grilling—my feelings were a bit hurt."

"We questioned everyone," said Grissom.

"I told you, mate—no worries. You've got a killer who seems to know all about bugs, one who blows into town the same time we do—I'd do the same in your boots. But things are a little different now, eh? Charong's in the clink and Quadros is dead. Guess that means me and Vanderhoff are up for the silver and gold."

"You were already cleared for the Harribold killing, Jake."

"And then there was one. You've got Nathan all locked away, then?"

"No. Things aren't as clear-cut as that."

Soames picked up his beer and took a drink—just a sip, not his usual enthusiastic gulp. "Course not. That's why you're here, right?"

"I suppose it is. How well did you know Quadros?"

"Laid eyes on him for the first time at the conference. Swapped a few files over the interwebs; he hung out in some of the same discussion groups you and I do. I thought you and him were the best of e-buddies."

"We did correspond, yes. But I was meeting him for the first time at the conference, too."

"Beginning to sound like I might have to settle for the bronze. You think Quadros was the Bug Killer all along?"

"I can't say. The investigation is still ongoing."

"And despite the dime-store badge you pretended to give me, I'm not really part of that. Never was, was I?"

"I'm sorry, Jake. I did . . . I did what I thought was necessary."

Jake stared at him. "We all do, mate. We all do . . . You probably wonder what I've been up to while I wasn't at the conference."

"I assumed you were enjoying Vegas."

"And that's exactly what I've been doing. Haven't been going quite as wild as you might think, though—can't knock back the pints the way I used to. I've been seeing a lot of shows."

"Which ones?"

"Well, a number of the ones that feature beautiful women in various states of undress—what a surprise, eh? But I've caught a few others, too—like this bloke who did impressions of damn near everybody from Elvis to the Pope. He was very entertaining. And the show I just got out of had a cross-dressing magician." Jake laughed. "Nothing's ever as it seems in Vegas, is it? Everybody spends all their time trying to convince people they're somebody else, or that something that isn't so really is. No place for a serious scientist."

"I'd say just the opposite. I can't think of a place that needs a serious scientist more."

Jake shrugged. "Fair enough. And maybe an entomologist is the perfect fit for Vegas, anyway. After all, who's better at pretending to be something else than our little many-legged meal tickets . . . they're the illusionists of the natural world, or maybe the impressionists. Hide in plain sight, right under your nose . . ."

13

GRISSOM MET WITH Nick and Riley in his office. The tox report had come back on the sample of Roberto Quadros's hair, and the first thing he did was hand copies of the report to both of them.

Riley responded first. "According to this, Quadros had the homobatrachotoxin in his system as far back as six weeks ago."

Grissom nodded. "And in levels high enough to induce paralysis."

Nick frowned. "But . . . we had Quadros in here, walking and talking. He wasn't paralyzed then."

Riley gave her report back to Grissom. "Snake handlers will dose themselves with small amounts of venom over a long period of time in order to build up a tolerance. Maybe he did the same thing."

"In that case," said Grissom, "we would have seen a gradual buildup. That didn't happen—a fairly high level simply appears at around the six-week mark and stays consistent until death. That suggests something else entirely."

"Captivity," said Nick. "Someone was using it to keep him immobile for the past month and a half."

Riley shook her head. "So if Roberto Quadros was a prisoner, unable to move—who was it we interviewed?"

"The motel room the body was found in was registered to Larry Wheeler," said Grissom. "LW—the same initials he used online to lure Keenan Harribold."

"So Quadros isn't our killer," said Nick. "LW is still out there."

"Yes," said Grissom. "Presumably with a large amount of HBTX that he still intends to use. And we have no idea where or when."

Riley and Nick surveyed the various items spread out over the surface of the light table. They included a tent, a sleeping bag, and several heaps of unwashed clothes, everything they'd confiscated from the last-known location of Robert Ermine, aka Buffet Bob.

"Okay," said Nick. "We didn't find anything obvious on the first go-round, so it's time to look a little closer. I'm thinking we concentrate on clothing; doesn't look—or smell—like he's washed any of it for a while, so it's possible something he wore while working for LW picked up some trace."

"Unless the killer decided he didn't want his drones wandering away from the hive. Could be that once Bob started working he wasn't allowed to leave—which is why no one's seen him for weeks."

"Yeah, but LW did send three of them on a field trip to obtain supplies at one point. Bob could have slipped back to his tent then, maybe for a change of clothes."

"I guess it's possible. You want tops or bottoms?" asked Riley.

Nick grinned. "I'll take anything above the waist."

"So I get socks *and* underwear? Lucky, lucky me."

Grissom studied the recorded interview with the man who'd called himself Roberto Quadros. On-screen, he was leaping to his feet and pointing an accusing finger at Nick Stokes, calling the entire process an outrage.

Defensive posturing. The larvae of the elephant hawk moth mimicking a snake about to strike.

"I didn't come here for the *hedonism*, Mr. Stokes," the imposter said.

Many insect species die after mating.

"I came for the intellectual stimulation provided by an exchange of ideas between men and women like myself . . ."

What was it he said to me when we first met? "We study arthropods, do we not? The biological equivalent of machines. They have no psychology, no culture, no advanced cognitive functions. Seeing them through the filter of human experience does nothing but distort data."

Were you really talking about insects? Or was that your opinion of the human race?

He watched the interview through to the end, then went back to something Quadros had said near the beginning.

"—at the very least Dr. Grissom could have talked to me *himself*."

He froze the image. Quadros had looked directly into the camera when he said it, knowing full well that at some point Grissom would be staring back.

Was that a trace of a smile hidden behind his bushy white beard?

"Think I've got something," said Riley.

Nick put down the T-shirt he'd been examining. "Fibers?"

"Yes. White, and very fine. They're all over the cuffs of these jeans."

Nick walked around to her side of the light table to take a better look. "Those don't look like they came from an animal. Could be plant matter."

"Well, you're the fiber expert."

"So they say. I'll check it against the database."

"You mind if I do it?"

Nick raised his eyebrows. "No, go ahead. I do something wrong?"

"No, no. It's just—you track down a fiber, it's business as usual. I do it—" She stopped.

"You do it, Grissom might notice. Funny, I didn't think you much cared what Grissom thinks."

"He's my superior—of course I care what he thinks. And this isn't about sucking up, either. I just want him to see that I'm competent."

Nick smiled. "I wouldn't worry too much about that. If there's one thing Grissom notices, it's how the job gets done. Just don't expect a lot of hearts and flowers—getting a 'good work' from Grissom is like three cheers and a parade from anyone else."

"I'm starting to get that."

"Don't worry, you're doing fine. Let me know what you find on those fibers."

This time, she smiled back.

In the end, Riley turned to Wendy Simms.

"Hey, Riley," said Wendy. "You look like you've got something on your mind."

Riley handed her the sample of the fibers she'd collected from the jeans. "I do. This."

"Fibers? I do DNA."

"I know. But these are plant fibers; I've searched through every botanical database I can find and can't get a match through physical characteristics alone. I'm hoping you can ID it for me."

"Well, plants have genes just like all living organisms. As long as this particular species is on file, I should be able to track it down."

Riley noticed Hodges in a corner of the lab, hunched over a piece of paper and muttering to himself. "No, no, that's too big . . ."

"What's Hodges doing?" asked Riley. "I've never heard him talk to himself before."

Wendy sighed. "Oh, you will. But he usually only does it when in the throes of creativity."

"What's he creating?"

"I'm not sure. But he asked me for my measurements—including hat size—so I'm a little worried."

"I can hear you, you know," said Hodges.

Riley and Wendy looked at each other, then approached Hodges together. He quickly turned over the large sheet of paper he'd been working on.

"Are those crayons?" said Wendy.

"*Pencil* crayons," said Hodges. "I was working on the color scheme. I was originally going to go with something that went with your eyes, but then I realized nobody'd be able to see your eyes anyway . . ."

"Do I even want to know?" said Wendy.

"It's still in the planning stages," said Hodges. "But maybe I need a female perspective; fashion isn't really my thing. Tell me what you think—but sign these first." He handed each of them a piece of paper.

"What's this?" asked Riley, scanning it.

"A nondisclosure agreement. Standard boilerplate, just says you won't talk to anyone else about what I'm going to show you."

Wendy rolled her eyes, pulled out a pen, and signed it. Riley shrugged and did the same.

"Okay," said Hodges. "Now, give me your gut-level first impression of both of these." He held up two large sheets of paper in front of him. "I'm calling the one on the left Trudy Transfer and the one on the right Buddy Bloodspatter."

Wendy blinked. Riley frowned.

"Trudy seems like she'd be cold," said Wendy. "Even though she's covered in . . . What is all that stuff? It looks as if she was practicing Dumpster diving in a bikini."

"Well, it's all kinds of things. Paper, fabric, bodily fluids—"

"And why's her head so big?"

"Because it's made out of foam rubber. It'll be lightweight, with oversize eyes and a biiiig smile. Very *anime*—just in case our new owners are Japanese."

Wendy crumpled the NDA into a little ball and threw it at him. "For the last time, Hodges—the lab isn't being sold. Don't you have real work to do?"

"Actually," said Riley, "I kind of like the other one. What's that big necklace he's wearing, though?"

"DNA," said Hodges. "I know, I know. But *you* try drawing a double helix and making it both accurate *and* artistic."

"Got a result on those fibers for you," said Wendy.

Riley looked up from the file she'd been scrolling through. "Yeah? What is it?"

"If you were a cat, you wouldn't have to ask."

"Catnip?"

"Not quite. It's *Teucrium marum*, a plant commonly known as cat thyme. Some cats react to it the same way they do catnip."

"Where's it grow?"

"Well, it's native to Spain and the western Mediterranean but does well in dry, sandy soil with a lot of sun—so it wouldn't be hard to grow it here. Maybe your guy's a cat lover."

Riley frowned. "Maybe."

She sat and thought about it after Wendy left. Somehow, she couldn't see the Bug Killer cozying up to a purring tabby—it didn't fit his *modus operandi* at all. So what was the connection?

She turned back to the file she'd been reading. It was the arrest record of Robert Ermine, who it seemed hadn't been entirely successful in his career as Buffet Bob. In fact, he'd been arrested five times and barred from at least a dozen places.

She wondered how the Bug Killer had chosen him. Had he trolled the homeless corridor, looking for subjects who fit a particular profile, or had he viewed his workers as interchangeable drones? Had all of his choices worked out, or had there been rejects? If there had been, some of them might still have valuable information.

Riley had always had good instincts as a street cop. Right now, they were telling her that someone out there had talked to the mysterious LW and could be persuaded to talk to her.

She printed out a picture of Roberto Quadros and headed downtown.

Riley talked to half a dozen homeless men and women before she found one who seemed to recognize the photo of Quadros.

"Do I know him?" the man with the blanket wrapped around his shoulders said. He was somewhere in his thirties, missing one of his front teeth, and very dirty; his beard was gathered into a kind of chin ponytail, bound by what seemed like dozens of rubber bands. "I don't know. Who knows anyone? I don't know *you*. *You* don't know you. I don't know *me*."

"Okay, you don't know him," said Riley. "But have you *seen* him?"

Rubber Band Man thought about it. "Yes. I have seen him. Not that picture—no, I've never seen that picture before—but I have seen that man, the one *in* the picture. Yes."

"Uh-huh. When?" Riley's hopes stayed firmly in the basement; she doubted she'd get anything approaching reality from this particular subject.

"Fifty-one days ago. It was a Tuesday. I like Tuesdays and sometimes give them their own name. That was Humphrey Tuesday, and it was very friendly."

She did some quick calculation in her head. Fifty-one days ago had, in fact, been a Tuesday—Humphrey or not. Maybe Rubber Band Man was more credible than she'd thought. "Did you talk to him?"

"Yes." The man stared at her without blinking.

"What about?"

"He wanted me to work for him. He noticed me counting the bottles I'd collected and said I was very focused. He liked that."

"What did you tell him?"

"I told him I already had a job. I pointed at the bottles. He said he understood."

"Did he say anything else?"

The man tugged the blanket tighter around his shoulders. "He said he'd give me food. Place to stay, too. That was when I knew there was something wrong with him."

A chill went through Riley. "What was wrong with him?"

"Eyes. Cold, cold eyes. Didn't see me, no, didn't see me at all. Like he was looking at a bug."

"Did he tell you anything about the job? Where it was, what you'd be doing?"

"Farming. Said we'd be farming. Making plants happy. Making happy plants. I told him no thank you, I have my bottles, and today's name is Humphrey. Other people went with him. Buffet Bob went. He never came back."

"No. No, he didn't."

"I liked Bob. He gave me food. More people used to give me food, but now they don't. Or water. Water is life, but you can't give it to people like me, because we're dying. I'm thirsty. All the time."

Riley hadn't quite acclimated to the dry air of Nevada, either; she always tried to keep some water handy. She took the bottle she had with her out of her bag and handed it to the man. "Here."

"You can't do that," the man said. "You're the law. You're breaking your*self*."

"Wouldn't be the first time. Take it, please. You won't get in trouble."

The man did. "This is not a Tuesday, but it is a happy day anyway. I think I will call it Hortense."

"Works for me," said Riley.

"Cat thyme?" Grissom asked.

"That's what we found," said Nick. He tapped a few keys, calling up a picture on the monitor. "Don't know what it means, though. It's not in-digenous, it's not a commercial crop—you can get it easily enough from nurseries, but it's not so rare that a purchase would stand out. I've made some phone calls to local greenhouses and importers, but no one seems to have ordered any in large quantities."

"If he's growing it himself, it's to hide his trail. It also suggests a fairly large facility."

"Yeah, but why? Is he planning on getting every cat in the city stoned? I just don't get it."

Grissom stared at the picture of the plant on the screen. "Have Hodges run a chemical analy-sis of the plant sample. There's something we're missing."

"Will do."

"Where's Riley?"

"She said something about conducting a few more interviews in the homeless corridor, showing a picture of Quadros around. Thinks someone may have seen or overheard him recruiting his workforce."

"That's good thinking."

Nick grinned. "I'll tell her you said that."

Riley ended up talking to the Rubber Band Man—who eventually volunteered that his name was Orson—for quite a while. His mind, while fractured, still housed a pretty good memory—a memory that worked mainly on whatever Orson considered important, but one that worked nonetheless.

Orson had considered the man with the cold eyes important.

The place the fake Quadros wanted to take Orson to didn't seem to be in the city limits, but it wasn't far outside them—less than half an hour's drive, anyway. Nobody would bother them there, meaning it had to be fairly isolated. And perhaps most important of all, they wouldn't be working outside—which meant a greenhouse, barn, or warehouse.

Riley hadn't gone back to the lab. Instead, she'd parked her Denali somewhere she could get a decent wireless connection, turned on her laptop, and called up Google Earth.

She still found the application amazing. It wasn't real-time observation, but it let you zoom in on almost any patch of real estate in the world, giving you an instant feel for the layout of the area: buildings, roads, geographical features like rivers, lakes, and valleys. You had to be careful how you used it, but it was still a very, very useful tool. And what she was looking for should be fairly distinctive: a large outbuilding of some kind, probably on a farm or a ranch, one that appeared deserted.

Sadly, those criteria were a little too easy to meet. Las Vegas bore the distinction of holding the number one spot in the country when it came to abandoned property; people here found it easier to simply walk away from a bad mortgage or loan, leaving everything from private homes to places of business empty. The rural sector didn't seem to be any exception.

After half an hour she had four possibilities. All were within range, title searches indicated all were in foreclosure, and none had shown any livestock, people, or vehicles when the satellite shots were taken. It was entirely possible LW had set up shop in a place that had been abandoned after these pictures were taken, but Riley figured he had to have been there for at least two months; his laborers had disappeared off the streets six weeks ago, and he would have needed a few more to get properly set up. The chances he was in one of the properties she'd narrowed it down to were good.

But was it good enough to tell Grissom?

She stared at the screen, tapping her finger on the edge of the case. Then she started up the Denali and headed for the highway.

"Okay, Hodges, I got your page," said Nick, striding into the Trace lab. "What have you got?"

Hodges handed him a printout. "This."

Nick took the sheet. "What, no guessing games, no wordplay? I figured you'd do ten minutes on the phrase *cat thyme* alone."

Hodges sighed. "Sorry, I'm a little down. I found out the lab isn't really going to be sold."

"And that's a bad thing?"

He shrugged. "It is for Buddy Bloodspatter." He walked away, shaking his head.

"Hodges, you get a little stranger every day," Nick murmured. Then he headed for Grissom's office, scanning the sheet as he went. By the time he reached his boss's doorway, he was shaking his head himself.

"Got the results back from the GC mass spec on the cat thyme," said Nick. "Maybe you can see something here, but I don't."

He handed it to Grissom, who scanned it quickly. "Almost ten percent dolichodial," he said. "There's a monoterpene dialdehyde called anisomorphal that's a diastereomer of dolichodial. Presumably, you could process one into the other."

"So you think he's producing anisomorphal? What is it, a poison?"

"Not exactly." Grissom turned to his workstation and called up a file. "The chemical anisomorphal was discovered in 1962 and named after *Anisomorpha buprestoides*, the Florida walking stick insect." He swiveled the monitor to give Nick a better view. "It's the primary component of a defensive spray they aim at predators. But even though it can cause intense pain—and even temporary blindness if sprayed in the eyes—it's not lethal."

Nick studied the picture on-screen. The Florida walking stick's body and legs were so thin that if you didn't know what you were looking at, you could easily mistake it for a twig. "Cryptic camouflage *and* a chemical defense," said Nick. "That definitely fits with LW's pattern."

"Yes—but again, we have to think in terms of his objectives. Since exposure to anisomorphal isn't fatal, why is he producing it?"

Las Vegas was an artificial paradise, a manufactured oasis created by money, vision, greed—and most of all, water. The lush greenery that fronted many hotels, the palm trees, the fountains, the ersatz canal that flowed through the interior of the Venetian resort . . . none of it was possible without plenty of water. Even so, the plants that lived and breathed in the hot, dry air of the city needed regular tending, and that meant there was an entire horticulture subindustry dedicated to their welfare.

The greenhouse that sprawled in front of Riley

was a branch of that industry—or had been, until the economy's free fall had turned it into an empty glass bunker. The sign over the front door read TROPICANA BOTANICA, and from the painting of the brilliant, multicolored flower beside it Riley guessed they'd planned on supplying exotic tropical blooms to the hotels, casinos, and restaurants of the Strip. But while the water still flowed, the money had dried up—and so had one entrepreneur's vision.

She got out of her vehicle, closing the door quietly. The previous two places she'd visited had been dead ends, but this one seemed different. There were fresh tire tracks on the dirt road that led to the place, and they led to a sliding steel door that was probably where delivery trucks had once been parked.

The front door was sealed with a large padlock and chain, a peeling notice of foreclosure pasted to the wood above it. The greenhouse itself was set back behind the offices, its transparent roof gleaming in the sun. She couldn't see what was inside, though; the wall panels had been covered with sheets of newspaper on the inside, floor to ceiling.

She walked around the side of the offices and got close enough to check the date on the nearest paper. Just over two months ago.

The wind was kicking up, blowing dust in her eyes. She leaned in close to the glass, listening intently and trying to shut out the sound of the wind.

Something moved inside.

*   *   *

Grissom got on the elevator of the Embassy Gold flanked by four security officers. It seemed Athena Jordanson's vow to demand increased security hadn't been forgotten.

The queen of soul was eyeing herself critically in a full-length mirror while a seamstress made final adjustments on her dress. It was a long, slinky affair, slit high on one end and plunging low on the other.

"Thank you for seeing me," said Grissom. "I realize you must be extremely busy."

Athena glanced at Grissom and smiled. "I am, but that's a good thing. Helps keep my mind off recent events."

"I apologize if my department's search of your new hotel inconvenienced you—"

She stopped him with a wave of her hand—a move Grissom suspected she was rather practiced at. "No, no, no. Couldn't raise a stink about security and then bitch when someone actually *did* something, could I? Well, I could, but that's a little *too* diva for me." She went back to studying the contours of the dress in the mirror.

"That's what I wanted to talk to you about."

She looked back at him sharply. "You find something?"

Grissom shook his head. "I wish we had. Unfortunately, all our searches came up negative."

"Unfortunately? Guess you're not a fan, huh?"

"On the contrary—I enjoy your music a great deal. But if we'd found what we were looking for, I could safely say you're out of danger. Finding nothing . . . proves nothing."

"Maybe there's nothing to find. After all, isn't the creep who sent me all those letters dead?"

"I don't believe he is, Ms. Jordanson. And that's why I'm here—to ask you to postpone your show."

"Postpone my show?" She frowned. "I can't do that, Mr. Grissom. Contracts work both ways—I squeezed this hotel for all I could, and in return they want their money's worth. I try to back out now, I'll spend the next ten years in court instead of on the stage."

"I'm not asking you to cancel—just push it back."

"Why? You think you'll find something the second time you didn't the first?" She turned back to the mirror. "I appreciate you trying to cover all the bases, but it's just not gonna happen. I mean, can you give me any solid proof that the person who killed Paul is still alive and trying to sabotage my show?"

Grissom hesitated. "No."

"Then I can't disappoint my fans *or* the people who sign my paycheck. Sorry, Mr. Grissom."

"So am I," said Grissom. "Thank you for your time."

The guards escorted him back to the elevator and down. He walked out through the lobby, then turned around and surveyed the front of the hotel. It was a massive structure, curving like a sine wave, and the front of the property was dominated by a series of stepped waterfalls surrounding a huge reflecting pool. The dancing fountains were as good as those in front of the Bellagio—some said even better.

Water, Grissom thought. *In the middle of the desert, water is more than just life—it's gold. And in Vegas, the more water you can waste on sheer spectacle, the more gold you obviously have. We treat the Strip more like a river than a street; we build bridges over it rather than disrupt the flow of tourists in their cars.*

He walked toward the parking lot and his own vehicle, then stopped and turned around. On an impulse, he took the escalator up to where the nearest pedway crossed over the street.

No, these aren't bridges. They're aqueducts, piping visitors from hotels and casinos on one side of Las Vegas Boulevard to the other. In a town so dry we build escalators outside, water is a metaphor for wealth—but the real wealth is still in people's pockets. Until, dazzled by the sights and sounds and carefully created atmosphere, they make their contribution to the local aquifer.

He stopped in the middle of the pedway. A homeless man was slumped against the wall at the halfway point, a hand-lettered cardboard sign propped up on his lap. It read WHY LIE? I NEED A BEER.

In another town people would have ignored him as an alcoholic. Here, he was just trying to join the party.

An image popped into Grissom's head. When ants traveled in large numbers and needed to cross a stream, they formed a living bridge by holding on to each other's bodies with their jaws. Once the rest of the group had crossed, they would let go, dissolving into individual drowning units. Their society had sacrificed them for its own needs, throwing them away once their usefulness had expired.

It was that image, of an ant bridge eroding under the relentless pressure of water, that somehow seemed important.

But he didn't know why.

14

CATHERINE AND GREG STARED up at Mount Pele. Impassive, it ignored them, burbling away to itself softly.

They went back to work.

They were still searching for obsidian. They scoured the floor, the interior and exterior of the artificial mountain, the gantry. When nothing turned up, they disconnected the pumps and hoses that the wax flowed through and checked them.

They came up empty.

"Let's rethink this," said Catherine as they took a break. They sat on the couch in the lounging area, eating cold pizza that Greg had brought along and drinking coffee from a thermos. "We know Kanamu was here; we know he was high. We know that the chunk of obsidian that knocked him out was hot, but we don't know why."

Greg chewed and swallowed. "Right. And none of our suspects has burns on his hands, so the killer used gloves or something else to pick up the obsidian."

"We've found work gloves, but nothing charred or singed." She finished her piece of pizza and washed it down with some coffee. "Maybe gloves weren't necessary. What if the obsidian was in some kind of clamp or vise—something to let the person handle it without getting burned?"

"Like tongs or vise grips?"

"Yeah. The killer grabs the tool and smacks Kanamu in the head with it, and the impact drives the shard into his skull."

Greg nodded. "That could work. Then Kanamu either topples over into the volcano and asphyxiates, or he gets dumped in by someone trying to make it look like an accident."

"We can take a closer look at all the tools we found on-site."

They finished their lunch and went back to work. Vise grips, tongs, monkey wrenches—anything that might have been used to grip the obsidian was collected. Some showed indications of having been exposed to intense heat, some didn't. They tested all of them for blood, hoping there might have been some spatter, but didn't find any.

"Back to the lab," Catherine sighed. "We're going to have to examine these a little closer—maybe one of them has some trace at a microscopic level."

They found no trace of obsidian on any of the tools.

Catherine looked up from the microscope. "So

no murder weapon—except for the volcano itself."

"Maybe that's who we should be considering," said Greg. He leaned back against a stainless steel counter and crossed his arms. "Pele, the volcano goddess. She got angry at Kanamu for creating a mockery of her natural glory and decided to punish him for it."

Catherine arched an eyebrow. "Uh-huh. And I suppose she magically transported a shard of obsidian all the way from Hawaii to do it, too."

Greg shrugged. "I'm just saying that a red-hot shard of volcanic rock isn't fake lava—it's pretty close to the real thing."

"And I think you've seen that special episode of *The Brady Bunch* too many times."

He grinned. "Okay, okay, I'm not serious. But if there is a bigger chunk of obsidian involved, I don't think it's in that warehouse—we've been over the whole thing. Which means the killer took it with him and got rid of it someplace else."

"Thereby getting rid of our best chance of discovering his identity." She frowned. "You know, that's not the only thing missing from this puzzle. There's also Kanamu's fingers."

"Well, at least we know who to ask about that . . ."

"Mr. Wornow," said Catherine, taking her seat on the other side of the interview table, "how are they treating you at County?"

Wornow, dressed in a standard-issue orange jumpsuit, shrugged. "Okay, I guess. My lawyer tells me he'll have me out on bail soon, and I can probably plea-bargain down to community service."

"Maybe you'll get to go to Burning Man this year after all," said Greg. "Of course, any recommendation we make to the judge will be part of your sentencing. You might get house arrest, which would severely limit your traveling options."

Wornow looked glum. "Great."

"But that doesn't have to happen," said Catherine. "Cooperate with us, and we'll put in a good word for you."

"What do you mean, cooperate? I already told you everything."

"Not quite," said Greg. "You admitted to cutting off Kanamu's fingers, but you didn't tell us what you did with them afterward."

Wornow looked uncomfortable. "Oh. Is that, you know, really important?"

"It might be," said Catherine.

"Well, I, um, kind of got rid of them."

"How?" asked Greg.

"I stuck them in a container full of acid. Then I buried the container."

"Belt *and* suspenders, huh?" said Catherine. "Where did you bury the container?"

"Out in the desert. I can give you directions, though."

"All right," said Greg. "Now, here's the really important question: what kind of acid?"

"Hydrochloric. I think. I mean, it wasn't mine, I borrowed it from a Burner friend—"

"Was it in a glass bottle or a plastic one?" asked Greg.

"Plastic."

"You're sure?" asked Catherine.

"Yeah, I'm sure."

"Is it possible it was a different kind of acid?" asked Greg.

"I don't know. Maybe. It had one of those warning labels on it, you know? With the symbol of the fingers being eaten away. So I figured—"

"That whatever the chemical formula, it was exactly what you needed," said Catherine.

Catherine drove while Greg consulted the directions Wornow had given them.

"Hydrochloric acid can be stored in glass or plastic," said Greg. "It's a relatively weak acid, but it will dissolve flesh in high enough concentrations."

"So will a lot of other things. Let's face it, most likely what we'll find is a bottle of very acidic soup."

"Maybe, maybe not . . ."

Another ten minutes of driving brought them to their destination, a fork in the road marked by a large, reddish boulder on one side. Catherine pulled over and they both got out.

"Lucky for us he decided to memorize the spot," said Greg. "If he'd just picked some random area off the road, we'd never find it."

"Well, he was nervous. He planned to come back when he figured the fingers were fully dissolved and then dump the whole thing somewhere else."

They took spades from the back of the Denali, then started digging carefully at the base of the boulder. It didn't take long for Greg to hit pay dirt.

"Got something," he said, putting his spade aside and kneeling. He used his hands to clear away the rest of the sandy soil. "One large plastic jug of . . ."

"Well, what do you know," said Catherine. "We just got lucky again."

Back at the lab, Catherine and Greg estimated the amount of liquid in the jug, then very carefully cut the top third of the jug away. What they hoped to collect would be delicate, and they didn't want to risk breaking it up by simply pouring the jug out.

What they found, floating on top of the acid, were four perfectly shaped finger casts made out of wax. The wax on the thumb hadn't detached from the corroding flesh yet and had settled on the bottom.

"Hydro*fluoric* acid," said Catherine. "Which will eat through glass just fine but leaves paraffin alone."

"It got rid of the fingers—well, mostly—but left us with something else," said Greg. He picked the casts out one by one with a pair of forceps, laying them on a plastic sheet on the worktable. "A record of the condition of Hal Kanamu's fingers just before he died."

"The tips of the forefinger and thumb were deformed. There was a single large, irregular bump on both of them."

"Could be a bubble caused by impurities in the wax. It's a real mixture, after all."

"I don't think so. Look, although both are irregular, they match—like two sides of a symmetrical object."

"You're right. Which means those aren't bubbles in the wax."

"No," said Catherine. "They're blisters. Blisters on the tips of our vic's fingers."

Back to the warehouse. But this time Catherine and Greg had a better idea of where they needed to look.

"You know," said Catherine, "Wornow said he used the pulley to get Kanamu's body from the cone of the volcano to the floor. But what if the gantry was on the wrong side? It's on wheels—he would have had to move it closer to the pulley."

"Meaning our crime scene isn't accurate. So what position was it in when Hal Kanamu went lava surfing?"

Catherine walked over to the base of the gantry. "There's a faint but discernible trail. It goes back in a curve around ten, twelve feet before stopping."

"Well, let's put it back where it was."

They did, the gantry's wheels squeaking as it rolled. When they were finished, one side of the gantry butted up against a thick wooden support beam that ran from the floor to the ceiling.

"There," said Catherine. "So if it was positioned *here* when Kanamu died—"

"Then this post is suddenly part of the picture," finished Greg. "Shall we?"

"After you."

They clambered up the side of the gantry and onto the platform at the top. Greg spotted something almost immediately. "Well, hello," he said. "Look what's visible at this height and angle."

Catherine saw it, too—a slender, doubled length of chain hanging from a nail pounded into the beam. She got up close and examined it. "Looks like a necklace. Metal's fairly unreflective—it was practically invisible up here, disappeared right into the grain of the wood."

"It's broken, too. The bottom links aren't connected."

"No, but they are blackened. And there's a significant burn mark on the wood, in an odd shape right at the bottom."

"That's the same shape as the blisters on Kanamu's fingers."

"Yes, it is." Catherine studied the equipment on the table at one side of the platform. A grinding motor, a toolbox, a butane torch on its side, and a partly disassembled pump were scattered around. She looked from the chain to the table, then to the edge of the platform that abutted the volcano itself. She pulled out her flashlight and shone it up at the roof.

In the shadows of the rafters, something glinted.

They had to go back to the lab to get an extendable ladder tall enough to reach the ceiling. When they returned and used it, what they found embedded in the ceiling right next to a support beam was a small chunk of obsidian. Greg pulled it out with a forceps and admired it for a second before depositing it in an evidence bag. "Ladies and gentlemen, we have a winner," he said. "Or in this case, a rock."

He climbed down and handed the bag to Catherine. She held it up and examined it through the clear plastic. "Looks like the same shape as the burn on Kanamu's fingers."

"Yep. But how did it get from there to where we found it?"

"I've got an idea, but there's still one piece of the puzzle missing." She climbed the ladder, then stepped across to the gantry. She bent over the worktable, peering at each of the pieces of equipment in turn. "This electric grinder motor has an exposed flywheel," she said. "And the power cord is duct-taped to the side of the gantry. Not plugged in right now."

"But it could have been—plenty of extension cords on the floor. If Wornow moved the gantry from here to where we found it, the power cord could have pulled free."

"Greg, find the most likely cord and see if you can run it up here."

He did, climbing up the side of the gantry with the cord in one hand. It reached, just barely.

"Now plug it in."

When he did, the motor hummed to life. "Still turned on," said Catherine. "So it was running when Wornow discovered the body."

"And when he moved the gantry, the plug pulled free and it shut off. He was so freaked a little detail like that didn't register."

Catherine opened the top drawer of the rolling tool chest beside the table and rummaged around. "I think it's time for a little reverse engineering . . ."

She found the tools she needed and used them to take apart the motor's housing. By the time she was finished, Greg had climbed up to join her. "Any luck?"

"If there's anything here, it's going to be tiny . . ."

"I've got an idea. Hang on." Greg climbed back down, got something from his kit, and came back. He handed it to Catherine.

"Magnetic fingerprint brush. Good thinking—the housing is full of metal shavings, most of them iron. But what we're looking for isn't."

She used the brush carefully to pick up shavings,

then gently move them to a white sheet of paper. Greg used a second magnetic brush to sort through them again, lifting and dropping them, looking for anything that wasn't adhering to the magnet.

"I think I've got something," said Catherine after a few minutes. She put down her brush and picked up a pair of tweezers, using them to pluck a tiny sliver from the bottom of the housing. "We'll have to get it under the microscope to be sure, but I think we're finally ready to re-create the crime scene."

"Hey, Monkeyboy," said Greg. "I see you made bail."

Bill Wornow stepped inside the warehouse, closing the door behind him. He wore a hooded sweatshirt and jeans and looked more than a little cautious. "Yeah. Did you find the, uh—"

"The fingers?" said Catherine. "Yes, they were exactly where you said they were. Thank you."

"Sure. I just want you to know—I've never done anything like that before, okay? I mean, I was panicking. Thinking back on it, I feel kinda sick."

Catherine smiled. "You were in a tight spot. You didn't want all your hard work going to waste."

"Yeah. This project, it just means so much to me . . . So, why'd you ask me to come here?"

"We just thought," said Greg from the top of the gantry, "that you might want to see how your partner actually died."

Wornow stared up at him. "Really? You know what happened?"

"Pretty sure," said Catherine. "Come on up, we'll show you." She climbed up the ladder beside the gantry. Wornow hesitated for a second, then followed her.

"Okay," said Greg. "So it's late at night. Hal's up here, tinkering away. He's wired on meth—no surprise there—so his attention maybe isn't what it should be."

"Did Hal usually wear a necklace?" asked Catherine. "One with a black chunk of rock on the end of it?"

"Yeah, he did," said Wornow. "He got it in Hawaii, never took it off."

"Well, he did that night," said Greg. "Maybe it was getting in his way, maybe he didn't want to get wax on it—but whatever the reason, he took it off and hung it on a nail, right there." He pointed.

"Then he went back to whatever he was doing," said Catherine. "At one point, he was using one of these portable butane torches—maybe to smoke some more meth, even though we didn't find a pipe. Of course, that's the sort of thing that might get disposed of if someone else noticed it . . ." She cocked an eyebrow at Wornow. He swallowed but didn't say anything.

"But when he was done with the torch," said Greg, "he didn't bother turning it off. He just set it down. At the edge of this table—and right beneath the necklace."

"Did you know about the cyst on Kanamu's spine?" asked Catherine.

"Cyst? No. I knew he had a bad back, though. He said he hurt it in a fall back in Hawaii. Someplace called Hualalai—he was always complaining about it."

Catherine nodded. "Well, that fall resulted in a condition called syringomyelia. One of the symptoms is an inability to detect extremes of temperature with the hands or feet."

"Which is exactly what was being produced," said Greg, "in the chunk of obsidian dangling from the end of the necklace. It got hotter and hotter, until the solder that attached it to the chain melted. At that point the rock dropped to the table. It probably made a noise when it hit, which got Kanamu's attention."

Catherine walked over to the table. "So he came over. He saw the rock lying on the table but didn't understand how it had gotten there. So he picked it up."

"Normally, you pick up a really hot object, you drop it right away," said Greg. "But Kanamu's syringomyelia had destroyed his ability to detect temperature. He actually turned around and took several steps toward the rim of the volcano. That's when he noticed the smell."

Catherine pointed at the disassembled grinder.

"He'd been using the grinder to work on something, because the motor was running. When he realized that what he was smelling was his own flesh burning, he reacted instinctively—he flung the obsidian away."

"And right into the flywheel of the grinder," said Greg. "Which spat it back at him much harder than he'd thrown it. So hard that when it hit his forehead, it not only ricocheted but splintered—leaving a very hot shard in his skull, while the rest of the obsidian went straight up."

"And Hal Kanamu went over the edge," said Catherine. "Despite the heat, it knocked him cold. And into the volcano he went."

Wornow stared at Greg, then Catherine. "So it was an accident?" he said. "A one-in-a-million accident?"

Greg shrugged. "That's what it looks like to us. And that's what we're going to be putting in our report."

Wornow shook his head in disbelief. "Man. I can't . . . I mean, yeah, okay, I guess you've got all the facts. But still, it all sounds so . . ."

"Unlikely," said Catherine. "Believe me, Mr. Wornow—in our line of work we run into the unlikely all the time."

"And it was all because of that damn chunk of rock," said Wornow. "You know, this project has had all kinds of bad luck from the beginning. I used to joke that we were cursed, but Hal didn't like that." Wornow walked over to the rim of the volcano, stared down into its now empty mouth. "Hal told me that anyone who removes lava from the islands was said to be cursed by Pele. He thought he could get away with it, though. Told me we'd be fine as long as we were respectful—that she'd protect us. He was going to put that rock into the volcano itself when it was done, had a whole ritual all planned out. Guess he waited too long . . ."

"I know a little bit about Hawaiian mythology myself," said Greg. "And the curse you're talking about? It isn't part of it. It was invented by a park ranger who was trying to stop tourists from taking souvenirs."

"Urban legend, as opposed to volcanic," said Catherine. "Your friend was the victim of bad judgment, not an angry goddess."

Wornow sighed. "Yeah, I know. But either way, he's still dead."

Riley drew her gun and advanced on the abandoned greenhouse.

She knew she was exposed. The smallest tear in the newsprint covering the windows was enough to let anyone watch her without being seen, and if they had a gun . . . well, out here in the desert there was no one to hear a shot.

She went back the way she came, ducking around the corner of the building housing the offices and flattening herself against the wall.

Quickly, she considered her options: she could call for backup, she could check it out herself, or she could leave.

Calling for backup because she simply heard a noise would get her branded a rookie forever. Leaving just wasn't an option.

She changed direction, creeping past the locked front entrance and the rolling steel door and around the other corner. She could see a long brick wall with windows set into it; keeping her head below the level of the glass, she kept moving.

At the far end of the wall, she peeked around the corner. Most of this side of the greenhouse was also covered with newspaper, but the first third had sheets of plywood nailed over it instead. Shards of broken glass lay scattered on the ground beneath. One of the sheets looked as if it had come loose at one end or been torn partially free.

The wind gusted, catching the plywood like a sail. It strained one way, then swung back with a loud *thump* as the gust died away.

Riley replayed the noise in her head, compared it to the one she'd heard a moment ago. They matched.

She sighed. It was a very quiet sigh, though, and she didn't put down her gun. Instead, she moved closer.

There were footprints in the dirt around the opening.

She peered through the crack, pushing it open

wider with one hand. The smell that met her nostrils was immediate and powerful: decomp, but mixed with something else. Something herbal.

She sneezed violently and backed away from the opening. Whatever was in there, she wasn't going any farther without a respirator.

She headed back to her vehicle to call it in.

"Well, well," said Brass, leaning against the fender of one of the black-and-whites parked outside the greenhouse. "The gang's all here. Doc, good to see you up and around."

Doc Robbins nodded at Brass and Grissom. "Good to be back. You're sure this guy hasn't left any surprises behind?"

"We've cleared the site," said Brass. "Nothing in there but DBs—I can't make any promises about what's in *them*, though. Maybe this time they're stuffed full of balloon animals."

Grissom put on the hood of his hazmat suit. "We're not taking any chances," he said. "Nick, Riley, and I are going in to examine the bodies first. I know it's a breach of protocol, but these are unusual circumstances."

"I have no problem with that," said Robbins. "In fact, I brought my own hazmat suit. Excuse me while I get ready." He limped away, muttering under his breath. "Stupid spider, turning me into a goddamned tripod . . ."

* * *

Nick and Riley walked up, already suited up. "We're good to go," said Nick.

"Riley?" said Grissom. "You were the one who found it."

Riley took a deep breath. "Follow me," she said.

They mounted the steps to the entrance. Police bolt cutters had sheared the chain in half; it lay discarded to one side. They walked in.

The front office held only a counter, with a rough slit hacked into the front of it. Grissom went behind it and peered underneath, then reached down and rapped one interior wall. It rang hollowly. "Reinforced with metal cladding."

"A shooting blind?" said Nick.

Grissom straightened up. "A guard post. Hives always post guards at the entryway . . ."

A short hall connected the lobby to the greenhouse. There were two offices on either side of the corridor; their doors had been removed. Grissom looked in the first one to the left.

A mattress lay on the floor. It was the only thing in the room, other than a large, half-empty jug of water. The other rooms were exactly the same.

They continued on to the greenhouse. Plastic trays holding nothing but dirt lined tables down either side of the room, while in the center, four bodies were sprawled around a burned-out can of Sterno. A blackened, bent spoon and four syringes lay on a piece of newspaper next to it.

"Big Johnny, Paintcan, Zippo, and Buffet Bob,"

said Riley. "Looks like they were having a little party."

"Celebrating the harvest," said Grissom. He walked over to the nearest tray. "Whatever was growing here was yanked out by the roots. And it appears they were growing a lot of it."

Nick knelt by the bodies. "Four needles, no waiting. Looks like they just ODed."

Riley stepped past the bodies, continuing on to the far end of the building. "I've got some kind of equipment. Looks like a distillery—piping, large drum, filters."

"We're too late," said Grissom. "He harvested the crop, processed out the anisomorphal, then disposed of his workers."

"How about the HBTX?" asked Nick. "That's the real threat."

Grissom joined Riley at the far end of the room. "This was probably his base of operations, but he would have needed different equipment to process the homobatrachotoxin—like a centrifuge. He may have taken it with him when he left."

"I don't know," said Riley. "This whole agriculture angle doesn't seem to fit the Bug Killer's methodology. This could just be a grow op."

"Actually," said Grissom, "there are several kinds of insects that raise crops. Termites, ants, and bark beetles all cultivate fungus as a nutritional source—ants were the first animals on Earth to deliberately grow their own food."

Nick was examining the bodies, one by one. "These guys are in pretty good shape for six weeks of captivity—no ligature marks or bruising."

"He kept them well fed, too," said Riley, peering into a large, open garbage container. "If your idea of well fed is canned chili and beef stew."

"Of course he did," said Grissom softly. "They weren't prisoners, they were workers. He gave them food, shelter, and purpose, and they performed the duties he assigned them."

"And none of them bolted?" asked Riley. "I mean, from what I understand these guys were pretty hard-core street veterans—wary about anything that might threaten their independence. Six weeks is a long time to work for a screwball for free stew and a mattress."

Grissom shook his head. "Slave-raider ants will stage massive invasions of other nests in order to steal pupae. When the stolen young emerge from the pupal state, chemicals released by their captors imprint them as part of the new colony. They think they belong, so they do whatever work they were born to do."

"Chemicals," said Nick. "You think the Bug Killer kept them in line by feeding them drugs? Or by making them feel like they belonged here?"

"What's the difference?" said Grissom. "Either way, he found a way to meet their needs."

"Yeah," said Riley. "Until he didn't need them anymore."

* * *

Grissom knew the anisomorphal was the key.

The walking stick insect used the chemical as a defense to ward off predators, but that didn't make sense; the only workable defense for the Bug Killer was to not get caught.

Maybe it is a defense—a diversion to make us look one way instead of another. A type of cryptic camouflage, like the walking stick itself—appearing to be one thing while being something else.

That simply didn't ring true. Too much time, too much sheer biological energy had been expended on this project. That wasn't what insects did; they were models of efficiency. Whatever LW had planned, the anisomorphal was a necessary element.

Secondary influences. Everything he's done has been in order to trigger a larger effect. Kill a quarterback to incite a riot; kill a helper to panic a queen. Threaten a lab to unnerve an opponent . . .

He's like a kid playing with a magnifying glass. Seeing which way he can make the ants run, pulling the wings off flies. By turning people into insects, he turns himself into God.

"Hey, Grissom!" Brass's voice on the walkie-talkie. "I said, one of your associates is here and asking for you. Can you hear me inside that hood, or should I get a bullhorn?"

Grissom grabbed the walkie and responded. "Sorry. Who is it?"

"Jake Soames."

Grissom walked back outside, pulling off his hood as soon as he was outdoors. "Jake? What are you doing here?"

Jake Soames leaned against Brass's car, a white cardboard box on the hood beside him. "Told your dispatcher I had something important to show you, convinced 'em to cough up your location. Not interrupting, am I?"

Grissom frowned. "We're in the middle of processing a crime scene, Jake. You shouldn't be here."

"You haven't seen what I've brought you yet. Look." He picked up the box and held it out. The top was transparent, with a small intake vent on one side and what looked like a tiny fan to draw air into the box. Five wasps crawled around the interior.

"Braconids?" said Grissom.

"That's right," said Jake proudly. "They're parasitic, lay their eggs in the living bodies of caterpillars. They use their sense of smell to find their prey. They're sensitive to not only the chemicals emitted by the caterpillar but the volatiles released by the plant the caterpillar is feeding on. Like a rent-a-cop responding to an alarm going off, right? Attack the plant and get an armed response for your trouble."

"These are the ones you mentioned in your research?"

"The very same. These wasps can be trained to

associate particular odors with food in about an hour. The idea is to train 'em to replace bomb- or drug-sniffing dogs. Since you gave me a tin star and all, I thought I'd lend a hand in case the bad guys left you a nasty surprise."

"These wasps can detect explosives?"

"They bloody well better, or my grant'll disappear." Jake grinned. "Come on, Gil—chance to be in on the cutting edge of science, eh? Let me and my little mates have a gander at your crime scene. I promise I won't touch anything—you can put me in one of those all-body condoms to make sure."

Grissom thought about it. "All right," he said at last. "But stick close."

"Like Vegemite on bread . . ."

Once he was suited up, Soames followed Grissom inside. "So this is like, what? One of those warehouses they grow marijuana in? Can't smell a damn thing inside this suit except my own sweat . . ."

"Be grateful," said Grissom. "Four corpses don't exactly produce a pleasant bouquet."

Grissom explained to Nick and Riley what Jake was doing there.

"You really think there might be a bomb here?" asked Nick.

"I doubt it," said Grissom. "But there's no harm in letting him look. Just keep an eye on him while he's doing it."

Jake had already begun, walking slowly around

the perimeter of the room and stopping to take air samples every few feet.

Grissom joined him. "Anything?"

"Not so far. It's a big room, though—give 'em a bit."

As he followed Jake around the room, Grissom's thoughts returned to Athena Jordanson. She was still important. The Bug Killer had made a queen run, but that wouldn't be enough for him. What would? Killing her? He'd made that almost impossible by his own actions—security around her would be on high alert. The hive was buzzing with fear and anger, ready to attack anything that moved. All they needed to explode into fury was—

An irritant.

Abruptly, he knew what LW wanted the anisomorphal for.

Incentive.

"Well, that was a bust," Jake Soames said cheerfully. "Either there's no trinitrotoluene here, or my guys are asleep at the switch and you're all going up in smoke."

Nick glanced over at Grissom and raised his eyebrows.

"Jake," said Grissom, "I appreciate you sharing your expertise, but we really have to process the crime scene now."

"No worries. Give me a call later, Gilly—we'll

have a drink." Grissom walked Jake and his wasps to the exit.

Riley shook her head. "I can't believe Grissom actually let that guy into our crime scene. With a box of bugs, no less."

"Give him a break," said Nick. "We cleared him in the Harribold case, so he's not a suspect. He was careful not to touch anything. And even though his methodology is a little out-there, it's no stranger than some of the things I've seen Grissom do. Show the guy a little respect; he's a scientist, no different than us."

"Is there something I'm missing here? That whole exercise seemed pretty pointless—"

Nick put up a hand. "There *is* something you're missing. Not your fault; you don't know Grissom like I do. But—you know how back in high school, there was always that one geeky kid who never had any friends? Sat by himself during lunch, usually reading a book? That's Grissom in a nutshell. Not real good at socializing, would rather read a paper on the mating habits of the dung beetle than go to a party. It makes him real good at his job, but it's a pretty lonely place to live."

"How about his coworkers? You guys seem pretty close."

"We are. Matter of fact, I'd say we're a family. But there's a world of difference between family and friends; family's where you go when you need to feel safe, feel protected. Friends—well, friends are who you go to when you need to cut loose."

"I have a hard time imagining Grissom cutting loose."

"Maybe so, but it's a basic human need. Hell, it's the only reason Vegas exists in the first place. And Jake—I don't know him that well, but he's about the only person in the world I've ever seen convince Grissom to drink something stronger than beer." Nick paused. "It's been a hard year for him. For all of us. I think he needs all the friends he can get right now, and that includes loud, booze-guzzling Australians."

Riley shrugged. "Okay, I get it. Anybody that tightly wrapped is probably in need of a little loosening. I just hope it doesn't affect our investigation."

"It won't. If there's one thing Grissom never loses sight of, it's the case he's working on."

"I need to go back to the Embassy Gold," said Grissom.

Conrad Ecklie stared at him, lines of frustration on his face. "Gil, we've been through this. Quadros is dead. It's great that your people located that greenhouse, but four dead junkies and a bunch of dirt do not add up to an imminent terrorist attack."

Grissom hadn't bothered to take a seat when he entered Ecklie's office, and now he tossed a photo down on the undersheriff's desk. Ecklie picked it up with a frown. "What's this?"

"That's a picture from Togo. Four people killed at a soccer game when a power outage panicked the spectators and sent them racing for the exits." Grissom tossed another photo down. "This one's from Harare, Zimbabwe. Thirteen dead after police used tear gas on an unruly crowd." He added a third. "Kathmandu. Ninety-three people killed in a stadium while trying to flee a hailstorm." Another photo. "Accra, Ghana. A hundred and twenty-three fatalities after police set off a stampede by firing tear gas when fans threw bottles and chairs onto the field."

Ecklie stopped him with a raised hand before he could add a fifth. "What's your point, Gil? If there's a connection between soccer riots in Third World countries and a dead serial killer, I'm not seeing it."

"Panic. In every case, LW has used bugs themselves to provoke specific reactions in the public at large. He believes that in large groups, people and insects basically react the same way. And so far, he's been right."

"Even if that were the case, it's irrelevent. He's dead—"

"That may not matter. All a bomb needs to go off is a timer."

Ecklie paused. "A bomb?"

"Yes. And if I'm right about the effect he's trying to cause, I know where it has to be. We don't need to shut down the hotel for this; all I need is access."

Ecklie looked skeptical. "To what?"

"The ventilation system."

They started with the intake vents at ground level, massive chrome-louvered panels designed to suck in the dry Vegas air, figuring that they were the most accessible. When that proved fruitless, they moved to the roof and the huge air-cycling plant that pumped cool air into hundreds of hotel rooms as well as the restaurants, the bars, and the casino. After that, the only thing left to search would be the immense length of the duct system itself, literally miles of air-circulation piping that ran through the entire hotel like the capillary system of a living organism.

That turned out not to be necessary. They found what they were looking for on the roof.

The bomb disposal unit brought Grissom the parts when they were done. The BDU commander, Lieutenant Coombs, was a wiry, soft-spoken man with a bristly gray mustache. "It's all yours, Grissom," he said as his men carried the pieces into the lab. "Pretty simple mechanism, really. He just adapted an industrial-grade mister to aerosolize the liquid—probably got it from a greenhouse."

"Thanks," said Grissom. "We'll take it from here."

"Sure," said Coombs, a chuckle in his voice. "Now that there's no danger of anything blowing up, you show us the door."

Grissom eyed the tank now sitting on a lab table. "Don't go too far. Things aren't quite stable yet . . ."

Hodges found Riley, Grissom, and Nick in the conference room, staring at the large monitor on the wall. "Got the results you were waiting on," said Hodges. "Anisomorphal—highly concentrated, too. I also found traces of a second chemical, dimethyl sulfoxide."

"DMSO?" said Nick. "That's a topical solvent—absorbs right through the skin and into the bloodstream."

Grissom studied the report Hodges had handed to him. "And it can carry other chemicals with it, making it an efficient way to deliver a drug through skin contact alone."

"Combined with an irritant," said Riley, "that could produce an intensely painful reaction."

"It could," said Grissom, "but not in these amounts. I think we're looking at cross-contamination, not something that was deliberately added."

"I'd have to agree," said Hodges. "The amount was minuscule. If, however, dimethyl sulfoxide was added to a powerful toxin like homobatrachotoxin—"

"You'd have a compound you could use to kill someone by applying a single drop to their skin," said Grissom.

"Not great news, I know. Just don't kill the messenger," said Hodges.

After Hodges had left, the team turned back to what they'd been studying: a graphic of the Embassy Gold's ventilation system on the flat screen on the wall.

"Up here," said Grissom, tapping the screen, "is where we found the anisomorphal. As you can see, this area of the system directs air to the Canyon Amphitheatre."

Riley leaned back in her chair. "The same place Athena Jordanson is giving her debut performance."

"Yes. The timer on the device was set to go off at the beginning of the concert. In the ensuing panic, people certainly would have died."

"Sure," said Nick. "But he would have killed even more if he'd just used the HBTX, especially if it were mixed with DMSO. Why didn't he?"

"It wouldn't fit his pattern," said Grissom. "Just as sex is secondary to many serial killers, death is secondary to LW. For him, primary satisfaction is gained by manipulating people as if they were insects. It feeds not only his sense of power but his sense of superiority."

Riley nodded. "So he wants them to react with blind panic."

"Yes. But for the first time, we're one step ahead; we've deactivated his device without his knowledge—and Athena Jordanson's performance is tonight."

A slow smile appeared on Nick's face. "You

think he'll be on hand to watch the bugs scatter?"

"I do. But he won't be foolish enough to be inside; he'll be somewhere in the vicinity, probably in the crowd on the Strip. Brass will have plainclothes officers posted, but one of LW's demonstrated strengths is mimicry; I doubt we'll be able to catch him from surveillance alone."

"And if we don't," said Riley, "he still has the HBTX."

"He's been careful so far," said Grissom. "But his workers have made mistakes. The cross-contamination was probably due to an error on their part, not his. We need to take another look at the greenhouse and anything they might have come into contact with."

"You really think we'll find anything?" said Nick. "They may not have been prisoners, but he obviously kept them isolated."

"Believe it or not, social insects have social problems," said Grissom. "Parasitic species that invade the nest and pose as residents, even slave revolts. LW may consider human beings no more than glorified bugs—but even bugs can surprise you."

Grissom went to see Doc Robbins.

Robbins was in the middle of performing the autopsy on the fourth and final vic from the greenhouse. Big Johnny had been identified as John Christopher Farsten, an unemployed laborer with a string of arrests for petty theft. He'd been a large, burly man with a full beard and a large bald spot on the top of his head.

"COD?" asked Grissom.

"Still waiting for the tox screen, but I'm going to go with HBTX poisoning. Signs of excessive salivation and cardiac failure consistent with poisoning by homobatrachotoxin, plus all the bodies were found in contorted positions suggestive of convulsions."

"The syringes we found tested positive for a combination of heroin and HBTX. Looks like he gave them a going-away present."

"Too bad they didn't know they were the ones going away. I also found something a little unusual in this one's bloodwork: an elevated level of O_2."

"Hyperoxygenation? What could cause that?"

"In someone in this condition? Almost certainly direct exposure—I'd say he was getting it from a tank."

"We didn't find any oxygen tanks at the site. Were there signs of respiratory illness?"

"No—his liver was in pretty bad shape, but he wasn't a smoker."

"Maybe not," said Grissom. "But he was definitely inhaling something . . ."

Riley and Nick went back to the greenhouse. They'd already gone through it once; the only thing they'd found had been half a pack of cigarettes stashed under one of the mattresses. Now they expanded their search to include the surrounding area as well.

"Grissom said it himself," said Nick as they walked an ever-increasing outward spiral that centered on the building. "They weren't prisoners. And guys like that would get cabin fever quicker than most."

Riley knelt and peered at the ground, then straightened up again. "So they must have spent some of their free time outdoors. Makes sense."

"Yeah. No matter how good the drugs your boss is giving you are, there are always going to be times you want to get away from him." Nick gave her a wide grin. "Not that I speak from personal experience, you understand."

"Right. You can't get *enough* Grissom drugs."

Nick laughed. "Whoa, *that* sounded a little bitter. You having a problem with our fearless leader?"

"I have no problem with fearless. I just wonder what other exemplars the '-less' applies to."

"Well, 'brain' and 'heart' definitely aren't on the list. I know, he can take some getting used to—half the time he seems vaguely irritated and the other half he's barely aware you're alive. But you have to understand, Grissom lives in his head. And that's a big, big place." Nick stopped and stared at the water tower that occupied one corner of the property. "And after all the years he's put in on this job, a pretty scary one. You can't really hold it against him if he gets a little lost in there sometimes . . ."

"I've got cigarette butts," said Riley. "They look fairly recent, too."

Nick stopped and crouched down. "Same brand as the half-empty pack we found. Guess this is where one of them came out for the occasional smoke break."

"There's something else." She pointed. "Wheel tracks, fairly close together."

"Some kind of dolly or cart—and pretty heavy, too. They lead toward the water tower."

They followed the tracks, which ended at the foot of a wooden ladder that ran up the side of the tower. "Interesting," said Nick. "I can see a hatch from here." He started climbing the ladder.

"Aren't you worried it'll be full of poisonous water bugs or something?" she asked.

"If it is," he said, "tell Grissom I blame him."

They'd both been to the diner enough times to not need a menu; Catherine ordered a salad, while Greg had the breakfast special. Both had coffee.

"You have to admit," said Greg, "that this was a weird one."

Catherine glanced around the almost empty diner. "You think? Meth addict does something stupid and winds up dead. Seems pretty straightforward to me."

"You've got to be kidding. An artificial volcano? A cursed piece of obsidian? A string of events so unlikely that no one would believe they could actually happen . . ."

An old woman tottered in the front door and sank into a booth. Her hair was a wild white mane, and she wore an old sundress covered in bright red flowers. She carried a white shopping bag with the letters *ABC* on it.

"I don't know if I'd go *that* far," said Catherine.

"No? Then let me re-create it for you, via the magic of storytelling—because, let's face it, there is no way we could ever actually *duplicate* the events that transpired.

"Okay, first of all there's Kanamu's injury. Happens as a result of taking a piece of obsidian from Hualalai, which he isn't supposed to do. Despite this, he turns the rock into a necklace and brings it with him to Vegas—where he correctly predicts something so unlikely that the odds against it make him rich. *And* it involves a virgin."

"So? Statistically, she was going to lose her virginity someday—and she's a celebrity. The only real surprise is that she didn't announce it on Twitter."

Greg shrugged. "Well, maybe. But look at the accident itself. You saw how all the individual items were arranged; the necklace and the torch both had to be in just the right position for the link to soften and break; the rock had to fall just right to not drop off the edge of the gantry. Kanamu's syringomyelia was caused by the fall at Hualalai, and if Kanamu hadn't had syringomyelia, he never would have hesitated the few seconds it took to get just the right distance away from the exposed flywheel—and then he had to pitch the rock at exactly the right angle for it to hit the flywheel and kick back at him, nailing him right in the forehead and knocking him out. A chunk of rock from a volcano killed him, and did it using the only artificial volcano within a thousand miles."

"One of two, actually," said Catherine.

"Even so. Would you agree the entire sequence is so unlikely we couldn't re-create it if we tried?"

"If I do, will you stop using the word *virgin*?"

"Yes."

"Then I agree."

Greg's smile got wider. "And would you also agree that one of the basic principles of science is the repeatability of phenomena?"

"I could argue the point, but sure."

"Then, by that definition, what happened to Hal Kanamu wasn't *scientific* in nature."

Catherine sighed. "No, it wasn't. It was sheer bad luck. None of it was impossible, just improbable. So if you're trying to ascribe some sort of magic explanation to all this—"

"Hold on there, Scully. I didn't say it was magic. I just said it was nonscientific."

"What's your point? Assuming you actually have one."

Greg leaned back, blowing on his coffee and

looking pleased with himself. "I'm not sure I do. I just get a kick out of the fact that even with all our reliance on rational thought and deductive reasoning, there's still room in the universe for the mysterious."

She gave him a reluctant smile in return. "Yeah, well, just remember that it's rational thought and deductive reasoning that provide us with a paycheck. What happened to Kahuna Man was unusual and bizarre, but it didn't break any natural laws—it was just very, very unlikely."

Greg nodded. "I guess in a way that makes him a Vegas success story."

"How so?"

"Well, isn't that why people come here? To beat the odds?"

The woman in the booth by the door turned around to look at them. Her eyes were wide and bloodshot. She met Catherine's gaze and chuckled at some secret internal joke, her laughter a low, raspy rumble; a smoker's laugh.

Their food arrived. The next time Catherine looked over, the woman was gone.

15

NICK OPENED THE hatch of the water tower.

The smell that drifted out of the dark interior was cool and damp, refreshing in the heat of the day. Nothing buzzed or chittered at him. He pulled the Maglite from his belt and clicked it on, then shone it inside. The tank was about half-full; the water fractured the flashlight's beam, throwing it up on the walls in wavery shimmers. Enough penetrated the surface that Nick had a pretty good view of what was beneath it.

Nothing.

"Doesn't look promising," he called down to Riley. "I'm going to take a sample for testing, though."

"Be careful," she called back. "If Grissom's right about LW combining those two chemicals—"

"I know, I know. Any exposure to bare skin would be fatal. But I highly doubt this is where the Bug Killer decided to stash his cache of poison—the hatch didn't even have a lock on it."

"Who needs a lock," she pointed out, "when touching a single drop will make an intruder drop dead?"

Nick hesitated. "Good point."

It wasn't until after he'd taken the sample, closed the hatch, and started back down the ladder that Nick noticed it. He stopped, put a hand over his eyes, and squinted. "Hey, Riley? I think I just spotted something weird. Take a look on the ground, just on the other side of that sage. No, to the left, about five feet away."

She found what he was pointing at and crouched to get a closer view. "That's . . . not the kind of track you expect to see in the middle of a desert," she said.

Nick jumped the last few feet and trotted over. "Maybe not. But I think it explains the dolly tracks leading up to the ladder." He pulled out his cell phone. "Grissom is gonna want to hear about this."

When Nick told Grissom what they'd found and where, he understood the significance of his mental image of ants building a bridge across water—and knew what the Bug Killer's plan had to be. He talked to Nick very briefly, then hung up and made another call.

"Brass."

"Nick just found a flipper print outside a water tower at the greenhouse site."

"A flipper? As in snorkel-and-skin-diving, scuba-gear-type flipper?"

"Yes. I think LW was using the water tower to test his gear—and I know what he needed it for."

"Well, Lake Mead is the nearest large body of water—"

"His target is still the Embassy Gold. Specifically, the fountains right outside."

Brass understood immediately. "The pumps—they're all located under the water itself, just like the Bellagio's. They have to use scuba equipment any time they do maintenance."

"Extremely powerful pumps," said Grissom. "Capable of expelling a thick stream of water a hundred feet straight up. But if someone were to change the orientation of one so it was aimed at the crowd instead—"

"You've got the world's largest squirt gun. Except this one's going to be loaded with more than just water, isn't it?"

"Jim, the emergency doors for the Canyon Amphitheatre empty directly onto the plaza facing those fountains. And on a Friday night—even without a panicked group of Athena Jordanson fans pouring from the exits—it'll be full of tourists."

"I'll call the Grand right away. They only do fountain shows in the evenings—in fact, I think they time them to entertain people leaving the theater. We can get a diver down there to disconnect whatever he's set up—"

"Don't send a diver yet."

"Why not?"

"Because it'll tip him off. There's still an hour before Athena Jordanson's concert starts, and if he isn't in place to watch the chaos, he will be soon."

"Grissom, where are you?"

"In the field," said Grissom, staring up at the sinuous bulk of the Embassy Gold.

He won't be in the crowd after all, Grissom thought. *He won't risk exposure to the toxin. But he will be nearby. Behind glass, where he'll be safe. Studying the results of his experiment like a child with an ant farm.*

There were numerous hotels with views of the plaza, but Grissom didn't think LW would be in any of them. Too far away, too removed. He wouldn't want to be any farther than the other side of the street.

Grissom used the pedway to cross over. He thought again about water, how it was the dominant metaphor in Vegas for wealth. He thought about the bombardier beetle and how it combined two different chemicals into a spraying attack so hot it actually boiled. He thought about *Argyroneta aquatica*, a spider that spent its entire life underwater, emerging only to replenish its air supply and feed. Waiting patiently in a webbed diving bell for prey to brush up against it . . .

He thought he knew why the body of one of the greenhouse vics had such a high oxygen level.

LW had used the water tower to practice with the scuba equipment, but one of his workers hadn't been satisfied with his daily allotment of nectar; he'd supplemented the drugs LW had fed him with stolen hits of pure oxygen from one of the tanks, adding an O_2 high to the one he was already experiencing.

Grissom stopped at the end of the pedway before descending the stairs. He was almost certain LW would already be in place, and he didn't want to alert the killer to his presence. The high walls of the pedway shielded Grissom from casual view, but once he reached street level he'd be much more exposed.

LW himself wouldn't be at street level, though. Grissom could already tell that the constant traffic on Las Vegas Boulevard would block too much of the view. LW would want to be at least one floor up.

There was a restaurant on the second floor of the hotel directly across from the Grand. Instead of taking the stairs down, Grissom continued straight ahead—the pedway connected directly to the casino. Once inside, he made his way through the blink and chime of the slots and to the restaurant itself. It was called Bugsy's.

The man staring intently through the plate glass at the street outside hardly seemed to notice when Grissom sat down at his table. It took him a second to realize he wasn't alone, and when he turned to stare at his visitor, Grissom saw that he was sweating profusely and seemed to be having trouble focusing.

"Hello, LW," said Grissom.

The man Grissom had known as Roberto Quadros smiled. He'd shaved off his white beard and gotten rid of the heavy-framed glasses; his hair was now a glossy black. He wore shorts and a T-shirt with the name of a casino on it. "Excuse me?" he said. His Brazilian accent was completely gone. "I think you have me confused with—"

"Stop. It's over," said Grissom. "The anisomorphal has been removed from the ventilation ducts. The fountain has been deactivated. No one else is going to die."

LW met Grissom's eyes. "Are you so sure?" he asked softly. "This isn't like you, Grissom. Confronting the accused in a noncontrolled situation . . . Aren't you afraid I might pull out a gun and shoot you?"

"I considered that," Grissom admitted. "But I thought it highly unlikely; it just doesn't fit your profile. Also, I didn't come alone—there are police stationed at the exits."

"And a sniper, no doubt. In case I make any sudden movements."

Grissom shrugged. "I asked to be able to talk to you first."

LW chuckled, which turned into a wheeze. "Why?"

"Because no matter how careful a scientist is, there's always a difference between observing a specimen in captivity and one in the wild."

LW nodded and took a sip of his glass of water, his hand trembling. "Ah. Very good, Dr. Grissom, very good. I can respect that. You think you can get answers now that later will be unavailable. Perhaps so. You may try, in any case. The longer our conversation, the greater the delay in my incarceration, after all."

"You don't seem well."

"A touch of food poisoning, I suspect. This damn town and its unsanitary troughs . . . I despise this place, Dr. Grissom. Bread and circuses covered in sparkles and doused with alcohol. The masses herded from one glittering spectacle to another, all of it as devoid of meaning or substance as a swarm of locusts mindlessly devouring a field of wheat. Ants who play at being grasshoppers for a weekend, then return to their little cubicles in their concrete anthills."

"And that's all we're capable of?"

"We? You and I are not the same as *them*, Dr. Grissom. We see the patterns their behavior always defaults to. We see how they react when offered sex or drugs or food. Have I not demonstrated this? Have my subjects not reacted with utter predictability at every stimulus?"

Grissom studied the man for a second before replying. "No, they haven't. We found your greenhouse because of trace left behind on one of your workers' belongings—possessions guarded for two months by people who owned less than him, people who didn't even know his last name. Insects don't do that."

The Bug Killer stared at him. His pupils were tiny. "Do you know why I chose the initials LW? I wondered if you'd figure it out. If anyone could, it would be you—Soames is an idiot and Vanderhoff's far more impressed with himself than he should be."

"I didn't—not until you killed the real Quadros. It stands for *lacewing*, doesn't it?"

The killer smiled. He seemed to be having trouble breathing. "Yes. I remember how impressed I was as a child when I learned that some ants actually keep livestock—herds of aphids that they milk for honeydew. But not all aphids are cows, not at all. Some are sheep."

"The woolly aphid."

"Yes! It grows a waxy white coat of protective fibers . . ." He stroked his chin, seemed surprised to feel it bare. "But that adaptation pales beside the ingenuity shown by lacewing larvae. They will pick up discarded tufts of fiber and disguise themselves with it, literally becoming wolves in sheep's clothing in order to slip past the ants guarding the aphid flock and prey upon their charges . . ."

He trailed off, his eyes unfocusing. He began to shake, spittle flying from his mouth as he collapsed to the floor.

*   *   *

"So this is the guy who sicced a spider on me?" asked Robbins. "Can't say I'm sorry he's dead."

Grissom stared down at the body on the autopsy table. "We still haven't been able to identify him. His prints aren't in the system, and he wasn't carrying any ID."

"He just collapsed in front of you?"

"He presented a number of symptoms first—shaking hands, difficulty with his vision and breathing, profuse sweating. He went into convulsions, then vomited and became incontinent."

Robbins frowned. "Those don't sound like the symptoms of homobatrachotoxin poisoning."

"No, they don't."

"Well, the tox screen will be back soon. In the meantime, let's see what we can find out otherwise." He picked up a scalpel and began to cut.

Grissom sighed and took off his glasses. He put them down on top of the postmortem report, which he'd read and reread a dozen times.

HBTX fatalities were usually caused by cardiac arrest, the poison paralyzing the heart. LW, however, had died as a result of respiratory failure. The tox screen told Grissom why: while LW had been poisoned, he hadn't been killed by HBTX. He'd been killed by an organophosphate—specifically, parathion.

An insecticide.

Grissom reached for the phone.

*   *   *

Nathan Vanderhoff regarded Grissom quizzically from across the table. "I'm not really sure why I'm here, Gil."

"I need to ask you a few questions, Nathan. It won't take long."

"I hope not. My flight's this evening."

"Yes, I know." Grissom consulted the notes he had in his hand. "You and Quadros corresponded, correct?"

"Yes, of course. Only on a professional basis, though."

"What about Jake Soames?"

"I hardly know the man."

"But you've spent some time with him in Vegas?"

"Well, yes. He seems to thrive on the party atmosphere, though I'm beginning to find it a bit wearing. Perhaps he is, as well; the last time I saw him he seemed somewhat exhausted."

"Did you ever notice Jake and Quadros together?"

Vanderhoff frowned. "I saw very little of either of them at the conference, but all four of us—including Charong—sat down together after our visit to the lab. Charong left first and I followed about twenty minutes later; I don't know how long Jake and Roberto stayed after that."

Grissom nodded. "Did Jake ever say anything to you about Quadros?"

"What do you mean?"

"Anything about him personally."

Vanderhoff thought about it. "There was one thing that was a little strange," he admitted. "The last time I talked to Jake, he referred to an ongoing project. From the way he talked, it sounded as if he and Quadros were working on it together—but when I asked him about it, he just laughed and said I'd misunderstood."

"I see," said Grissom.

Jake Soames met Grissom's gaze without flinching. He seemed just as relaxed in an interview room as he did on a bar stool, the kind of easy acceptance of his surroundings that Grissom had never mastered.

"We caught the Bug Killer," said Grissom.

Jake smiled. "Is that right? Congratulations all around. Too bad Nevada doesn't use the electric chair—serve the bastard right to meet his end in a zapper, wouldn't it?"

"He's already dead, Jake. Poisoned by an organophosphate insecticide—not as flashy as being electrocuted, but just as ironic."

"Parathion."

Grissom studied Jake's face. The smile had faded, leaving only a look of weary admission.

"You killed him," said Grissom. It wasn't a question; Grissom had known before he called Jake in.

"I won't deny it. I snuck into his hotel room, the

one he was staying in after he killed the real Quadros, and put it in a water bottle."

Grissom wasn't surprised. Nick and Riley were executing a search warrant on Soames's hotel room as they spoke, looking for the parathion. Grissom had no doubt they'd find it, too.

"How did you know?" asked Grissom. "He had everyone else fooled."

"I did some investigating on my own, Gilly. I went out drinking with the man." He paused, then leaned forward with his elbows on the table. "You know, there's some things you just can't quantify, mate. Human nature's one of them. Charong's a pervert and Vanderhoff can be an arrogant prick, but neither of them's a killer. Quadros—well, the psycho dressed up as him—was different. Get a few drinks in him and you could see that under all that bluster was nothing but contempt—contempt for the whole human race. If it was any of us, it was him."

"So you decided to kill him?" Grissom shook his head. "That's . . ."

"Cold? Inhuman?"

"I was going to say impetuous."

"Ha!" Jake grinned. "That's what I love about you, Grissom—I'll bet you have a heart tattooed on your bum with *science* on the banner. But give old Jake credit for a *little* intelligence; I didn't act without testing my hypothesis first."

"You had proof he was the killer? Why didn't you come to me?"

"Because the way I got it might have run into a few difficulties in court. It was enough to convince me, but a jury is another matter."

"Would it be enough to convince me?"

"Judge for yourself."

After they had taken Jake Soames away to be formally charged with the murder of the man known as LW, Grissom joined his colleagues in the break room. They had all finished eating but hadn't gotten up to leave yet; they were waiting for their boss.

Grissom sat down at the head of the table.

"Well?" asked Catherine.

"Braconid wasps," said Grissom.

"Sorry?" said Greg.

"It's how Jake Soames determined LW's guilt."

Nick leaned forward. "How?"

"Soames suspected that Quadros was the Bug Killer. He'd been working with braconid wasps in his own research and decided to see how effective they were. He surreptitiously sprayed one of the training chemicals on Quadros, then waited to see if there was another attack."

"That's why he showed up at the greenhouse," said Riley. "The wasps. He wasn't using them to sniff out explosives—he was seeing if Quadros had been there."

"Yes," said Grissom. "And the wasps told him that he had."

"I get it," said Nick. "Not really that much different than planting an explosive dye pack in a bag of stolen money—except the dye's invisible, it works by smell instead of sight, and it leaves traces behind detectable only to wasps . . . Okay, maybe it's not that similar. But I understand the concept."

Greg shook his head. "So at that point he knew the killer had been posing as Quadros—something we'd already figured out. But how did he find him?"

"The same way. He knew that the killer would have changed his appearance—including his clothing—but had noticed earlier that his shoes were rather expensive. That's what he sprayed with the training chemical—he gambled that the killer would keep them."

"Undone by comfortable footwear," said Nick. "Warrick would have been proud."

"The rest was persistence and luck. He took the wasps up and down every hallway of every hotel on the Strip until he got a hit. That told him where LW was staying—he convinced a maid to let him into the room while it was unoccupied."

Greg nodded. "Which is when he slipped LW the insecticide. But why didn't he come to you instead of going the vigilante route? I thought you two were buds."

"We are. I asked him the same question."

"And?" prompted Riley.

"He didn't want his interference to screw up our case. The braconid method is still very new and has never been tested in court. He worried that his data would be misunderstood or distorted if we went to trial—damaging not only our case, but the credibility of the method. Especially since he wouldn't be around to defend it."

"Why not?" asked Greg. "I'm sure the LVPD would spring for airfare from Australia if the case called for it—"

"He's dying," said Grissom.

There was a moment of silence.

"Pancreatic cancer," said Grissom. "His oncologist tells him he has a few months left, at most."

"Wow," Catherine said quietly. "And now he's going to spend it in a prison hospital."

"He was repulsed by what LW did," said Grissom. "Jake has always been . . . a little larger than life. When he encountered someone who had nothing but contempt for everything he reveled in—everything he was about to lose—he felt it was appropriate to take action."

"So he took the law into his own hands," said Riley.

Grissom paused. "I can't say I agree with what he did. But he didn't try to hide it; he told me everything. I'm sure he could have covered his tracks well enough to at least return to Australia and die at home."

"Why didn't he?" asked Greg.

"Because," said Grissom, "a scientist uncovers information; he doesn't hide it. He wanted the last investigation he ever performed to be part of the public record, not a deception motivated by self-interest." Grissom got to his feet. "Or as Jake put it: the Bug Killer was wrong. Humans may act like insects some of the time, but we understand that our actions have consequences, good or bad. We get to choose accordingly."

Grissom paused. "And that's exactly what he did."

Nick shook his head. "No offense, boss, but—what is it with you and serial killers? I'm starting to think you attract them the way honey attracts flies."

"Honey isn't the only thing that attracts flies," said Grissom. "So do corpses."

"Speaking of which," said Greg, "Do we have an ID on LW yet?"

"No," said Grissom. "His prints and DNA aren't in the system. He didn't leave anything behind that might indicate his true identity. Even though he claimed to be superior to the mass of humanity, in death he's become as faceless and anonymous as any member of a beehive or ant colony. His history, his true motivations, will likely remain unknowable, as frustrating as that sounds." He paused. "I suppose that, in the end, it's what we leave behind that defines us."

He nodded once, as if to himself, and then got up and left the room.

About the Author

DONN CORTEZ is the pseudonym for Don DeBrandt, who has authored several novels. He lives in Vancouver, Canada.